DRIVE ME CRAZY

BETH BOLDEN

CHAPTER ONE

It was absolutely, totally, without a doubt in Tony Blake's mind, a setup.

Now, he might not normally *mind* a setup, but there was no question this was his brother's doing, and instead of Tony being mildly intrigued, he was a little pissed off. Was it not enough for Wyatt to end up married to a hot, funny, professional baseball player while Tony got his heart smashed into a thousand tiny little shards? Admittedly, it had always been Tony who did the leaving before, and maybe this time he deserved to find out how much being dumped sucked, but Wyatt taking pity on him by finding some random guy for Tony felt like a step too far.

Even if the guy was really cute.

"Tony," Wyatt said jovially, a touch too friendly even for him, which was the thousandth reason Tony needed to believe this was not only a setup, it was a *bad* setup, "meet Lucas."

Lucas smiled, the skin around his eyes crinkling. He was short, much shorter than either Wyatt or Tony, and had a *very* athletic build, complete with pecs and abs and biceps and quads that Tony might've been interested in exploring further, if Wyatt hadn't been the one responsible for all this.

"Hi," Lucas said, extending his hand. "It's great to meet you, finally."

"It is?" Tony questioned. People usually liked meeting him. He knew he was attractive, that he'd been hot with the short buzz cut he'd had back when he'd first moved to LA, to help Wyatt start his food truck, *What a Catch*, and that he was even hotter now that his hair had finally grown out, nearly to his shoulders. He had great hair; if the food truck business failed, he could always go on Instagram and become a hair model or something.

"Wyatt's told me a lot about you."

It could probably have been scripted by the Setup God, that's how fucking transparent it was.

"I'm sure he has." Tony crossed his arms over his chest, and glared at his brother, because he did not want anyone's fucking pity, okay? Nobody's leftovers, nobody's scraps, nobody's galling sympathy. He was *just fine*. He could be single, even though he hadn't been in many, many years, and yeah, maybe he'd done his share of moping around, when the breakup had happened, but it was his first broken heart! Didn't you deserve a little wallowing, a little pity party, when the man you thought was the love of your life casually dumped you and said, "someday you'll understand why we wouldn't have worked out"?

Yeah.

Tony thought of the dartboard he'd made of Brody's face that he'd tacked up inside the little cottage he lived in, set back from the main house Wyatt and Ryan owned, and felt a tiny bit better. He'd landed a great hit last night, right smack on Brody's annoyingly perfect nose, the one he was convinced Brody had had fixed. Nobody had a nose that perfect in real life. *Nobody.*

It was a nose that could've launched a thousand ships, and it had fucking launched Tony from the tentative idea that he *might* like guys into the full-on, no-holds-barred realization that he was absolutely not straight. It had taken some time, but he'd finally landed on the right label. Not that figuring out who he really was had convinced Brody to stick around.

Asshole.

"Tony, why don't you tell Lucas a little more about the truck?" Wyatt said, his glee evident and really fucking annoying. There were a lot of times that Tony kinda hated his brother, and right now was pretty high up on the list.

"The truck?" Tony asked in disbelief. That's what Wyatt wanted them to talk about? *Geez, you suck at this,* Tony wanted to tell his little brother. *How did you ever get a guy like Ryan Flores when your game has this much epic suckitude?*

Lucas leaned against the edge of the sofa in Wyatt and Ryan's living room. "Your food truck?" he asked, his own nose crinkling adorably. Damnit, he was pretty cute. And even worse, he was exactly the kind of guy that Tony had always guessed he might like. Brody was nothing like Lucas; his ex was tall with dark hair, and really dark, intense, penetrating eyes. There'd been more than once that he and Brody had been mistaken for brothers. Which, *gross*. But yeah, Lucas was definitely cute, and from the way he was eying Tony, the feeling was probably mutual.

What was even worse than a setup? A setup that fucking *worked*.

"That's what I invited him here to talk about," Wyatt said, his voice betraying a hint of frustration, as he called out from the kitchen where he was putting the final touches on dinner. "The food truck."

When Lucas With the Cute Nose left, Tony was going to have a real heart-to-heart with his brother on what you did during a setup. You didn't throw two people together and then *keep fucking talking*. You left. You kept your distance. You hoped, against all odds, magic and fireworks happened.

"Really?" Tony asked. "Well, okay. The truck is called What a Catch, and we serve, well, I guess . . . LA food? California casual? Tacos, the occasional burger, some fresh fish. We're most famous for our mahi mahi tacos, actually."

"Sounds pretty good," Lucas said, and he only sort of sounded like he meant it. Which made sense Tony supposed. Because everyone knew that Lucas hadn't come here to talk about their food truck. He'd come here because Wyatt had given him an invitation into Tony's pants.

"Dinner's just about ready," Wyatt called out again, and added, "Ryan should be here soon. Dodgers had an early afternoon game."

"Have you met him before?" Tony asked, because if Wyatt was going to continually interfere, then he would at least take advantage of the subject change.

"Met who?" Lucas asked idly. From the way he'd not-so-subtly looked Tony up and down, he'd been sure he was interested, but now he just sounded bored. Which was *fine*, and not at all insulting. *Nope*. Because Tony had been Not Interested first.

"Ryan Flores, Wyatt's husband," Tony said impatiently. "You know, the baseball player. The famous one." *The rich one*, Tony mentally tacked on. Maybe that was why Lucas had agreed to any of this in the first place, maybe he needed money. Maybe he really wanted to get to Ryan. Well, he would have to rethink that whole plan, because Ryan was pretty fucking devoted to his brother. And Tony was even more devoted to the pair of them. Nobody was going to take advantage of his brother's kindness and his brother-in-law's natural generosity, not while he was around.

Maybe Lucas stupidly assumed that because Wyatt and Ryan had money, that Tony had money too.

He managed a decent salary from the truck, because Wyatt's connections and their bomb food kept them pretty solidly in the black, and he could even save a big chunk of it, because living in Wyatt and Ryan's guest cottage meant his living expenses, especially for LA, were crazy low. Still, he hadn't always been the poster child for responsible decisions, and while he had some money saved, it wasn't exactly a fortune. It wasn't enough to go along with a setup, that was for fucking sure.

Lucas gave him a weird look. "No?"

"Ah well, you will. He's . . ."

"Stupendous? Amazing? The game-winning player of the century?" Ryan asked as he walked in, tossing his motorcycle helmet on the couch and giving Tony a quick hug, before turning to Lucas. "Hey there, you must be Lucas."

They shook hands, and Lucas seemed as vaguely disinterested in Ryan as he did in Tony, so it couldn't be the money, and he sure wasn't a fame whore, because Tony had seen plenty of those before, hanging off Ryan like he was God's gift to the world.

"That was you, then, who hit the winning walk-off today. I caught the end of the game as I was finishing my workout," Lucas said offhandedly. And Tony wasn't really surprised—how could anyone be that noticeably ripped and *not* care about sports—but he'd clearly not been impressed by Ryan in person. So that *wasn't* why he was here, after all.

"It was me," Ryan said with a face-splitting grin. "I'm going to go say hi to Wyatt, see where we're at with dinner."

As he walked into the kitchen, Tony rolled his eyes. "He means, he's going to go make out with my brother. We might eat . . . sometime this century."

"You're not cooking?" Lucas asked, and unlike Ryan and his walk-off hit that won the game, he actually sounded interested. Plain and simple, this guy was *weird*. Tony couldn't get a read on him at all.

Tony shrugged. "It's Wyatt's kitchen," he said, and then lowered his voice to add, "And sometimes my . . . *less than conventional methods* annoy him. He's all officially trained, you know?" He didn't mention that he'd had six months of culinary school under his belt before he'd dropped out. Of course, he'd barely gone to class in those six months, but still. Wyatt had not only graduated, he'd done so with honors, and then worked his way up to the highest echelon of restaurants, Bastian Aquino's Terroir.

"Unconventional?" Lucas sounded even more intrigued.

"I mean, I'm not formally trained. Not like Wyatt. He likes things . . . *just so.*"

"How does that work on the food truck, then?" Lucas asked. His greenish-hazel eyes had gone soft. Like he genuinely wondered how the two brothers got along when they worked in such close quarters with such different backgrounds.

"It didn't, at all, at first, but now we figure it out," Tony said. Then hesitated. "Do you want a beer? I'm gonna grab one, because like I said, we're gonna be waiting for dinner for awhile."

Lucas smiled again, and it was even warmer than it'd been just a moment ago. "Sure."

"Any preference?" Tony asked, but Lucas shook his head.

"Whatever you're having is totally fine."

Tony went to the small fridge built into the bar at the far end of the room and grabbed two Coronas. "I'd go into the kitchen for lime," he said apologetically, flipping the caps off with an expert motion, "but…I've interrupted them way too many times already."

Lucas grinned as Tony handed him one of the bottles. "Really? And they're married? How long?"

"Not long, almost a year, maybe?" Tony grimaced. "But Ryan hitting that walk-off hit…it's like a fucking aphrodisiac to them."

"Must be weird living with all that…" Lucas waved around. "You know. 'Happily ever after' shit."

Is it really shit? Tony wondered. *And if it's shit, why are you even here?*

Once upon a time, Tony might have agreed with Lucas, but that was before Brody, and before he'd known what it felt like to get his heart smashed. To watch the man he loved walk away and resume his life like Tony had never been part of it. Not only had it hurt like fucking hell, it had also made Tony resolve that someday, he'd have that again, and it wouldn't be with some ungrateful piece of shit who didn't really care about him. He'd have it with someone like Ryan, who gave a *thousand* shits, and who was loyal and true and wasn't going to just casually stab Wyatt in the back because he could.

He'd find a real partner, someone he could love, who loved him back.

Unfortunately, he was ninety-nine point nine percent sure that it was *not* going to be Lucas of the Cute Nose and Ripped Arms.

Wyatt would be disappointed, but secretly, nobody was going to be more disappointed than Tony himself. It was impossible to live in such close quarters with, as Lucas would put it, *all that "happily ever after" shit,* and not crave it for himself.

"It has its moments," Tony said.

"Does Ryan come around the truck often?" Lucas asked, picking at the corner of the label on his beer.

"I don't know how much you know about baseball, but it's pretty fucking crazy, the schedule they keep," Tony said. "He's not around much during the season. Sometimes Wyatt travels with him, and then it's just me."

"You run the truck by yourself?" Lucas questioned, looking surprised.

"I don't usually book us much, if I'm going to be by myself. And sometimes I get a friend or two in town who gives me a hand," Tony said. Hoping, even though he knew Lucas was *not* The One, that he was maybe a tiny bit impressed at how Tony could handle a kitchen, even when it was a really busy kitchen. What he didn't mention was that one of the friends, Jeremy, had just texted him a few months before, telling him he was making the move from Napa to LA permanent. He could work more hours now, Jeremy had said. Was Tony interested in hiring him? Tony was pretty sure he was, but he needed Wyatt's approval first, because that was how they'd figured out how to run the food truck—they did it *together*.

"Ah," Lucas said. "Could use a permanent set of hands, then," he added. So casually that Tony almost missed it. But then Wyatt and Ryan emerged from the kitchen, only slightly disheveled, which meant that Tony might not have to totally disinfect every flat surface this time, and Wyatt said, "Tony will really need your help, Lucas, when I start working on the cookbook and also traveling with Ryan this summer."

Everything shifted into sudden, painful clarity.

"What," Tony stated flatly. "You hired this guy?"

Wyatt shot his brother a lopsided grin. "Sort of? Let's call this . . . sort of an impromptu job interview? But yes, I'm hiring him. *We're* hiring him."

"I don't understand," Tony said. "This isn't a setup?"

Lucas shot him a slanted, knowing look. Maybe it could've still been, but of course Tony had just inserted his foot into his own mouth. Repeatedly.

"It's a job interview," Wyatt said sternly. "Geez, do you *ever* think about anything besides your cock?"

That might've been a fair assessment pre-Brody; Tony had definitely gotten around. He'd had a lot of sex and made zero apologies for that fact. The only thing he felt bad about when he thought about his former way of life was that he'd hurt some people; people who hadn't done a single thing to deserve that pain. But post-Brody?

Tony couldn't remember the last time he'd thought with his cock. He'd actually been surprisingly close this time, but only because Lucas was so goddamn cute, and Tony had been pretty interested in seeing just how ripped he was underneath those clothes.

"Yes," Tony muttered. "You'd be surprised."

"Well, I wouldn't," Wyatt said. "Yes, Lucas is going to be helping you out this summer. I'm gonna be super busy with the cookbook. I won't be able to work many shifts in the truck."

Tony had known it was coming, just the way he knew that this summer was going to be a big one for What a Catch. The food truck scene was really heating up in LA—there were so many opportunities, and most of them were opportunities they weren't taking because they didn't have enough staff. Tony, at least, had the desire, but Wyatt was distracted. Busy. It was something Tony had been dying to discuss with his brother, but he wasn't going to talk about it now, not in front of the guy who was apparently his new employee. He definitely wasn't going to bring up Jeremy now—that could wait til later, til they were alone.

Tony turned to Lucas. "And I'm assuming you have qualifications?"

"Tony," Wyatt warned, "don't be an asshole. I was going to tell you . . . I just got busy."

Probably busy in the sack with his husband, Tony thought. He tried—and succeeded most of the time—to not be jealous of Wyatt. Wyatt was an all-around good guy, a loyal brother, and deserved the happiness he'd found. *I just want a little piece of my own,* Tony thought before he could stop himself, *he doesn't even have to be rich or a professional athlete. He just needs to be . . .* nice.

Nice, after Tony's experience with Brody, was not something he'd ever take for granted again.

"I'm not being an asshole," Tony argued, "I just want to know what I'm dealing with." When he glanced back to Lucas, he'd set his beer down on a side table, and had a look in his eyes that practically screamed, *this isn't worth it! Where's the door?*

"Hey," he continued, taking a step closer to Lucas, and setting a quick reassuring hand on his shoulder. *That's not creepy at all, you finding a way to touch him before he goes running out the door—definitely not even close to creepy.* "Hey, seriously, I know we can be a little . . ." *Overwhelming, uncomfortable, too much to handle.* "We can be a little difficult, but this is going to be good. For us, and for you."

Lucas gave him a look. "You don't even know me; how do you know that?"

I could get to know you, get to know you better. Tony almost said it, but he'd already made a fool out of himself by assuming this was a setup. He wasn't going to make things worse when Lucas had *just* made it crystal clear this was going to be a business-only arrangement.

"Then tell me about your background," Tony said. He glanced over at Wyatt. "Is dinner almost ready?"

Wyatt nodded. "In a few," he said, turning back towards the kitchen. "And we'll be eating outside. Ryan—can you set the table?" Nobody needed any more evidence that Ryan Flores was whipped by his husband than his quick nod of agreement. When he'd first met Ryan, he'd definitely not been the "setting the table" kind of guy, but love, Tony realized, changed you. Realigned your priorities. Sometimes permanently.

"So," Tony repeated, his attention returning to Lucas, "your background?"

"I'm not formally trained either, but I've spent my whole life in kitchens," Lucas said, his jaw jutting out slightly, like he was challenging Tony to dispute that particular fact. "I can prep quick and keep up on the line."

"Then why aren't you lining up to work someplace good?" *Someplace not on four wheels*, Tony mentally edited. The LA food truck scene might be heating up, but the foundation of the valley was the brick-and-mortar restaurants.

"I want to work part-time," Lucas said, that chin growing even more belligerent. "Is that going to be a problem?"

That explained why he was looking at food trucks, not one of the higher-end Los Angeles restaurants—of course there was also Lucas' lack of culinary education, but here, it mattered way less. Lots of chefs worked their way up from the dish room and never went to culinary school. What they didn't do was work part-time.

Food trucks were a lot more flexible in that regard.

"Why part time?" Tony asked. LA was not a cheap place to live, and you definitely couldn't survive on a part-time food truck employee's salary. Obviously he had something else going on; Tony wondered if the something else had anything to do with those ripped arms he was having trouble *not* stealing glances at. Maybe he was some kind of aspiring MMA fighter or maybe even *hotter*, he was into the underground fight club scene. He'd heard rumblings of the intense, no-holds-barred fights, sometimes even held in cages. Tony had a sudden, inflammatory glimpse of Lucas pressing him up against the cage, the metal links digging into his skin.

He shook his head, trying to clear it. It turned out that the very worst kind of setup was a setup that was actually a job interview.

"Do you have a problem with part time?" Lucas demanded, instead of actually answering the question.

The only problem Tony had was that he'd never get to find out if he'd been right, and Lucas of the Cute Nose and Ripped Arms wasn't for him after all. He sighed. "No," he said. "I just wondered. You can keep your secrets, if you want to."

"I do," Lucas said. "It won't interfere with my ability to do the job."

"As long as you show up on time and work hard, I don't give a fuck what you do the rest of the time," Tony said. Managers had said this to him all the time, and he'd *mostly* kept up his end of the bargain. Not always, but then he'd always been easily distracted, and sometimes it hadn't mattered that he'd given his word. Now, Tony looked back on past Tony and was annoyed despite himself. Why had he been such a fuckup? Why hadn't he made the most of the skills he'd worked his ass off for?

"Good," Lucas said, and it seemed the two of them had finally agreed on something.

"Dinner," Wyatt called out from the kitchen. "Come and get it."

Tony looked at him. "Do you want to stay for dinner?" Suddenly he wasn't sure that had been part of why Wyatt had asked Lucas to stop by. He'd only assumed because Lucas had come by around dinnertime.

Lucas shrugged. "I've got someplace to be," he said. "But thanks. And thanks for the beer." He drained it and set it back on the side table. "Wyatt has my number. You can text me if you want to get in touch."

For professional reasons only went unsaid. Tony inwardly grimaced. He'd been complaining about Wyatt's awkward game, but it turned out that nobody's was worse than his own. "Sure. And if you want to try the truck out this week, I've got a couple of shifts you could fill."

"Yeah, I think we could work something out. Text me the schedule," Lucas said, and then he was gone, exiting through the door like he was afraid Tony would drag him back by his teeth. And yeah, that would've been fun as fuck, but Tony knew better than to get involved with someone (*again*) who didn't give a crap.

After disposing of Lucas' empty beer bottle and grabbing himself a second one, Tony wandered out onto the patio attached to the back of the house.

"Hey," Wyatt said, setting a platter of ribs onto the table, "where's Lucas?"

"He left," Tony said. "I think we scared him off. You with your casual interview tactic and me with . . . *well*, you know."

"Your insistence that I was trying to set you up on a date?" Wyatt asked, amused. Ryan appeared on the doorstep, balancing a bowl of potato salad and another filled with some of the homemade quick pickles that Wyatt was famous for.

"Yeah, I think that was more of it," Ryan agreed as he set the bowls down onto the table and took a seat next to his husband. "He probably thought you were a real creep."

"Thanks," Tony said shortly, because that was *exactly* what he'd been afraid of. Looking like some kind of bro horndog who couldn't keep it in his pants. "But it must not have scared him off too badly, because he said he'd take some shifts this week, try to figure out if he's a good fit."

"Great," Wyatt said enthusiastically. "That works out because I have a bunch of cookbook meetings this week and I couldn't work, anyway."

"Oh, so you're going to leave me alone with him? Are we sure that's a good idea?" Tony asked sarcastically as he grabbed a few ribs and dropped them onto his plate.

"It'll be fine," Wyatt said. "Unless you were planning on accosting him during his shift?"

Tony rolled his eyes. "Besides," he said, "I was going to ask Jeremy to cover, anyway. He said he wanted more shifts, that he would be spending more time in LA. I thought we'd just hire him on semi-permanently? But then you brought this new guy in."

He'd actually really wanted to hire Jeremy, and he'd sworn that Wyatt had known that, but then he must've forgotten because he'd still hired Lucas. Tony trusted Jeremy, knew him from way back when he'd worked at the Napa Tavern, before he'd moved to LA. Lucas? Could've been anyone off the street.

"I . . . I don't really know about Jeremy," Wyatt said cautiously.

"He's sketchy," Ryan added, even though Ryan probably wouldn't know sketchy if it ran up and punched him in the face.

"Seriously?" Tony said, more than a little shocked. "Jeremy? Sketchy? Are we talking about the same person? Never speaks? Always on time? Does everything he's asked to do?"

"I don't know," Wyatt said with a shrug as he scooped up potato salad. "It's just a weird feeling, like a prickling on the back of my neck when he's around."

"He's so quiet," Ryan added. "Sometimes I feel like he wants to take me into a dark alley and skin me."

"Oh my god," Tony said. "You two talked about this." It was stupid to even say it, because of course they had. Wyatt and Ryan talked about *everything*. They were totally *that* couple, and Tony would've hated them on principle, except they were actually really fucking cute, and Tony was happy his little brother had ended up with someone who was so great.

And someone who could get them free Dodgers tickets. That part was definitely an extra benefit and not any kind of requirement, but it sure could be nice.

"Of course we talked about this," Wyatt said. "That guy's been giving me the creeps from the very beginning."

"Why is this the first I'm hearing about it?" Tony asked testily, tossing a gnawed rib bone onto his plate with more force than was really required.

"I don't know, because he was just a temp, and I thought he'd eventually move on."

"And you'd never need to tell me," Tony said. "Because you knew I liked him."

"Honestly, you kinda like *everyone*," Ryan added.

Tony wanted to deny this, but Ryan was annoyingly right, and so he kept his mouth shut.

"Seriously, just give Lucas a chance. He seems like a good kid. And he could use the job."

"The *part-time* job?" Tony questioned.

"Yeah," Wyatt said sheepishly. "I knew about that. That's why I thought it'd be a good fit."

"How did you even meet this 'kid'?" Tony asked.

He watched as his brother and Ryan exchanged looks and knew he wasn't going to like the answer before Wyatt even opened his mouth. "Uh, the restaurant supply store?"

"You met him at the *store*? And just *gave him a job?*" And they thought Jeremy was creepy! Tony couldn't fucking believe this bull-shit.

"Tony," Wyatt said calmly. "He's a good guy. I checked his references, and everything."

"Oh, and *everything*," Tony snarked back. "Jeremy didn't even *need* references, because I know him. I trust him."

"I know you do, and I hope he never gives you a reason to *not* trust him," Wyatt said, "but the truck is half mine, and I want to set us up for success this summer. I think Lucas is going to be an integral part of that. I'm sorry I didn't tell you he was coming or that he was coming for a job, but I like the guy."

Tony still thought this was total bullshit. Three years ago, when he and Wyatt had barely seen eye to eye, when they could barely be in the same room without their mutual animosity flaring out of control, he might have said so, *again*, but they'd learned how to be better brothers, and even better friends since then. And then there was Nana; it was hard to push Wyatt hard, when Tony remembered some of her last coherent words to him so well—"Take care of your brother, Tony, he needs you. And you need him." It had absolutely been a guilt trip of a trap, and Tony had walked right into it and hadn't left because how could he? Maybe Wyatt was settled and happy and things were good, but Tony had also learned in the last few years that a really great place to be was right by his brother's side.

So instead of saying a word, Tony fell silent and ate his dinner, trying not to sulk, and mostly succeeding. And that was fine, because Ryan had clearly been looking forward to performing, with hand motions and expressive gestures, what had led to his walk-off hit this afternoon. And Tony loved Ryan too, and not just because he was rich or a professional baseball player, and so he let him have his moment.

After, when he and Wyatt were cleaning up, he brought it up again, for hopefully the last time. "If I'm going to hire Lucas," Tony said as he scrubbed down a pot in the sink, "then I'm going to hire Jeremy, too."

Wyatt gave him a single piercing look and then turned back to the leftover ribs he was wrapping up in plastic. "If you want to," he said. "The truck's half yours, you know. I don't get to make all the decisions."

"I know," Tony said. He'd been totally prepared to drag out their partnership agreement, so he was pleased that Wyatt had brought it up first. "I just want . . . I want us to agree."

Wyatt gave him a tap on the shoulder with his fist as he passed by him on the way to the fridge. "You really are getting to be a softy," he said. "But yeah, me too."

"It's just . . . better that way," Tony said. And maybe he *was* becoming a softy, or maybe this was how he'd always been, deep down. He'd just tried to hide it for a long time with black leather and fast cars and too many girlfriends and not showing up to work when he was supposed to. But the truth was, his heart had never really been in any of those things. Well, *maybe* the fast cars. And the leather. Those were pretty badass.

Marco, their younger brother, was headed down that road now, and Tony knew he wasn't the only one concerned about him.

"Agreed," Wyatt said. "Okay, hire Jeremy too. But keep on eye on him, okay?"

"Sure, of course, like I wouldn't." Tony would, because he took his job seriously, took the truck seriously, but he was honestly more worried about Lucas. The guy looked like he could fucking bench-press a semi and Wyatt was worried about mousy, quiet Jeremy? Something about that just didn't add up.

"Good," Wyatt said, and pulled him into a quick, soapy hug. "I trust you, you know."

"I know," Tony said, and while maybe Three Years Ago Tony wouldn't have appreciated that *at all*, he appreciated it now. He hadn't always had Wyatt's trust, but he did now, and he wasn't going to fuck it up.

CHAPTER TWO

LUCAS WASN'T SURE WHAT he'd been expecting of the food truck, but this definitely wasn't it.

He'd met Wyatt at the local restaurant supply store, when they'd both wanted the last set of hotel pans on the shelf. You couldn't live in LA and not know who Wyatt Flores was—or his husband. They were ubiquitous, especially if you had any interest in either the food or the sports scene, and Lucas was into both, so when he turned down the aisle and spotted Wyatt Flores standing next to the hotel pans, blond hair mussed and a frown on his face as he considered the selection, he'd known exactly who he was. There'd been a definite part of him that had thought, *maybe this is it, maybe this might be your big break,* and another, far less mercenary part of him that had thought, *maybe he could use a friend.* It was ridiculous, because Wyatt Flores probably had friends coming out his ass, but he'd still given him a friendly smile and said, "Are you going to get those?"

Wyatt had looked up from the shelf, and smiled back, so friendly that you'd never guess he was rich and married to someone who was even richer. He'd heard that about Wyatt. That he was friendly and nice, and amenable to getting involved in charity events, speaking engagements, culinary demonstrations, anything that might help showcase his skills and also bring attention to a platform that needed it.

"Are these all the pans they have?" he'd asked, and Wyatt had smiled again. "I'm afraid so," he'd replied. "You wanna split them?"

That mercenary voice in the back of his head—the one that said, *do it, do it, do it! You might get to work slightly less insane hours if you say yes*—had been loud enough he hadn't been able to ignore it. Also, it wasn't like splitting the last set of hotel pans in the store, two for each of them, would mean anything in the grand scheme of things. Wyatt wasn't promising friendship or loyalty or even any monetary assistance. Still, after they'd checked out, and Lucas had handed over a handful of creased bills to the blond man, he'd surprised Lucas by striking up a conversation.

"What do you do?" he'd asked.

"A lot of things. I've done some cooking on the line," Lucas had been able to answer, honestly. "But mostly right now I'm looking to rent some commercial kitchen space for my energy bar business. Trying to take things to the next level."

Wyatt had nodded seriously, like this was also now an important move to him. Even though he'd had no idea what it had taken for Lucas to align the planets to even get *this* far. "You make energy bars?"

"Good for you, while actually tasting good." Lucas grinned.

"I've got a food truck," Wyatt had said casually, and it wasn't like Lucas *wasn't* aware of it. He was. He knew it was often parked by Dodger Stadium. He knew they catered a lot of the team's charity events. "It's not big, but it might do." Wyatt hesitated. "And I've got a part-time opening, actually, helping out with the truck this summer. You interested?"

Lucas' eyes had narrowed. He'd wondered if one would be available without the other. Would the tiny food truck even have enough space for him to work? It might, but Lucas already knew if it was free, he would find a way to make it work.

"What's the job?"

"Helping my brother run the truck, mainly. He's really good, the menu's solid, but he needs help, and"—Wyatt flushed—"I'm really bad at saying no to people, which means I'm overbooked."

That was a state of affairs that Lucas understood a little too well. "Salary?" he'd asked.

Wyatt had named a very reasonable hourly rate, and then added, sealing the deal, "I'll throw the kitchen rental in, free of charge. Just use it in the mornings and late at night, okay?"

They'd exchanged a quick handshake and then numbers, and agreed that Lucas would come over the next evening to meet his older brother, Tony. He was the one who apparently ran the food truck.

A quick Google search while Lucas had taken a lunch break the next day had yielded very few results. Tony had an Instagram that he barely ever used. One of the last pictures on it was of a tiny pansexual flag tattoo, nestled right next to a bright red broken heart. So, Tony Blake was queer like his brother was. That was interesting. Lucas didn't quite know what to make of the heart, but the one thing he *was* sure of was that he'd never be dumb enough—or have the time—to devote himself to a relationship that might break his heart. Hookups and *only* hookups, that was how Lucas Barnes blew off steam, and he didn't see that changing anytime soon.

There weren't any selfies on Tony's Instagram, so he'd been slightly surprised when he'd walked into Wyatt and Ryan Flores' house and Tony had been standing there. Both brothers were tall, but that was where any and all similarities ended. Wyatt was the typical Cali boy, blond hair, blue eyes, tanned skin, way-too-white teeth. He was cute, but *obvious*. He wasn't the kind of guy that Lucas would have felt compelled to watch, if they were in the gym together, or turn his head to look at if he'd seen him walking down the street. But Tony? That was a different story. Tony was lean, his hair long and dark, and his eyes were an intense deep blue, and when he smiled, his whole face lit up. He was arresting and captivating, and then he opened his mouth, and Lucas thought for a split second, *I should leave, I should just get out of here, before I do something I'll regret.*

Even worse, Tony seemed to think Lucas' arrival was something it wasn't, and Lucas inconveniently remembered both the pansexual flag and the broken heart.

He'd escaped, *barely*, and then later that night, Tony had texted him with the hours for this week's shifts. He'd kept it strictly professional, but Lucas' fingers had still hovered over the keyboard, wondering if he should say something else. Say something that he'd absolutely, one hundred percent regret later.

But he'd shoved the phone away, and gone for a hardcore workout, pushing himself further than he usually did, hoping that it would help keep the way Tony's eyes crinkled near the edges when he smiled, out of his mind.

It didn't quite work, but then, by the time he fell into bed, he was so exhausted it didn't matter anyway. He was out like a light.

The next afternoon was his first shift at the truck, and he showed up expecting one thing—to constantly fight the attraction humming between him and Tony—and getting something else entirely.

The truck itself was shiny stainless steel, brightly painted with the name, and it appeared to be friendly and welcoming. Inside, the atmosphere was a little chillier.

"Hey," Tony said brusquely as Lucas stepped inside. "Glad you're here." He didn't sound glad at all, and if Wyatt hadn't promised him free—*free!*—commercial kitchen space, Lucas would have walked out and not looked back. Well, maybe he'd have looked back a *little*. It was just hard to be in the same general vicinity as Tony and *not* look.

You're not here to look, you're here to work, he told himself sternly. Usually the reminder it was not playtime was enough to keep Lucas focused. He'd worked hard from the moment he'd been old enough to, and he was close enough to see the fruits of his labor paying off, that usually was all the reminder it took. But Tony was another kind of distraction entirely.

Today he was wearing a pair of loose cargo shorts, emphasizing the long leanness of his legs and exposing well-defined calf muscles that Lucas wanted to nibble on a little bit, and a t-shirt. It wasn't the kind of outfit that would have normally made Lucas look at anyone twice. But the t-shirt was tight in all the right places. Tony wasn't ripped; he clearly didn't work out like Lucas did, but he was undeniably fit and his hair was fucking stunning, and those eyes? Lucas was dying to see what they'd look like, fluttering closed as pleasure overtook him.

It was a huge problem.

The second, slightly less huge problem? Standing next to Tony, eyes covetous and hand fluttering like it was just about to settle on one of those muscled forearms and *grip*.

"This is Jeremy," Tony continued, "he's our other part-time employee."

Jeremy's reception was even chillier than Tony's. "Nice to meet you," he said, obviously not meaning a word of it. Lucas wondered if Tony knew that his other employee had a massive crush on him, and also that he seemed to be fairly possessive. But Tony was one of those guys who seemed like he didn't catch many of the undercurrents in a room—normally Lucas might have written him off as dumb or oblivious, but there was a fierce intelligence in his face, and that obliviousness only weirdly seemed to add to his charm.

"Great," Lucas said, even though he didn't mean it either. *Free kitchen space,* he reminded himself again. *Fucking* free. Only something he'd wanted, and dreamt of, and worked for, *forever.*

"Let's get started," Tony said. Normally Lucas would have appreciated how Tony wanted to get down to business. He didn't have time to hang around, or goof off, or perform some kind of ridiculous idle social experiment in chitchat, but something about Tony's brusqueness today bothered him.

It's because you want him to like *you, like he did yesterday.*

Lucas brushed the thought aside. He really, *really* didn't have the time to deal with that kind of fairytale, "happily ever after" bullshit. He was here to do a job, and he'd do it, even though Jeremy kept shooting him weird glares. It was no longer as charming that Tony seemed oblivious to Jeremy's . . . *weirdness.* Lucas didn't want to keep calling it that, but there was just something *off* about this dude.

"This is the menu," Tony continued, pointing to a piece of paper tacked up on one of the gleaming stainless steel cabinets above their head. Lucas scanned it, and none of the items surprised him. The collection of burgers and sandwiches and tacos were just as Tony had described the night before. But . . . *seriously,* Lucas thought, *no vegetarian or vegan options? Who were these guys? Cavemen?*

"Hey," Lucas said before he could decide he was being stupid and potentially throwing away his fucking *free* commercial kitchen space, "you guys don't seem to have either a vegetarian or a vegan option here."

Tony stared at him like he'd grown a second head—not mad exactly, but definitely confused. "What?"

"A vegetarian or vegan option?" Lucas repeated. This wasn't fucking rocket science; this was *LA*. How long had Tony been here, anyway?

"Are you going to bring your hipster bullshit here?" Jeremy asked belligerently, which was more than a little nuts. First off, it wasn't *his* menu, and second off, a hipster? Lucas almost laughed, but didn't because he was on thin enough ice as it was.

"A hipster?" Lucas said slowly. He glanced down at himself. He was wearing something very close to what both Tony and Jeremy were wearing—an old t-shirt, emblazoned with a local punk band whose shows he'd gone to when he was younger and he'd had the time and the money, and a pair of ripped jean shorts, paired with his favorite pair of old, stained Converse. He'd doodled a rainbow on the toecap of one, and Lucas stared at it. "Sorry," he said, "no bow ties or black-rimmed glasses or self-important opinions here."

Jeremy made a scoffing noise. "Are *you* a vegan?"

"Actually, no," Lucas said honestly, wondering why Tony was just standing there, *staring*, like suddenly Lucas was a different fucking person. "I try to watch what I eat. But I know the food truck scene here pretty well, and people are gonna want both of those—vegetarian *and* vegan options."

"No," Tony said resolutely, finally abandoning his silence. "The menu stays."

"But . . ." Lucas began to argue, but the look on Tony's face shut him up. He was already on thin ice, and it was getting progressively thinner.

"The menu stays," Tony repeated, and Lucas shut his mouth because nobody wanted *his* opinion. It wasn't the first time, and it wouldn't be the last. This was one of the biggest reasons why Lucas worked so hard—eventually he would be his own fucking boss, and nobody would get to tell him to shut up ever again.

"*So,*" Tony continued, "this is the menu. We sometimes run a special, but mostly it stays the same. I have prep lists here; I like to get totally prepped for the event before we ever get to the event space, because sometimes . . ." He trailed off. "Well, sometimes things are a little unorganized. I always want to be sure we're all set before we show up."

Lucas kind of thought Tony was an idiot—the vegetarian thing was ridiculous, honestly—but this was good. Tony's clear dedication to organization was the first inkling that this wouldn't just be painful from start to finish.

"The bins are all marked with what we're going to use them for," Tony said, indicating scribbled-writing-on-masking-tape labels that had been stuck on the stacked bins next to him. "I'm going to prep the pulled pork, Jeremy will take the fish, and Lucas, since you like vegetables so much, you can take all that prep." Tony said it with a glimmer of a smile, but Lucas wasn't dumb. He'd been around kitchens long enough to know that he was not only being put in his place, he was being deliberately stuck with the worst job. Maybe he would've been anyway—Jeremy had worked with Tony before, and Lucas was brand new to the truck—but it still stung.

This is why you work so hard, he reminded himself. Of course he also realized that working for himself basically meant doing every single job, even the really shitty ones. But it was different, doing them yourself, when it meant you were working towards something bigger and better. It wasn't just your boss being an asshole.

And Tony might not *really* be an asshole, but he was edging dangerously closer to that territory, and Lucas was really fucking glad he hadn't done something stupid and texted him last night like he'd wanted to.

"Salsas first," Tony said, indicating the flats of fresh vegetables set in the corner before handing him a whole Leaning Tower of Pisa of plastic bins. "We'll see how good your knife skills are."

"Fine," Lucas said, and Tony glanced over, apprehension on his face. "They're fine," Lucas amended. "I can chop with the best of them. Small, even dice, I'm assuming?"

Tony nodded, looking like he wanted to say something else. Apologize, maybe? But then the look was gone, and Jeremy was calling him over to talk about the fish that had been delivered.

"Recipes are written out here," Tony said, pointing at a bunch of scribbled pages stuck up on the wall in front of him before he turned away. "Let me know if you need anything else."

"Sure thing," Lucas said. He pulled out his roll of knives, picked his favorite one, sharpened it quickly, and got to work.

Usually he could lose himself in the reassuring, calming rhythm of prep, but this time, he felt uneasy. Like someone was staring at him. But every single time he looked up, Jeremy was bent over the fish and Tony was absorbed in browning several huge pork shoulders.

Finally, annoyed with himself for being so jumpy, he pulled his AirPods out of the pocket of his shorts, one of the few indulgent personal purchases he'd made over the years, and started up the latest episode of one of his favorite podcasts. It helped to distract him just enough, even though the fine hairs on the back of his neck kept prickling, like someone was definitely staring at him. It was probably Jeremy, Lucas decided, and if he let the other guy get to him, he would never be able to keep this job, and the free space Wyatt had promised. He'd just have to learn to deal with Jeremy's odd behavior. Maybe as soon as he figured out that Lucas wasn't interested in Tony, he'd leave him alone.

Except that you're not really not *interested in Tony*, that sly voice in the back of his head reminded him.

Maybe Tony wasn't even single, maybe he and Jeremy were already hooking up, which was why Jeremy kept glaring at him like he was some kind of interloper.

That thought wasn't a pleasant one, and frankly, made him think way less of Tony. Jeremy was kind of cute, Lucas supposed, if you could ignore the weird looks and the way he stared at Tony like he owned him. He was about Lucas' height, with sandy blond hair and brown eyes. *Unobtrusive*, Lucas thought, *you'd never remember he was there after he leaves a room.* Unlike Tony, who seemed larger than life, and even though his actions were methodical and efficient, as he browned the meat and then set it into the pressure cooker, filling it with various spices and sauces, not even glancing once at the recipe posted above him. He'd clearly done this a bunch of times before, and that made sense, because this *was* his truck.

Lucas returned to his chopping, breaking down a ton of pineapples, then mangos, then red bell peppers, and finally moving on to the jalapenos. There was a box of gloves on the counter, but he didn't bother with them, quickly slicing the peppers open, and then emptying their seeds and membranes into the garbage with a twist of the tip of his knife.

He was in such a groove, seeding the jalapenos, that he didn't even notice when Tony came over. He jumped when Tony touched him briefly on the shoulder. It reminded him a little of the night before, when Tony had touched him, trying to reassure him. But this touch had been so quick, like it almost hadn't happened. Like Tony was afraid, like he didn't want to touch Lucas too much.

Lucas pulled out one of his earbuds. "What's up?" he asked.

"You've done this before," Tony said, pointing to Lucas' sharp knife, poised to dig out the guts of another jalapeno.

"I told you I've done this for a long time," Lucas said. He was annoyed—it was either because Tony didn't trust that he knew what the fuck he was doing or because he hadn't wanted to touch him.

"Yeah, but lots of people say that, and then it turns out they're . . . not very good," Tony said. "But you're good."

It was faint praise, but at least it was something. Tony could've booted him off the truck, and then he'd be back to square one, trying to find something cheap and clean and certified for food prep. But this space, while small, was really well organized, and Lucas knew it would be perfect. If he could just keep his fucking mouth shut about the menu and avoid any other temptations to text Tony something totally unprofessional.

He's your boss. Plus, he's probably fucking Jeremy.

It was a real statement on how much Lucas hated the chain of command that the latter bothered him way more than the former.

"Thanks," Lucas said shortly. *You're not here to be friends.*

"You didn't wear the gloves," Tony said, surprising Lucas. He'd seemed averse to idle chatter when Lucas had arrived, but *now* he wanted to talk? Lucas would never fucking understand people.

"I didn't," Lucas said, reaching in his pocket and pausing the podcast on his phone. They were having a particularly good conversation on risk versus reward, and Lucas didn't want to miss it while he was trying to suck up to his new boss. "Waste of time."

"And you know well enough to not touch your face until you've washed your hands."

Lucas looked up at the guy, befuddled. "Doesn't everyone fucking know that?" You made that mistake once in your life—and you never, ever made it again.

Tony laughed, and Lucas' heart literally hiccupped at the way he looked—bright and happy and way too fascinating. No wonder Jeremy walked around half the time like he wanted to plant a flag that proclaimed "Property of Jeremy" on Tony's back—anyone who saw this guy would want him, desperately. He was seriously dangerous.

"You'd be surprised," Tony said, and leaned closer, close enough that Lucas could smell the roasted pork smell hanging around him, and underneath, the citrus of his cologne, and even deeper under that, the spicy scent of man.

Lucas swallowed hard.

"Maybe I would be," Lucas said, even though he couldn't imagine anyone working in a professional kitchen and *not* knowing about the searing pain of pepper oil in an eye. It didn't even feel like idle chitchat anymore, the kind of bullshit gossip he was used to from hanging around kitchens for over ten years. It felt way more intimate than that, even though they were technically talking about food.

"Hey, Tony," Jeremy said, breaking the mood that had fallen between Tony and Lucas. Lucas turned away as Tony went to see what Jeremy needed, viciously twisting his knife, and sending another shower of seeds and jalapeno guts into the trash. If he'd needed any more evidence that Jeremy was unhappy about Lucas being a third wheel, that was it right there. He'd been watching, waiting for the moment that Tony went over to Lucas, and then had immediately needed him to come back.

It was stupid, and Lucas was annoyed that he was even annoyed by it. He didn't creep on another guy's hookup. There were so many guys out there, and if Lucas wanted one, all he needed was to open one of his many apps and find one for the night. And if Tony wanted Jeremy, he definitely wasn't going to stand in their way.

Still, instead of finishing up the jalapenos, or even more smartly, restarting his podcast, Lucas watched as Tony walked over to where Jeremy was prepping the fish for the day. And it was crystal fucking clear that there'd been no issue—at least not with the fish itself.

"I told you," Tony said patiently—way more patient than Lucas would've been, "we want these to all be about the same size. Same thickness, same width."

"They are," Jeremy retorted stubbornly, but Lucas already knew that while Tony might be more understanding with a guy he was hooking up with, he was also a perfectionist in his kitchen. He might talk about Wyatt being the exacting one, but it was clear Tony ran this show, and he ran it really well. Everything was put away in its place. Every surface was spotless. The produce was good quality, the meat and fish had seemed to be the same, at least from where Lucas was standing. The only one who wasn't living up to expectations was Jeremy, and Lucas turned away. Jeremy was Tony's problem to deal with—all he had to do was prep the veggies.

He clicked the play button on his phone with a knuckle and fell back into his same rhythm. A few minutes later, he was running his knife along the last of the peppers, mincing them into a fine, even dice.

When he looked up, Tony hadn't come back, but he was definitely still looking at him, as he tended the flank steaks he was currently grilling. But Jeremy wasn't in the truck anymore.

He finished up the last of the dicing, and then brought his knife over to the small sink, scrubbing his hands carefully, and then cleaning his knife. "Where's Jeremy?" he asked casually, even as he knew just how bad an idea it was to get involved in what was very likely a lover's spat.

"He took a break," Tony said. "I think he's grabbing a smoke outside."

Smoking was not terribly unusual for kitchen workers, but Lucas had never picked it up. His body was a freaking temple, and he liked to keep it in perfect form. "Ah," he said, and wondered, even though he really shouldn't, if Tony was a smoker, too. He hadn't smelled it on him earlier, but that didn't mean anything necessarily.

He'd meant to sound neutral—not getting involved, not this time, and not ever—but his tone came out nothing like that.

"Yeah," Tony said with a heavy sigh. "I'm going to have to try to fix the fish. Really, Jeremy should."

Don't do it, don't offer, Lucas screamed at himself, but he was already opening his mouth to do it, anyway. "I can fix it," he said.

"No," Tony said, "not that I don't appreciate it, but Jeremy needs to figure out how to fix his own mistakes."

It was exactly what the best chefs would have said, and Lucas' opinion of Tony rose a little higher—and it was already getting way too fucking high. It was the way he smiled, with his entire face, the way it lit him up from the inside out.

"Are you sure you didn't take a turn at one of those big-shot places?" Lucas asked casually as he wiped down his cutting surface. "That's kind of a Bastian Aquino sort of attitude."

Tony grinned, and it hit Lucas right in the solar plexus. "My brother worked for him."

"Wyatt?" Lucas said. He'd known that, of course, and that was why he'd brought up the Bastard. But then again, Aquino *was* notorious. It wasn't like Lucas was trying to lure Tony into another one of those quasi-flirtations. No way, he was definitely not going to be that stupid.

"Yeah," Tony said. "I've got another brother, Marco, too, but he's into cars, not food."

"That's cool." Lucas turned towards him. "I'm done with the salsas," he said. "What do you want me to do next?"

"Already?" Tony sounded surprised. Maybe Jeremy had been assigned to veg prep before, and he'd done a shitty job of it, which was why Tony kept expecting Lucas' standards to be so goddamn low.

Lucas shrugged. "I said I knew what I was doing," he reminded Tony.

"Right, you did." Tony grimaced. "I just . . . well, I'm glad you're on the team." He hadn't seemed particularly glad this morning, so Lucas took that as a good sign. Of course, it was clear it was not going to be very difficult to run circles around Jeremy. Anyone even semi-competent could've done that in their sleep.

"Me too," Lucas said, and discovered he meant it. Maybe the menu wasn't perfect, and maybe Jeremy sucked, and maybe he was a little too tempted to get into Tony's shorts, but this could be a good gig for him. And not just because of the free kitchen space Wyatt had offered.

The door opened, and Jeremy climbed back into the truck. "J," Tony said, his voice not softening even a little, "fix the goddamn fish. And don't fuck it up again. That shit's expensive."

Gross, Lucas thought, *he even has a pet name for him. I fucking hate those.*

Jeremy nodded sullenly and went back to his station.

"And you," Tony said, pointing at Lucas, "can help me with these steaks. And then we need to sauté the veg for the cheesesteaks."

Jeremy shot him a glare, and Lucas knew that was the job he'd wanted to do next, probably because it meant working more closely with Tony. Shit, he'd just painted a target on his back. Maybe this *wouldn't* be a great gig for him after all—no matter how hot he thought Tony was.

"Sure, boss," Lucas said, and enjoyed, probably way too much, how Jeremy frowned.

CHAPTER THREE

"You're home early," Wyatt said, looking up from his spot on the couch. He had his laptop out, balanced on his knees, and the TV was tuned to one of the Dodgers' away games, the volume muted.

It wasn't early; it was just past ten o'clock, but Tony supposed it was early for them, considering that they usually shut the truck down after nine and cleanup almost always took more than an hour, because both of them were semi-fanatical about making sure everything was perfect when they closed up.

Tony flopped down on the opposite couch. He kinda wanted a beer—it had been a *long* day—but once he was sitting down, he really didn't feel like getting back up again. "I had Jeremy *and* Lucas today," he told Wyatt. "And they got the truck cleaned up in no time. It practically fucking sparkled." Truthfully, it had been mostly Lucas. Tony briefly considered telling his brother he'd annoyingly been right about the guy, but Wyatt could already be insufferable. He wasn't going to give his head any reason to get bigger.

"It worked out okay, then," Wyatt said, looking up from the laptop. He was typing in a Word document, probably working on recipes and ideas for the cookbook he'd recently signed a contract to write. He hadn't wanted to do it, but Tony had encouraged it. "It'll bring a higher profile to the truck," he'd cajoled. "It's practically free publicity."

Of course Tony hadn't taken into consideration that the cookbook would also mean that Wyatt was basically unavailable to work for the summer, and he'd end up not only hiring Jeremy, but a stranger, too.

Tony didn't know which circumstance was most frustrating—that he'd had to welcome Lucas, who was annoyingly attractive, into their tight-knit circle, or that Jeremy, having finally gotten the job he'd been begging for, had spent the whole day basically fucking up.

"It worked out fine," Tony said.

Wyatt raised an eyebrow. "Just fine?"

"Lucas is good. He knows his shit," Tony said. He really, really didn't want to give Wyatt an opportunity to tell him *I told you so* about Jeremy. He'd been better about prep when they'd worked together. Maybe he'd just been nervous and unsettled because Lucas was there, and because it wasn't just him and Tony, like he'd expected. He'd calm down and get his shit in order, and if he didn't, then Tony would make *sure* he did. The one thing he couldn't stand was a slouch he knew could do better. Maybe because a few years ago, that had been him.

"I'm not even a little bit surprised," Wyatt admitted. "He acted like he had his shit together."

The biggest problem about Lucas, the problem that Tony really didn't want to share with his brother, was that he liked him, probably too much. But after his first disastrous assumption that Wyatt had been setting them up, Tony had promised himself firmly that he would keep things professional. Yeah, maybe there was a cute little rainbow doodled on the toe of Lucas' Converse, and he'd barely blinked when Wyatt and Ryan had swallowed each other's tongues in front of him, but that meant nothing. He might not even like guys. And even if he did, that definitely did not mean that he liked *Tony*.

"He also showed up and immediately wanted to change the menu. First fucking thing," Tony complained. That was maybe a little unfair, because as soon as he'd shut down Lucas' suggestion, he'd been unable to do anything *but* take a closer look at the menu, and he'd realized the exact same thing—somehow when they'd revamped for the summer, he and Wyatt had totally forgotten to put a veg option down. They'd had one earlier, in the winter, and in the fall, and even two the summer before. But Wyatt's new cookbook was about grilling and different ways to prepare meat, and since he was using the truck as a sort of proving ground, they'd gotten carried away and spaced on offering an option for people who weren't interested in that.

It was really stupid, and Tony had felt embarrassed that they'd made such a rookie mistake. How could you ask someone to listen to you, and follow you, when you couldn't even get the fucking basics right? He would have to figure out a way to correct it somehow and do it without admitting to Lucas he'd been right all along.

That was going to be a challenge.

"What did he want to change?" Wyatt asked mildly. This was why he'd never have been a great head chef; he was way too laid-back and had so little ego, Tony often wondered how he'd ever managed to go toe-to-toe with Bastian Aquino.

"He pointed out that we missed a veg option," Tony said with a grumble.

Tony watched as his brother mentally perused the menu and noticed the moment he realized that Lucas was right.

"Oh shit," Wyatt said. "We're gonna have to fix that."

"I've got it under control," Tony said.

"Are you sure?" Wyatt asked, which was annoying. Yeah, Tony liked their collaborations, but he was totally capable of coming up with some vegetarian options for the menu on his own. He'd work on it tomorrow, in fact, because the truck wasn't booked for tomorrow, and he could use some time in the kitchen, *alone*, to sort his fucking thoughts out.

Like, why he was so hung up on Lucas when he didn't seem even vaguely interested in Tony.

He'd already sworn to himself he would *not* do this again—pine after some guy who didn't give a crap about him—and so he was more than a little perturbed that the very first chance he got, he'd headed right down that same path. What was wrong with him? After being the one who did the leaving for his entire adult life, was he now cursed to always see something he wanted, but couldn't have?

"I'm sure," Tony said. "I'll work on it tomorrow."

"Okay," Wyatt said. "And that reminds me, I'm going to add a veg section to the cookbook. Yeah, it's supposed to be about meat, but what about sides? What if you have a vegetarian friend? What if you have someone watching their cholesterol? I need to diversify."

"Ugh," Tony said.

"What? You think I'm wrong?" It meant something that the first time tonight that Wyatt had sounded even mildly concerned was at the possibility that he and Tony might not agree on something. And on *his* cookbook, no less.

"No, of course not. You know you're right. I know you're right. Even Lucas knows you're right." Tony lifted himself off the couch and went to the fridge. "You want a beer?"

"Yeah, sure," Wyatt said. And reached for the remote, flicking the TV off. The Dodgers were up 9 to 2 in the eighth inning, and clearly he didn't feel any husbandly obligation to continue watching. "Why don't we take them outside? I've been cooped up all day in meetings and then working on some ideas."

"Sure," Tony said, grabbing two bottles from the mini fridge in the living room. "Let's go out to the patio."

Wyatt followed him out the back door, and maybe on another night, a night when he didn't feel so exhausted, maybe he'd have lit a fire in the fire pit built into their patio, but for tonight, he just sat back on one of the Adirondack chairs and popped open his beer.

"The new neighbors moved in," Wyatt said, craning his neck to see to the next property over. The house had been empty as long as Tony had lived there, but recently it had finally been sold and now a new couple was moving in. They didn't know much about them yet, despite Wyatt's curiosity and Ryan's digging.

"You should plant some new trees," Tony said, leaning back and closing his eyes. It hadn't been the work that had really exhausted him, but the prior night, when he'd tossed and turned and wondered if he'd made the right choice in inviting Lucas to work at the truck. Letting Wyatt get his way, when all evidence pointed to this being something he should've stood his ground on. Lucas turning out to be wildly efficient and a total pro should have relaxed him, but instead he felt even more keyed up than normal. Maybe it was the way Lucas held himself aloof, always sticking in his earbuds when he didn't need to be listening. The way he seemed to not want to talk to Tony at all, even though Tony had done his best to keep a professional distance, to not be a fucking creep.

"Why?" Wyatt asked, popping open his own beer.

"So you don't have to potentially see your new neighbors," Tony said. *"Duh."*

"There's those bushes there, though," Wyatt said, gesturing at the fence-height bushes that mostly blocked the back of the neighbors' yard from Wyatt and Ryan's own.

"Trust me, if they suck, that is not going to be enough," Tony said. He knew something about shitty neighbors, though all his experience was from cheap-ass apartment complexes, where the walls were paper thin, and it felt like you were living *with* a bunch of inconsiderate strangers. But Ryan was rich, he didn't need to put up with any of that shit; he could block them out, and he *should*.

"Okay," Wyatt said uneasily. "We can plant some trees. I'll talk to Ryan when he gets back."

"Good." Tony took another drink of his beer, mostly satisfied that not only would Wyatt and Ryan continue to have their peace and quiet, he'd get his. Frankly, after having to watch Jeremy like a fucking hawk today, he deserved it.

"So," Wyatt said, breaking the silence that had fallen between them. "You wanna talk about Lucas?"

Tony rolled his eyes. "Why would I want to talk about Lucas?"

"He's gay, you know," Wyatt said.

Great. That's just fucking great. Now I know it's just me *he doesn't like.*

"I didn't know that, but I don't see why it matters," Tony said. He really, really did not want to have this conversation. Even more than he hadn't wanted Lucas to be a setup—and then he had.

"It matters because you like him," Wyatt said patiently.

"I barely know the guy; how could I like him?"

"When he showed up at the house, you thought he was a setup. It's pretty much a given that you like him," Wyatt said reasonably, and even though it was a perfect night, just a hint of a breeze on the warm air, and his beer was the perfect ice-cold temperature, Tony considered getting up and going into his little cottage, just to get away from his brother's prying.

"He came *at dinnertime*, and he sure as fuck did not say he was there about a job," Tony said. "Anyone would have assumed that."

"Only if you *wanted* him to be a setup," Wyatt argued.

"I didn't. Trust me, I really didn't. And maybe I thought he was sort of cute? But it doesn't matter now, because we're keeping it strictly professional."

"Oh?" Wyatt asked slyly. "You discussed it?"

"Fuck no," Tony said. The last thing he wanted was for Lucas to shut him down to his face—or even worse, to quit the truck because Tony couldn't stop being a creep. Maybe he hadn't wanted to hire him, and he'd been unsure about it despite Lucas' obvious skill, but with Jeremy suddenly fucking up hourly, having someone who was rock steady working next to him might not be a bad thing.

"Then how do you know you're keeping it strictly professional?" Wyatt wondered.

"I just *know*," Tony said.

"Ah," Wyatt said, a wealth of insinuation in the single word.

Tony drained the rest of his beer. "I'm going to bed," he said, standing up.

"Sure thing," Wyatt said. "Have a good night."

As he headed towards the cottage, typing in his key code in the front door lock, Tony thought darkly that he wouldn't be having a very good night. He was too tangled up with too many distractions. But maybe he was tired enough that he could sleep tonight—and maybe he'd be even luckier and none of his dreams would be about Lucas.

He did sleep slightly better, but Lucas showed up twice in his dreams—once, laughing at him, as the truck parked at a vegan convention and everyone threw rotten tomatoes at it, and the second time, when Lucas had pressed his much smaller body forcefully against Tony's own much larger one, bracing it against the stainless steel work counter in the truck. "I know you want me, you can't take your eyes off me," dream Lucas had whispered, right in his head, before he'd leaned in just a little bit further and bit the lobe of his ear, just hard enough to send a spike of mingled pain and pleasure through Tony.

It had woken him up with a jolt, and he'd lain there in bed for at least an hour, both wishing he could go back to sleep, and also dreading it, because surely Lucas would figure out another way to torture him while he was unconscious.

It wasn't Lucas' fault that he was unbearably attractive or it felt like every time their eyes met, sparks seemed to dance along Tony's skin. It wasn't Lucas' fault that he was the first person—guy or girl—that he'd met since Brody, who'd made him want to drop everything and then drop to his knees.

"You look tired," Wyatt observed, walking into the kitchen and pouring himself a cup of coffee from the carafe on the counter. "Not sleep well?"

"I slept fine," Tony said shortly, taking a drink of his own coffee—his second of the morning, but then Wyatt didn't need to know that. He didn't need to know everything, even though he had an annoying habit of butting in where he wasn't wanted *or* needed.

"I never sleep very well when Ryan isn't here," Wyatt confessed, leaning over and propping his elbows up on the counter. "It's kinda sad."

"Sad that you're so attached you can't sleep if he's not there, or sad that he's a baseball player who spends a hell of a lot of the year on the road?" Tony asked.

"Yes?" Wyatt said meekly.

Tony laughed.

"You wanna help me with this recipe?" Tony asked as Wyatt stood up and, grabbing a bagel, threw the two halves into the toaster. "It could use your touch."

Two years ago he'd never have offered, and he definitely never would have admitted to his younger brother he might be able to do a better job than Tony himself. But that was good, solid partnership, Tony figured. Plus discovering that your own capability wasn't even remotely diminished by accepting help from someone who was better than you were—it turned out that only made you smarter, not dumber.

"Sorry," Wyatt said, turning back from the toaster. "I've got meetings."

"Of course you do," Tony grumbled.

"Sorry," Wyatt repeated, sounding like he genuinely regretted it. "I'm going to have to take some kind of class, *how to say no and mean it.*"

"I know you'd rather be here, and not listening to some big-mouthed, bloated-ego jerk waste your time in a bland conference room," Tony said with a grin. "Right?"

Wyatt nodded, grabbing his bagel from the toaster. "What are you making? Testing stuff for the veg option?"

"Yeah," Tony said. "Thinking of a roasted veggie panini with a spinach walnut citrus pesto."

"Hmmm," Wyatt said, and he sounded just about as enthusiastic as Tony did about the possibility. It was a variation of what they'd done last summer, and didn't feel exactly fresh, but then neither of them was really an expert if they weren't using some kind of animal protein. "Save me one, I'll swing by around lunchtime."

"Sure," Tony said.

"See you in a few hours," Wyatt said, pouring the rest of his coffee into a to-go mug, munching on the bagel as he left the kitchen.

For the rest of the morning, Tony tried to ignore his instincts and stop thinking, *Lucas would be good at this*, because he would. He was the one who'd noticed the gap in the menu, and he'd told Tony he tried to eat "clean." Whatever that meant. Probably that meant no bacon and no fat and nothing even remotely sweet. Tony didn't really have much of a sweet tooth, but cookies were hard for him to turn down.

He roasted the eggplant and zucchini in careful slices, and then blistered the red peppers on the open flame of the stove, quickly breaking them down once they became cool enough to handle. When he finally finished the panini, he took a bite, and it was exactly as he'd expected—it was *fine*, but it wasn't anything particularly special. The last thing Tony wanted to do was show up with an uninspired veggie menu option, after claiming just yesterday that he wasn't going to change anything. It needed to blow his mind; it needed to blow *Lucas'* mind. Tony didn't examine that too closely, because the truth was, Lucas was a transient part-time employee who he probably shouldn't worry about so much. He'd be long gone in a season, and the food truck would endure. At least it would if he and Wyatt could keep this good thing going.

He saved one of the paninis for Wyatt, even though he already knew he would have to come up with something else. Something sensational. Something that Lucas couldn't forget once he put it in his mouth.

A quick scan of his favorite food blogs while he was eating his own lunch didn't spark any inspiration, so Tony turned to his next possibility: the enormous bookcase full of cookbooks he'd been collecting for years. For a long time he'd never bothered unboxing them, but when he'd moved to LA and into Wyatt and Ryan's guesthouse, his brother had taken one look at all the big, heavy boxes and demanded that he at least get to *look* at what Tony had collected over the years. When Wyatt had seen them all out, most of them pristine, their bindings never cracked, their pages clean of any splatter, he'd insisted on finding a bookcase big enough that now sat in the living room of Tony's new living quarters.

Tony went there after lunch, plucking a handful of vegetable-themed books from the shelves, settling down on the couch with his favorite sticky notes to make notes and remember pages of interest. Recipe development was painful sometimes, and always difficult, but this was especially hard because it *wasn't* something he was good at. There was a reason Wyatt's cookbook was almost entirely about meat: it was a significant part of the Blake family diet.

But as he was skimming through the first book, Tony felt his eyes growing heavy, his abbreviated night of sleep catching up with him.

He woke up much later, startled awake by his phone dinging insistently. Yawning, Tony reached for it and was not surprised to discover that he'd been sleeping for at least a few hours. His neck felt like it was permanently wrenched, and tomorrow was a big event that would mean almost a whole day on his feet, bent over the counters in the truck. That wasn't going to help—and the last thing he could ask Lucas for was a neck rub with those undoubtedly strong, talented hands.

Down, boy, Tony thought. At least he'd been tired enough that his sleep had been dreamless.

He didn't need Lucas invading any more thoughts than he already was.

When he went back into the main house, using the back door that connected to the kitchen, Wyatt was there. He'd cleaned up and was putting the plate Tony had left his sandwich on into the dishwasher.

"You're here later than I expected," Tony said, heading to the fridge and grabbing a bottle of water off one of the shelves. "I thought you'd be swinging by at lunch."

Wyatt rolled his eyes. "I thought so too. But the blowhard in the bland conference room? An understatement. He fucking loved to hear his own voice, and he got a lot of love in today."

"Yuck," Tony said.

"Did you take a nap?" Wyatt asked, his eyes narrowing in on Tony's messed-up hair.

"Fell asleep looking for some inspiration."

"Yeah, the sandwich was okay." Wyatt didn't usually mince words, but he was being *nice,* a particularly terrible sign.

"Not something I want to put on the menu," Tony said firmly.

"Why don't you ask Lucas to help?" his brother suggested slyly. "He's the one who noticed we were missing a veg option, after all."

"He's an employee," Tony said, which was true, but he was more of the democratic sort, and so was his brother. It had never mattered before where a contribution came from. But Lucas was a totally different story. Tony wanted to blow his mind, wanted to impress the shit out of him, wanted to make him crave Tony's food—and *Tony.*

Ugh.

Wyatt's expression made it clear how stupid he thought that was. "Who cares?" he asked and Tony didn't want to say, *me, I care. I want to make an impression, not remind him I'm a total idiot.*

"You . . . you *like* him, don't you?" Wyatt said when Tony didn't answer. "Oh my god, you do. That explains why you thought I was setting you up."

"I thought you were setting me up because a guy *randomly* showed up to our house right at dinnertime, and you knew him and I didn't," Tony said stiffly.

"You still like him," Wyatt said, and the fact that he'd morphed from question to statement was not a good sign. Tony considered running away, back to the cottage, but that'd only be a confirmation that Wyatt had guessed right, and Tony still had a sliver of plausible deniability.

"He's fine," Tony grumbled, and yeah, that was the fucking truth, Lucas was *fine as hell*.

"Yeah, sure," Wyatt teased. "Totally fine. So fine you wanna get up on that."

Tony dumped the cookbooks he'd been holding onto the island countertop. "How about, instead of prying into my personal feelings, we figure out what we're going to serve tomorrow for a veg option?"

Wyatt's grimace told him the whole story—he had another meeting, and he had to leave soon—but then he shook his head. "Fuck that guy, I'm not going to any more of these meetings. He can fuck off."

"What guy is this?" Tony wondered, flipping open David Leibovitz's book on vegetables. He was maybe a little classier than their food truck clientele might appreciate, but maybe one of the recipes would jog his brain.

"Oh, some marketing guy at the Dodgers," Wyatt grumbled. "He wants me to do more charity outreach with Ryan next year. Wants us to be the 'face of the franchise.'"

"I thought that was Ryan," Tony said, as he watched his brother pull his phone out and type out a quick text.

"Apparently," Wyatt grumbled, "we're a matched set, these days."

There was no way that didn't suck. Tony knew, *obviously*, that not everything between his brother and Ryan was sunshine and roses. You couldn't be one of LA's most visible couples and not deal with some shit. But it was rare for Wyatt to look so visibly frustrated by it. "What kind of stuff does he want you to do?"

"The charity stuff is fine," Wyatt said, pulling another cookbook towards him. "I got him to consider some LGBT charities, *finally*, so that was good. But the rest? I don't want to make appearances at clothing store openings."

"Not really your brand, either," Tony pointed out. Two years ago, Wyatt would have bristled at the thought that he and Ryan, either separately or together, had a *brand,* but that ship had sailed. Now, Wyatt mostly seemed to want to protect it fiercely, and not compromise it with any kind of bullshit commercialism.

Tony could appreciate that.

"Yeah, no kidding," Wyatt muttered. "Like either of us gives two shits about designer clothing."

"Well, Ryan more than you," Tony said. He was glad that Wyatt liked his old jeans and threadbare t-shirts because a lot of the stuff Wyatt got, he didn't want, and Tony was the same size, so he was the recipient of most of it.

"He still wouldn't want to go to store openings," Wyatt said, and he wasn't wrong. Neither Ryan nor Wyatt was into the celebrity lifestyle. Not the way the Dodgers wanted them to be, it seemed like.

Tony flipped through the Leibovitz book, but nothing zinged at him. He pulled out an old *Chez Panisse* cookbook next. "What are you looking at?" he asked his brother.

"French Laundry's second book," Wyatt said, and stuck a sticky note to a page. "We could also call Xander. He does so much farm to table at the Barrel House, he'd have some good ideas for us."

"If you want." Privately Tony thought Xander's stuff was a little too high-brow for the truck, but then he was the one who'd picked up David Leibovitz's book.

"Eh," Wyatt said. "He'd probably suggest we do something really fucking fancy." He glanced over at Tony and grinned. "He would, wouldn't he?"

"He totally would," Tony agreed, and then sighed.

"What should we do? You really don't want to ask Lucas?" Wyatt asked.

"I don't," Tony admitted. "I . . ."

"You like him," Wyatt said, grinning again. "I get it. You want to impress him; you don't want to go running to him for help."

Tony considered denying it. He could keep on denying it, even though Wyatt had already figured out the truth. But he trusted his brother; even *mostly* trusted him not to interfere.

"Yeah," he said, feeling himself flush. "Yeah, I don't. I want . . . I don't know what I want."

Except he did—*exactly*, with bonus explicit detail.

"Yeah, I get that," Wyatt said, wrapping one arm around his shoulders, and giving him a quick squeeze. "Well, let's come up with something to impress Mr. Picky, huh?"

"Okay," Tony said, grateful that his brother understood exactly what he needed—and when he needed to lay off on the mostly inevitable teasing.

CHAPTER FOUR

Tony was early to the truck, armed with an actual decent recipe for the day's veggie special. Hopefully, if it sold well, it would end up permanently on the menu. Tony had high hopes, anyway. And not just for the special to sell out.

But, to his surprise, he wasn't the earliest to the truck. Lucas was already inside, starting the salsa prep for the day without being asked, even though Tony had mostly decided that he would switch Jeremy and Lucas around. Even Jeremy could do veggie prep without fucking it up.

"Hey," Lucas said. He'd covered up his hair today with an old Roxy cap. He was wearing it backwards, and it had more doodled rainbows on the brim. It made him look young with his face exposed like that, and frankly, too fucking delectable. Tony took a deep breath.

"Hey," he said. "You're here early."

"Yeah, I hope that's okay. I know we have a lot to do prep-wise," he said.

"Yeah," Tony said. And then he glanced down as the phone in his hand dinged with an incoming text. "Oh well, *shit*, we really do now. Jeremy's sick."

"Sick?" Lucas said, and he didn't have to move his hands from his knife or the red bell pepper in his grip, the air quotes around the word were unmistakable.

"Yeah," Tony said in a hard voice. This hard day had just gotten a lot harder. But then, if Lucas had been the one to bail, Tony wasn't sure they'd have been able to handle it—at least with Lucas on board, Tony felt vaguely confident.

"That sucks," Lucas said, and even though he knew how many plates they were hoping to serve today—at a major music festival's food truck court—he didn't sound all that disappointed. "I hope you don't catch it, too."

"Catch what?" Tony asked, distracted, because he was so busy tearing through one of the shelves. He knew he'd left some cash here to pick up incidentals on the way to the festival—he *knew* he had, and now it was gone.

"Jeremy's 'sick,'" Lucas said patiently.

"Why would I?" Tony asked.

"I don't know, because you're close and all," Lucas said, and his voice sounded slightly more defensive.

"Close? Jeremy and me?" Tony didn't know what he was more baffled at—where his money had gone, or why Lucas thought he and Jeremy were "close." "Wait, you don't think . . . seriously?"

"Think what?" Lucas challenged.

"I'm single," Tony said firmly. "Very single."

He watched as Lucas swallowed, his Adam's apple bobbing hard. His voice was carefully neutral. "Okay. Me too."

"Yeah, Jeremy and I are friends from way back. Some-times"—*more than sometimes*, Wyatt's voice in his head correct-ed—"he can be a little territorial. But it's not like that."

"Good to know," Lucas said, and both his face and his voice were frustratingly opaque. *Tell me you're relieved*, Tony wanted to beg, *even if it was ridiculously dramatic and way too serious, considering he barely knew the guy, tell me you let out a breath you weren't even sure you were holding, because you make me do that, every fucking minute of every day we spend together. Like I forgot how to breathe and you remind me, all the time.*

"Hey," Tony asked, because even though it felt like he was sud-denly overwhelmed because Lucas had *thought about it*, at least as far as thinking he might not be available, he also needed to find this fucking cash, "did you get into this cupboard at all?"

Lucas glanced up from where he had moved on from bell peppers to mangos, his knife slicing confidently right up to the pit. "What cupboard?"

"This one," Tony said impatiently, pointing to the open, empty shelf in front of him. "I had some petty cash in here. In a plastic container." Both the container and the cash were gone. He didn't want to think Lucas, who had been here, unobserved, had taken it, because that would be so much more than a fucking disappoint-ment. It would feel like a betrayal, even though they weren't friends, and they definitely weren't anything else.

"Yeah, no," Lucas said. "And the truck was locked up when I came here this morning."

"How did you unlock it?" It suddenly occurred to Tony to ask. Both he and Wyatt had keys, but Tony hadn't given Lucas one yet, even though he'd come here today intending to do so. The extra key was rattling around on his keychain right next to Tony's own. Nestled together like Tony had hoped he and Lucas might be, someday.

Now, he just felt really fucking stupid.

"Wyatt gave me a key," Lucas said matter-of-factly, "when he hired me."

"Oh," Tony said. Surprised that Wyatt had done it without mentioning anything to Tony, and also realizing that when Lucas had come by the house the other night, it hadn't really been an interview, because Wyatt had already hired this guy, without ever consulting Tony.

He felt a surge of annoyance against his brother. Was he med-dling? Was he just busy and distracted and forgetful? It was hard to say. But that kind of frustration required a lot of time and energy that Tony knew he didn't have—not since Jeremy had texted.

"Well, we're gonna have to swing by the ATM and get some more," Tony said with exasperation.

Lucas looked up from his mangos, his expression suddenly softer. Like he was actually concerned, just as concerned as Tony. "Was it a lot of money?" he asked.

"Not a lot. Under a hundred dollars." Suddenly Tony couldn't remember how much it was. It hadn't been nothing, but at least he was good about always taking the cash box in at the end of the night.

"Still not great to lose," Lucas said.

"No," Tony agreed. He paused. "Also," he said, "we've got a new special."

He'd stayed up way too late the night before, both prepping the recipe for today, and also wondering the best way he could present it to Lucas. "Oh?" Lucas asked, sounding vaguely interested, but he was still paying most of his attention to the mangos on his board, his knife flashing in the early morning sunshine streaming into the truck's interior.

"Spinach artichoke jalapeno grilled cheese," Tony said, praying that Lucas would look up. See the apology in his expression. "Kind of a mashup of the dip plus jalapeno poppers. So we'll need double jalapenos chopped today."

"Spinach artichoke jalapeno?" Lucas said, not even glancing up. "Sounds good. Vegetarian?" His tone was casual, like they hadn't just had a confrontation about this very topic the other day.

"Yeah," Tony said, his throat suddenly dry. He looked away, pulling a box of fish out of the fridge. "Yeah, it is, actually."

Lucas said nothing, but when Tony found his courage to look over at him, he could've sworn there were the remnants of a smile playing around the edges of Lucas' full lips.

After prep was done—which they finished so much faster than Tony could have imagined—they swung by the ATM on the way to the music festival. Tony had texted Wyatt, letting him know the money was missing, and he'd been surprised but not unconcerned. Also, he specifically ignored the part of Tony's message where he'd mentioned that he hadn't realized that Lucas had a key.

It wasn't like he *wanted* to believe that Lucas had taken the money, but there just weren't very many options. Wyatt had not taken it himself, as he was as surprised as Tony to find out it was missing. He was sure Jeremy wouldn't, because he knew how much Jeremy wanted this job, and if you wanted something that much, you'd hardly do anything to jeopardize it.

Still, even though he was essentially the only suspect left, Tony didn't want to think Lucas had taken the cash. Maybe because he looked so damn cute today, in that backwards baseball cap and the loose-fitting tank that showed off a pair of gorgeously ripped arms, and even a little sliver of even more gorgeously ripped torso.

Focus, Tony reminded himself, as they set up in the lot advertised as the food court. It was still early, not quite ten, but people were already milling around, waiting to see which trucks had shown up.

Tony himself was a little curious—he knew some of the other truck owners, but there were so many in LA that it was impossible to keep track of all of them.

"Looks like we'll have a crowd," Lucas said, sticking his head out the door. It might only be his second day, but he already knew the routine, even though Jeremy had worked at the truck on and off for several months and Tony still had to remind him of the setup process sometimes.

That's just going to make it harder to fire him, at the end of the day, Tony thought. *You know he took that money. Nobody else could've done it.*

Except Tony wasn't quite convinced. Either Lucas was a very good actor, or he'd been just as surprised as Tony that it was missing—actually, Tony corrected, he'd been surprised that it was even there at all.

As Tony set up the menu board, he glanced over at where Lucas was laying out bins of plastic ware, napkins, and condiments. "Hey," he said, trying to be casual, but it wasn't really a casual question. Not really. "So, when you opened the truck up this morning, was there any sign someone broke in?"

Lucas looked up, and if Tony wasn't mistaken, a look of concern crossed over his features before it melted right off. "No," he said. "Everything was locked up. Nothing looked out of place."

Tony had already, as unobtrusively as possible, checked the door, and it looked pristine, no scratches or gauges from someone trying to break in. Same with the metal around the lock mechanism. He wasn't exactly a detective or a cop, but surely if someone had broken in, there'd have been a sign?

Lucas tried to deep breathe and unwind the sudden tension that was building in his chest. It had been a weird morning. First, finding out that Tony and Jeremy weren't together in any way, shape, or form had made him way too fucking happy. But then, the issue of the money had cropped up, and now was cropping up again. He knew Tony suspected that he'd taken it. He was new. He had been there first this morning. Of course he had a *good reason* to be here before anyone else, but somehow he had a feeling that Wyatt hadn't informed his brother of that particular fact. Why? Lucas wasn't really sure. He wasn't really the type to volunteer info, but if Tony came at him later, accusing him of stealing, he wasn't going to hold back the one thing that might exonerate him.

At least, give him a very good reason for why he'd been at the truck at the crack of fucking dawn.

He also thought it was totally one hundred percent suspect that on the day of such a big event, *plus* the day where Tony would discover the money was missing, Jeremy had called in "sick."

If Jeremy was sick, then Lucas was a freaking monk. And, from the way his dick twitched every time Tony came close, Lucas knew *that* was pretty far from the fucking truth.

Still, although Jeremy had left them in the lurch, he wasn't exactly disappointed that he wouldn't have to share the space today with that weirdo.

Tony was muttering as he climbed back into the truck.

"Gabriel's here," he said, "and so is Ash. *And* the fucking picnic truck."

Lucas didn't know who Gabriel or Ash were, but he *had* heard of the famous—or apparently in Tony's mind, *infamous*—picnic truck. It was called Basket, and it specialized in all kinds of stuff you'd bring to a picnic or a cookout: ribs, hot dogs, potato salad, deviled eggs. Lucas had ordered from it once and had been surprisingly impressed by their macaroni salad. *Macaroni salad,* that fucking mainstay of middle-class American potlucks and grocery store delis. Completely reimagined and absolutely crazy delicious.

But it sounded like Tony was not exactly thrilled they were here, which kind of made sense, because they definitely seemed to grab the lion's share of attention wherever they went.

"They're new," Lucas said. "A novelty."

"Ross is a dick," Tony grumbled, "and Aaron is an even bigger dick."

That surprised Lucas. Tony didn't seem like the kind of guy who'd trash his competition. "Really?"

"They stole our onion dip recipe," Tony said. "Well, *Wyatt's* onion dip recipe. And he thinks it's funny, but it's really not, because then *we* had to take it off the menu."

"Why?"

"They claimed theirs is an 'old family recipe' which is total bull-shit, but somehow it was basically identical to ours, and Wyatt didn't want us to look like we were copying them, even though we'd had it as a side, nearly from the start. That was when we decided we'd do more salsas, lean into the fish tacos and stuff."

"You should make it for me sometime," Lucas said. He hadn't intended for it to sound like an invitation or, god forbid, *a date*, but Tony glanced over in surprise, like he'd just propositioned him. Over *onion dip*, for god's sake.

"Next big event, we'll add it as a special. At least if freaking *Basket* isn't around."

Lucas told himself that he wasn't disappointed in the way Tony dismissed him. He probably wouldn't be around for the next big event, and Tony knew it.

Returning to his final set of prep, Lucas tried to let it go, but the way Tony had said it was weird. *Stole*. Money and a recipe were totally different beasts, but there was a weird similarity there that kept bothering him, piquing his curiosity. Finally, even though he knew better than to bring up what was clearly a sore subject, Lucas put his knife down and turned towards Tony, who was working on the spinach artichoke mixture for the grilled cheese, wilting spinach in a huge pot on the stove.

"What do you mean, they *stole* it?" Lucas asked.

Tony looked up, surprise etched on his face.

"Like, did they break into the truck and *steal* the recipe?" Lucas continued, gesturing to where the vague recipes were written out in bold, slashing letters that he'd discovered was Tony's handwriting. "Or did they just buy some and duplicate it?"

"I don't know," Tony said. "I wish I did, but fuck if I know how they got it. I guess they could have recreated it. But . . ."

"It was totally identical," Lucas finished. "Fuck, that sucks." He knew how hard it would be to recreate a recipe *that* closely. It'd take dozens of attempts, and tons of time. Not the kind of time that anyone would waste in the food truck business. Tony was probably right; somehow the Basket guys had stolen the recipe.

Tony looked at him again, this time with way more surprise. Like he genuinely thought Lucas had already stolen from him once, and so why would he actually *care* if someone else did it?

"Thanks," Tony said shortly. "You almost done over there?"

Lucas nodded.

"Okay, good. Me too." Tony glanced at his watch. "Just in time, it's almost eleven," he added with a grimace, giving a last stir to the spinach mixture, before lifting the enormous pot effortlessly and scooping it into a hotel pan to keep warm.

Tony might be lean, but he was strong, and *fuck*, if that wasn't something that cranked Lucas up effortlessly. He wanted to know just how strong Tony was, how well he could put him through his paces. How his muscles bunched and tightened when he was trying not to lose control.

Not helping, Lucas reminded himself. *You can fantasize about him when this day is over,* and *after he's fired you.*

There was no way around it—it was a bitch of a day.

It was crazy hot, dust clouds swirling around the empty lot they'd set up in, and inside the food truck? It was hot enough that even the fans they'd set up felt like they were sluggishly pushing around the boiling air. It was also busy, which wasn't so much a surprise, but an expectation. Even though it was back-breaking, frantic work, trying to serve the huge line that kept queuing up outside the truck, Lucas caught Tony eying the number in their line compared to the other trucks, especially Basket. What a Catch held their own, and even though they weren't exactly the fastest in the world at getting the food out, they kept it moving. When the lunch rush faded into late afternoon, and they finally had a chance to catch their breath, Lucas leaned against the counter and pulled his shirt up, wiping at the sweat on his forehead.

"Fuck," he said. "It's so fucking hot."

Tony had pulled his hair back in a cute little bun—before, Lucas would have *died* before ever admitting that the man bun thing was anything even remotely cute, but Tony made it work. Frankly, Tony could make anything work. He had that kind of animal magnetism that stole everyone's attention. Lucas had caught more than a few guys and girls in the line checking him out. Tony hadn't even seemed to notice, not because they were slammed, but because he just didn't seem to care. Like it happened so often that he couldn't be bothered by it. It should have been annoying, to know that he wasn't alone, that everyone who met Tony wanted him, but all it made Lucas want to do was grab him by that stupid bun and yank him down, brand his name across his lips, so everyone fucking knew who Tony belonged to.

He took the bun down now, shaking out all that hair like a fucking influencer shampoo commercial, and despite the heat and the awkwardness that had grown between them, Lucas still burned, still wanted to see that hair spread out against his sheets. It wasn't ever going to happen, but at least the thought distracted him from the way his back and his feet ached.

As he wiped his face again, he caught Tony staring at his exposed abs. He worked hard, and he looked good, and Tony was just admiring because he was right there, and it was unavoidable.

Except that wasn't quite true, and Lucas knew it. He'd felt the spark of attraction between them from the very beginning, and it was growing stronger. Getting stuck together, with no Jeremy as a buffer, in this wretchedly hot truck wasn't helping.

Every time Tony brushed up against him, his long legs eating up the small interior of the truck, Lucas felt his breath catch. It was fucking distracting, and it also made him want to fight the inevitable.

"Hey, you want to try this sandwich?" Tony offered. "I made an extra." He slid a paper plate over, the bread perfectly grilled, glistening with butter on its browned edges, gooey cheese oozing out of the center, speckled with the finely diced jalapeno, and Tony's spinach and artichoke mixture.

"Oh, thanks," Lucas said. It was almost too hot to be hungry—all he seemed to be was a well of unquenchable thirst—but he needed to keep up his energy. He could always pull a bar from the cooler he'd hidden in the cab, one of the batch he'd made just this morning. But the sandwich smelled good, and if Lucas could tell anything from orders that had crossed his station, it had been popular. Picking it up, he took a bite, and then another. It wasn't fancy; it definitely wasn't healthy, even though it was the vegetarian option. But it really was fucking delicious.

"This is . . . really, really good," Lucas said and watched as an even more delicious smile spread across Tony's face.

"You think so?"

"Hell yeah. It's tasty. A hit too, I think."

"Yeah," Tony said, and his chest practically puffed out underneath the thin cotton of his t-shirt, "it seemed to be."

"I could . . ." Lucas had told himself after their argument a few days ago, when Tony had shut him down, that he wouldn't volunteer any of the expertise that Tony and Wyatt didn't have. Maybe Tony hadn't apologized, not in words, but this was an olive branch. He'd listened anyway, and he'd come back, maybe not with a perfect option, but a very good one. Lucas was touched even though he told himself that it meant nothing. It was just a sandwich. But you couldn't be in the food business for long with that kind of attitude, and he knew very well it wasn't *just* anything. "I could help you out, I have a fantastic recipe for jackfruit pulled pork. We could do an alternate of the pulled pork sandwich as a vegan option. The slaw is dairy-free, already."

"Jackfruit?" Tony sounded dubious, but Lucas reminded himself that most people were, until they tasted it.

"Yeah. You cook it right, with the right spices, and it's *just* like meat. I could even bring in a sample." And even though this was going to be a long-ass day, and he had another full day tomorrow, he found himself offering time and energy he didn't have. Why? He wasn't sure. It might have been the effortless way Tony smiled, or the way he really seemed to love this business and this truck and his calling. Lucas understood that all too well.

"That'd be great," Tony said, and suddenly he was way less enthusiastic, and it wasn't hard to guess why.

Tony was going to fire him, not because he really *wanted* to, but because he'd decided that Lucas had to be to blame for the missing cash.

"I didn't steal the money," Lucas said, putting down the half-eaten sandwich.

Tony was in the middle of putting his hair back up and he froze, hands twisted up in it, and stared at Lucas.

"I didn't," Lucas continued with all the certainty he could pour into his words. *Because he fucking hadn't.*

"I . . ." Tony stammered. Caught off guard by the fact that they were talking about it. Like he'd thought Lucas would go down easy, without a fight. Would take his knives and go, even though he'd never done anything wrong. And maybe, maybe Lucas might have. If Tony was slightly less appealing, if he didn't enjoy this work as much as he did, despite how hard it was. And then there was the *other* issue—Wyatt had made it clear that the free kitchen space depended on him helping Tony out this summer.

That was the other, incredibly surprising thing—Lucas *wanted* to help him. Wanted him to pull in more tickets than Basket. Wanted to help him rub it in the dick and the even more of a dick's faces. The commercial kitchen space, that was a great bonus, but somehow that'd become secondary. That realization should've sent him running, but Lucas was intrigued, and intrigued enough that he wasn't just going to take Tony's dismissal sitting down.

"You thought I did," Lucas said calmly. "And I get why. I was here alone this morning. You don't know me."

"But you didn't." Tony didn't sound as sure as Lucas hoped he might, but he sounded a hell of a lot more conflicted.

"I didn't," Lucas confirmed.

"Then who did?" Tony said, and finished putting his hair up, rubbing a hand across his face with a bandana he'd grabbed from his back pocket. *"Fuck."*

"You said you know Jeremy really well . . ." Lucas said, carefully, because he was still on shaky ground. Tony still didn't quite trust him, might not believe him yet, *and* he and Jeremy were friends.

"Yeah," Tony said warily. "I do."

"And you trust him," Lucas said. This might get him fired faster than lying and admitting he stole the money.

"I . . ." Tony suddenly looked unsure. "I think so. I'd vouch for him. I would."

"Someone must have broken in and taken it," Lucas said. "Just like the recipe."

"You think those are related?" Tony sounded astonished, like he'd never connected them before, which made sense. The recipe stealing was petty sabotage between competitors, but the money? That was someone who was desperate. Someone who was willing to break in on the chance there was some cash hanging around.

Lucas shrugged. "When did Basket show up with the onion dip?"

"A month ago," Tony admitted. "I can't believe I didn't . . . *ugh*."

"I mean, I don't *know* for sure, I'm not like an investigator or anything, it just seems pretty fucking coincidental, you know?"

Tony nodded. "Yeah, it kinda does. Shit, I wonder if I should report it."

"Cops will do jack shit," Lucas said with an eye roll. "They'll fucking laugh you out of the station. Especially if you bring up the recipe thing. And by itself? Less than a hundred dollars in cash? They aren't going to do anything."

"Yeah," Tony said with a nod. "Okay. Well, I guess I'll have to do something about it."

Lucas didn't know he was going to say it, but his mouth opened anyway and out came something he'd never, ever expected to fucking say. "I could help you."

Tony must have been surprised too, because his jaw dropped a little. "You?"

Maybe Tony still thought it might be possible that this was all Lucas' way to deflect suspicion.

"Yeah," Lucas said, doubling down. Because why the fuck not? He'd already gotten himself part of the way into this mess, why not jump right in? It would end in disaster, but he'd offered anyway. He knew, because he didn't do hearts and family dinners and happily ever afters. He did hot sex and then disappearing acts right after. And even though Tony had never said it, it was so fucking clear that he wanted more than what Lucas could ever give him. Which was why this was a colossal mistake, and yet Lucas was making it anyway, with eyes wide open.

It'd be fucking amazing until it wasn't.

"You really want to help me find who stole the money?" Tony questioned.

Lucas stuck his jaw out. "Gotta clear my name, don't I?"

Tony laughed. "I guess so. So, what's your story?"

"My story?"

"Yeah," Tony said. "Why you were at the truck early? Because I know it wasn't to fucking impress me."

"Maybe it was," Lucas said flippantly. He held his secrets close to his chest, *always*, and yeah, all Wyatt had to do was tell his brother the arrangement they had, but Wyatt hadn't. Which meant maybe he was waiting for Lucas to do it. It wasn't like Lucas didn't want to share, but sharing always led to *more*. Like friendship and camaraderie and fucking *feelings*. Which was why Lucas almost never shared. Why would he? He had his life, and he'd built it, brick by brick, until it was nearly perfect.

Now Tony was here, with his stupid food truck, threatening to demolish it all.

"I don't believe you," Tony said, but he was still smiling. Like he knew just how much Lucas didn't want to tell him, yet he knew Lucas would do it anyway.

"Fine," Lucas grumbled. "Wyatt and I have an arrangement, I guess. I use the kitchen space when the truck isn't in use."

"What do you want the space for?" Tony wondered.

Of course he wouldn't be satisfied with even a fraction of the truth. Like he'd dug deep into Lucas' chest *already*, and knew he was holding back, and refused to accept it. "I have a business," Lucas said, hedging. "I make energy bars. And a couple of places I want to sell to, they require them to be prepared in professional kitchens."

Tony's smile suffused his entire face, like he'd finally figured out something, a little corner of what made Lucas tick, and it *thrilled* him. Which didn't exactly make Lucas want to walk away. It made him want to get closer. "That's so cool," he said. "Why didn't you tell me?"

This right here was why Lucas hadn't told him. The sparks flaring between them, tying them together. "I thought Wyatt told you."

"Liar," Tony teased. "You knew he didn't."

"I . . ." It was Lucas' turn to flush. And it wasn't just the muggy, oppressive atmosphere in the truck. "I don't like to share my shit, normally."

"Why not?"

"Because of *this*," Lucas said, finally losing it and gesturing between them. "Because shit gets complicated and messy and I don't like that."

"Well," Tony said with an irrepressible grin, "we'll just have to make sure we keep our shit clean, then, won't we?"

Tony wasn't entirely sure that he trusted Lucas. He *wanted* to. His story made sense. He'd even ducked away for a few minutes and called Wyatt to double-check Lucas' story.

Wyatt had annoyingly been surprised that Tony had ever suspected Lucas of taking the money.

"What?" he'd exclaimed. "Lucas, really?"

Tony had rolled his eyes. "We don't know him at all," he'd said to his brother. "You found him in a *parking lot*."

"And? I checked his references. He's doing what he says he's doing. Starting an energy bar company."

"I just don't get why you didn't *tell* me," Tony said, and hated how plaintive he sounded. "And you say *I* like everyone."

"You do," Wyatt said matter-of-factly. The only real positive was that at least he hadn't brought up Jeremy or his no-show today. Of course that might have been because Tony had neglected to mention it.

Still, he wasn't *quite* sure he trusted Lucas' story. Not the energy bars. That much was true, because Lucas obviously hadn't wanted to tell him about his business.

But he told Wyatt, that annoying voice in the back of his head echoed, *and he offered to help you find the person who's stealing from you.*

Tony had been really shocked when Lucas had offered, but deep down, he was way too interested in spending more time with the guy to turn him down. Plus—he had no idea where to even begin. If it wasn't Lucas, and it wasn't Jeremy, then who was it? The guys from Basket? They might've taken the recipe, but why would they break in to steal less than a hundred bucks? Especially when they were practically having to turn people away? It didn't make sense.

"You look like your mind is going a hundred miles an hour. Which . . . I'll add . . . is not what you're *actually* doing right now," Lucas said with a teasing edge to his voice. "Can this hunk of junk go *any* faster?"

"Hey," Tony said, giving her a nice tap to the dash, "be nice to Belinda. She's trying her hardest."

"Belinda? You named the truck?" Lucas scrunched up his nose in bewilderment, and it was way cuter than it should've been.

"I did," Tony said, finally pulling into the lot where they stored their truck.

"Nice change of subject," Lucas said as he opened the door that separated the cab from the kitchen in the back. "What were you angsting about over there?"

Tony's first thought was to tell him he didn't reveal his secrets to people who were so averse to sharing their own, but then Lucas *had* tried. And he'd offered to help Tony find the culprit. That was sharing—maybe not exactly the kind of sharing he wanted, but it was a start.

"I hate the thought that someone is targeting us," he admitted. "It feels . . . ugly."

"The recipe and the money might not be related," Lucas pointed out, as he began to clean out the fridge. The final cleanup step that Tony hadn't even had to prompt him to start. Maybe it was stupid, and maybe he'd regret not firing Lucas later, but god, he'd been a saving fucking grace today.

"They might not," Tony agreed. "But I think they are. I think . . . I just think someone wants us to fail."

"Then they're going to have to do a hell of a lot worse," Lucas said firmly. "And we're going to catch them, so it won't work in the end."

Tony leaned against the counter opposite the fridge. "How are we even going to do that?"

"I don't know," Lucas had to admit. "But we'll figure it out."

Tony let out a big, exhausted yawn. "I'd ask you if you want to head to the Funky Cup for a beer, but I'm fucking dead on my feet."

He'd heard of the Funky Cup—that it was a chill, great place to grab a drink post-shift, especially for industry workers because they stayed open super late, but he'd never been there. He wondered if Tony often invited Jeremy for a beer, after a long day in the truck.

"Me too," Lucas admitted. "And I've got an early morning."

Tony looked over at him, a curious expression on his face. "Coming back here, to make your energy bars?"

"No," Lucas said. "I do personal training, too."

"Oh," Tony said. He sounded flustered now. "Well, if you ever need to change your shifts, just let me know. What days are better than others, etcetera."

"It's fine." Lucas' clients were used to needing him to shift his schedule around. "My friend Ria, I work at her gym, and she's chill."

"Okay, just . . . I'm glad you're on board and I don't want things to be hard on you," Tony said, rubbing his neck, eyes sheepish. "I want you to be part of this team."

Lucas tipped his head back. God, Tony was so goddamned tall. If he hadn't just disinfected this counter, he'd have been tempted to jump on it and grab Tony and pull him over—reel him in with just his feet around those lean hips. Chase Tony's mouth with his own.

And he *was* tempted. He wanted it, even though he knew it'd be a mistake. Tony deserved more than a hot hookup every once in a while—though Lucas would probably want it to be a little more often than that, fuck his insane schedule.

"Well"—Tony cleared his throat, glancing away—"just let me know."

It'd be a lot easier if this was a one-sided attraction. It'd be so much fucking easier to keep pushing it away. But Lucas knew Tony wanted him too.

"I will," Lucas said, tilting his head back, still imaging how simple it'd be to pull Tony close. To take what they both wanted.

It wasn't like Tony could read his mind, but it felt like he had, because suddenly Tony was stepping away, too far away, and ducking his head. "I'll clean up here, you get going. You've got an early thing tomorrow."

"Are you sure?" Lucas usually just took what people gave him, because people rarely gave him much of anything, and he certainly wasn't going to spit on a little goodwill. But something stopped him. He didn't really *want* to leave, no matter how tired he was.

"Yeah," Tony said definitively.

"Okay," Lucas said, reaching out to smack him lightly on the shoulder. The cotton of his t-shirt was damp, and his fingers wanted to dig in, feel Tony's sweat smeared on his own dewy skin. "Yeah, probably better."

But before Tony could ask what that meant—because he would, and that wouldn't lead to *anything* good—Lucas scooted out the door, grabbing his cooler on the way out of the lot.

They'd narrowly avoided temptation tonight, but Lucas had a feeling that it was just going to keep getting tougher.

CHAPTER FIVE

"So, someone stole the cash out of the truck?" Ryan leaned over the kitchen island counter and stole a piece of bacon from the tray next to him, prompting Wyatt to shove an elbow into his ribs.

"That's for brunch," Wyatt said.

"It's brunch *time*," Ryan retorted. "That's good enough. Plus, you wore me out this morning. I'm starving."

"Ew," Tony said. "It's bad enough that I know it's probably happening. I don't need details."

"Seriously," Ryan said, pulling everyone's attention away from the pilfered bacon and back to what *he* wanted to discuss. "Seriously, what's this about a break-in? Did you call the cops?"

Tony glared at his brother. He knew he'd tell Ryan—he told Ryan *everything*—but Tony didn't particularly want to get into the details of why he'd decided not to call the police. Probably because the first and last reason happened to be the exact same one.

"It was like eighty bucks," Tony said. "I don't think they'd be interested in helping me track that kind of cash down."

"True." Ryan tapped his fingers on the counter. Tony knew, from many weekend brunches, that he was watching and waiting for Wyatt to turn his back on the bacon pan, and then he'd strike again.

Wyatt knew it too, and when he turned back to the stove to flip the pancakes, he faked them both out, and reached back with the spatula, giving the back of Ryan's hand a sharp whack as it strayed towards the bacon again.

"No," Wyatt said calmly. "No bacon, not until brunch."

"Bah," Ryan said. "It's like you're not even happy I'm home."

"I made you bacon, didn't I?" Wyatt teased.

"You did," Ryan said with a heavy sigh. "I'll just take this outside." Wyatt smacked him again, before he could touch the bacon plate.

"*I'll* take the bacon outside. You can take the pancakes and the syrup. Make sure you grab the fruit too," he ordered.

"Sure thing," Ryan said with a sulky tone. Tony followed behind him and they quickly set the table on the patio, just finishing as Wyatt appeared outside with the big platter of bacon.

Tony had just filled his plate, drizzled on an unhealthy amount of maple syrup all over his blueberry pancakes, and was about to take his first big bite when the loudest, most obnoxious *squawk* interrupted him.

"What was *that*," Ryan said, sounding outraged. "Was that some-one *dying*?"

"I don't know," Wyatt said, his voice mystified. Then it happened again, and then again. Followed by a single phrase. "Ahoy, matey!"

"Oh my god," Ryan said, "it's a parrot."

"A *loud* parrot," Tony corrected. And after it squawked out again, "Walk the plank!" he added, "A very nautical parrot."

"It must be the new neighbors' parrot," Wyatt muttered. He glanced up from his plate and glared at *Tony*. "You must have known this was going to happen. You told me to plant some trees!"

Tony held up his hands. "Trust me, I had nothing to do with this. I was thinking maybe you wouldn't want to see some overweight grandpa lounging around in a Speedo or something. I didn't think they'd have a talking parrot who also happens to sound like he's being murdered, *slowly*."

"We can do something about this," Ryan said with determination. "There has to be something we can do. Something in the Homeowners' Association rules."

"Good luck with that," Tony said to his plate as he cut into his pancakes again. The parrot's obnoxious screeching punctuated every word that came out of his mouth.

"Maybe it's a noise violation," Wyatt said hopefully.

"It sure sounds like a noise violation. Emphasis on the *violation*," Ryan said, twisting around in his chair, trying to see into the neighbors' backyard.

"You could call animal control," Tony suggested slyly around a mouthful of bacon.

He loved his brother and his brother-in-law a lot, both separately and also together, but he already knew there was no amount of money, no threats, no coercion, that would shut that parrot up.

"I could always go over there and leave a poisoned fish," Tony suggested, grinning.

"You're . . . *fuck*," Wyatt swore. "You think this is funny!"

"No, it's definitely not funny," Tony said. "It's *hilarious*."

"I'm going to go over there," Ryan said, beginning to slide his chair out. But Wyatt put a hand on his arm, and Tony watched as a silent, complex conversation passed between them.

He wasn't often very jealous of his brother and his husband. He knew their lives weren't perfect—Wyatt's frustration with the marketing coordinator earlier in the week was a minor annoyance compared to some of the other shit they'd had to deal with—but they were so brimful of love that it was hard not to look at them sometimes and wish desperately that he could find that kind of no-holds-barred, all-in trust and love and partnership.

Before, he'd never wanted it. And then when he had, he always seemed to seek it from the wrong people. First Brody, and now, maybe, Lucas. Lucas, who was so sure he couldn't share his secrets, because he was afraid of things getting "messy." Well, *life* was messy. This goddamned parrot was evidence of that.

The only way to keep it clean was to not get involved at all, and how satisfying could that be?

"Fine," Ryan said in response to Wyatt's wordless entreaty, and sat back down. "But we have to do something about this."

"I'll go over there with a coffee cake later today," Wyatt said. "Tony, you still have Nana's recipe, right?"

"Of course," Tony said through a mouthful of pancake and bacon. "But you don't bake."

"I think I can make an exception." Wyatt flashed a sudden, killer smile. "I have to welcome our new neighbors to the neighborhood."

"I should help you," Tony said.

Wyatt glanced in his direction. "You're not any better at baking than I am. Besides, it's an easy recipe, how hard can it be?"

"Consider it a community service," Tony said. "Besides, I don't have any plans today."

"Not trying to hang around Lucas today?" Wyatt asked slyly.

"We're not working today," Tony said, trying to muster an innocent expression and failing. "Besides, it's not really like that."

"You *want* it to be like that," Wyatt countered.

"Yeah," Ryan added, "your eyes freaking light up whenever his name comes up. I don't . . . I'm not sure they even did that with Brody."

"We're not talking about Brody," Tony said. "This is a Brody-free zone. And new rule—it's also a Lucas-free zone. You guys are the worst when you interfere."

"Us? Interfere?" Ryan was *definitely* not as innocent as he sounded.

"We would never," Wyatt said, and Tony smacked him on the arm, hard.

"You absolutely would," Tony said, "and you *won't*." Lucas was already a little skittish; if Wyatt or Ryan interfered, he would go running for the hills, never to be heard from again.

And Tony already stupidly liked him too much; that was the very last thing he wanted.

"Fine, fine, we'll behave," Ryan said. "I promise." The bird squawked again, punctuating his sentence with a particularly vociferous cackle that echoed throughout the entire backyard.

"I'd feel bad," Wyatt said ruefully, "because it sounds like it's dying, but we couldn't be that lucky, could we?"

"I've missed the way this smells," Wyatt said, as he pulled the coffee cake out of the oven. "We need to not let this recipe die."

"Unfortunately, we don't run a dessert-themed truck," Tony said wryly. "Though that'd be a good idea. Like fucking Basket's concept, but with old-fashioned desserts."

"That sounds awesome. We should look into it," Wyatt said.

"Yeah, with all our extra time," Tony said, "and all our exceptional baking skills. Miles would laugh us out the door."

"He would, but he'd be a good consultant. Just . . . I've been thinking. We should start a second truck."

"We can barely handle one as it is," Tony objected. "We had to hire more staff."

"And we can keep doing that," Wyatt said.

"So, that's what you want? A food truck empire?" Tony didn't know how he felt about Wyatt's sudden aspirations. It wasn't like he *didn't* want to be part-owner of a food truck empire, but what Wyatt was talking about was a lot more involved than just "hiring some staff." It was branding, recipe development, more hands-on management, and possibly finding a more permanent home—at least a place they could regularly park and sell at.

"You'd be *managing* the food truck empire," Wyatt reminded him.

If they were successful, they'd make even more money. Tony would definitely have the money to move out of the guesthouse, maybe even buy his own condo. That should be something he wanted, but there was something good about his life now that he hadn't had before. He'd never been close to his brothers before, especially Wyatt, and he'd discovered that he actually really enjoyed hanging around his brother and his husband. That wouldn't have to stop if he moved to his own place, but all those late-night impromptu hangouts would end. He probably wouldn't end up sitting in the kitchen as Wyatt attempted to bake something.

But even so, it was important not to stand still, either. Especially not to use it as a way to keep change out or push away all those messy parts of life. Tony wasn't going to let himself fall into the same trap that Lucas had.

"We could think about it," Tony said.

"Okay," Wyatt said, with a quick approving grin. "I hoped you'd say that. I'm gonna go deliver this to the new neighbors."

"The neighbors who own such an obnoxious bird don't deserve such a delicious-smelling cake," Tony said mournfully, already regretting not telling his brother to make *two*. One for the neighbors and one for him . . . or *them*, technically, Tony conceded.

"Probably not," Wyatt agreed, "but I'm hoping if I butter them up enough, they might be more willing to listen to what an annoying menace their damn bird is."

"Good luck," Tony said. He knew that a coffee cake wouldn't help; he knew how much that house had cost, because *naturally* he'd looked up the listing. And anyone who paid that much for a house wasn't going to get rid of their bird for a coffee cake. No matter how good it smelled.

After Wyatt left, Tony pulled out his phone and, more than a little bored, scrolled through Instagram. He almost never posted anything—the last thing was probably the tattoo he'd gotten of the pansexual flag, accompanied by the little broken red heart—but he liked to use it to keep track of food trends and what some of the other trucks in the area were doing. It never hurt to keep a close eye on the newest innovations—and on the competition.

After scrolling through his feed for a bit, Tony finally gave up trying to resist temptation, and pulled up Lucas' Instagram. He'd found it the other day, when he'd been creeping around on the internet, and had been immediately struck by the aesthetic of Lucas' photos—almost all black and white, regular objects that were rendered fascinating by the angles and coloration he chose. And, additionally, there was the real attraction of his page: the shirtless selfies he liked to post.

Tony had barely resisted the urge to follow him, because he was absolutely worried about looking too creepily enthusiastic, so he was pleasantly surprised to see that Lucas had posted a new pic, just this morning. He was wearing the same hat he had yesterday, throwing the curves and planes of his face into sharp relief, the black and white emphasizing the bulges and valleys of his chest and abs. Tony let out a happy sigh. Fuck porn, he had found enough jerk-off material for a year, just in this one photo.

Then, just as he thought he might need to take a moment alone, he noticed that this time Lucas had tagged himself in a place. Ria's Gym, the tag said. Tony remembered what he'd said, just yesterday, that sometimes he worked as a personal trainer at his friend Ria's gym. This seemed to be the place, and when he googled it, he found it wasn't that far away, and seemed to be a popular destination. The reviews were all good, and they specialized in drop-in classes for spinning, yoga, aerobics. You could even drop in and get a consultation with a personal trainer—which Tony assumed must be Lucas.

Tony had never, not in any of his thirty-one years, ever been tempted to join a gym, or even to "drop by" one. It would be totally creepy to go and ask for a personal trainer consult—plus, he was sure that Lucas would torture him, and not in any of the fun ways—but he could always drop by for a class and just "happen" to run into Lucas. That would be *less* weird, right?

He pulled up the schedule for today and grimaced when he saw that the only class scheduled for this afternoon was a spin class. What did that even mean? What were they spinning? Were they making straw into gold?

He googled *that* and nearly gave up the whole idea entirely. It looked *absolutely fucking awful.* There were people who subjected themselves to this?

But how else was he supposed to just casually bump into Lucas? He couldn't just text him and ask him to hang out, not when Lucas had made it clear that his schedule was full.

This was the best way, Tony decided. If he had to be a little sore tomorrow, it'd be worth it. Besides, he'd kept telling himself that he needed to start working out. His metabolism and the hard work at the truck had always kept him slim, but that wasn't always going to be the case. If he kept eating shit like grilled cheeses and pancakes and bacon and coffee cake, he would definitely need to do something about his fitness level, and there was no better time to start than now.

The very first sign that this was a terrible idea happened when Tony approached the outside of Ria's Gym, and saw a bunch of very fit, very muscular people milling around the entrance. They were all dressed in skintight Lycra and looked so much more intense than Tony had expected. "Drop in" classes had indicated a kind of casual commitment, but none of these people seemed particularly casual about spin class.

Worse, Tony hadn't even gotten inside yet and had a chance to "run into" Lucas. He nearly chickened out when one of the Lycra-clad women gave him a look, taking in his baggy old USC shorts and worn-out tank top. He didn't really *have* workout clothes, but these had seemed fine when he'd thrown them on. Apparently, from the way she was looking at him, they were *not* fine.

But nobody ever said that Tony Blake was a quitter. He opened the door with a renewed sense of determination and marched over to the registration desk, where a woman with dark braids was bent over a laptop. "Hi," he said, "I'd like to register for the spin class."

She glanced up, her dark eyes narrowing slightly as she took him in. Her nose wrinkled, its gold ring winking under the lights. "Are you sure?" she asked. Her voice wasn't unkind, more *concerned*. And honestly, it wasn't like Tony wasn't feeling like this might be a huge fucking mistake, too. But instead of admitting that he shouldn't have set foot in the door, he nodded enthusiastically.

"Yes," he said. "Yes, I'm definitely sure." *Sure I want into Lucas' pants.*

"Okay," she said. "It starts in five minutes and it's twenty dollars. You might want to . . . stretch a bit, before. Our instructor Charles, he's a little notorious."

"Notorious?" Tony squeaked. But he handed over his credit card anyway and watched as she swiped it.

"Yeah," she said. "But don't worry. Everyone always comes back."

"They do?" Tony couldn't figure out why and the sadism hadn't even started yet. "Why?"

She shrugged, slim, muscular shoulders rising and falling. "I think a lot of people like the pain, you know? But," she added, "if that kind of masochism isn't for you, we have plenty of other classes. The aerobics is always fun, and our yoga classes are always packed. And, we also offer personal training." Her look told him he could probably use the latter more than any of the former, but if he said he'd changed his mind, and he actually wanted to be tormented personally, Lucas would probably pop his head out of the busy gym behind them, and the game would be up.

Instead, Tony just nodded, and let himself get swept up in the crowd heading towards a room filled with bikes. A terrifying guy with bulging calves and the most sculpted ass he had ever seen, wearing the tightest Lycra Tony had ever had the privilege to witness, was standing at the front.

"You can do this," he muttered to himself under his breath. "You can really do this."

Someone glanced over at him, clearly having overheard him, and gave him a sharp shake of her head.

Well, that's fucking supportive of you, Tony thought.

He picked a bike near the back, hoping that he might not get singled out by the guy at the front of the room. In his brief research foray earlier, he'd noticed that a lot of the videos he'd watched had featured a barking, yelling instructor who seemed to be able to pedal at fierce speeds *and* simultaneously emotionally destroy the people around them.

Tony was not here to be reduced to a sniveling puddle; he just wanted to see Lucas and not look like a creep while doing it. Also, there was the bonus of working out on his day off, something he'd known he needed to start doing for a while now.

The second (or twentieth) sign that this was a mistake was when the guy at the front started out the class by screaming, his voice carrying over even the suddenly throbbing dub-step music echoing through the room.

"This is fine," Tony repeated. "Just fine. You can do this."

Except that he was really not confident that he could. Especially when he climbed up on the bike, and a dizzying array of options flashed up on the screen in front of him. He didn't know what any of them meant, but he started pedaling as the instructor said, and was peeved to discover that whatever level he was supposed to be at—he wasn't even fucking close.

So he pedaled harder. And harder. He couldn't remember the last time he'd been on a bike, but it hadn't been like this, and honestly, he was pretty damn sure he wasn't ever going to get on one after this, if he survived it.

"Asses up!" the instructor screeched over the music. "I want to see those asses *bounce*. That's it, that's better! Get it, guys."

Then his gaze, roving the room, must have fallen on Tony, because suddenly it felt like he was under a white-hot spotlight. "Guy in the back, in the ugly *shorts*," he yelled, "I wanna see you move that ass."

"I am moving that ass," Tony muttered, pedaling even faster, annoyed that somehow the fact of wearing shorts was annoying to other people. He couldn't believe he'd paid money for this. He couldn't believe anyone else who'd done it once would ever voluntarily do it again. His lungs were already burning, his calves were cramping, and sweat was beginning to bead on his forehead. And it'd been approximately two minutes. He had no idea how he would survive forty-five minutes of this.

Yes, he hated going to the gym, but he did plenty of active stuff outside. He and Wyatt liked to hike Runyon Canyon, and they often went for long, casual jogs through Malibu, and sometimes even to Venice Beach, people-watching along the boardwalk. Wyatt had even dragged him surfing a few times, though that was definitely more a thing he shared with Ryan, and Tony often ended up sunning himself on the beach instead. But he *was* active, and that wasn't even counting the long labor-intensive hours he spent in the truck. But this spin thing was fucking insane, and the only thing keeping Tony on this torture device, otherwise known as a bicycle, was his pride.

Also, there was the possibility, growing dimmer and dimmer, that he might run into Lucas. Of course, the idea of seeing him now, when Tony was already a sweaty, incoherent mess, was not exactly the non-food-truck-related meet cute he'd envisioned. He'd imagined some flirty banter, him leaning slightly against one of the weight machines, maybe flicking a strand of hair out of Lucas' eyes. He hadn't been dripping, his hair had been fantastic, not pulled back and damp already, and he certainly hadn't thought he'd be limping. But that was rapidly looking like a pretty damn certain possibility, because his legs were already screaming, and Tony couldn't imagine them hurting *less* the longer this torture continued.

The hard drive techno beat segued into something . . . actually tougher and somehow *harder*, and Tony was tempted to actually groan out loud. Had that hell he'd just been through only been the *warm-up?*

There was no way around this—he was definitely going to die, and he'd be a punchline forever, because really, *death by spin class?*

Only the shreds of pride Tony had left kept him on the bike, pedaling away like his life depended on it, and maybe it did. The instructor alternatively sneered and barked at *the guy in the shorts hiding in the back* three more times and maybe someone else would have crumpled and fallen over—Tony already knew there was no getting *off* this bike, you were on it or you were off, probably crying on the floor—but he wasn't going to be that guy. He was already the guy in the shorts, hiding in the back. Fuck if he was going to be a quitter too. He dug deeper, and it didn't get better, necessarily, but he discovered that if he could focus on the beat, and on keeping the rhythm, the pain faded into the background, at least enough that he could *mostly* keep up.

Then it was over, the instructor was clapping, everyone was clapping, and it took a second for Tony to realize two things: *one*, it was finally over, and *two*, he was actually allowed to get off this death contraption. But . . . *could he?*

Gingerly, Tony let his feet come to a slow stop, and he realized as feeling returned to his legs, that he really wasn't sure walking would even be a possibility.

Naturally, as he lifted one leg gingerly over the bike, groaning as his thighs screamed, that was when he saw a flash of telltale messy blond hair and tanned skin. Fate hated him, because even though he'd come here with the express purpose of running into Lucas, he wasn't stupid enough to think he had any brain power left to deal with it now. He'd burned it all up, trying to keep up with the stupid spin class.

He ducked his head, but it was hard, because he was tall, maybe one of the tallest guys in the class, and even though his hair was pulled back, mostly covered with a sweat-slicked bandana, it was probably impossible to hope that Lucas wouldn't see him.

Or maybe he'd see him and think it was creepy and weird that Tony had come to his gym. Maybe he wouldn't even come over.

Tony had suffered through the last forty-five minutes with the sole idea that he *might,* but suddenly, when faced with the possibility, it sounded like an awful idea.

Groaning again, Tony reached down and grabbed his bag, pulling an old, worn t-shirt from its depths and using the soft fabric to wipe the sweat from his face.

"Hey."

Fate *definitely* hated him right now.

Tony looked up, and yep, Lucas was standing right there, a knowing grin on his face, like he knew exactly what Tony was up to, and exactly what Tony had suffered through because of it.

"Hey," Tony said sheepishly.

"I'd say, *imagine seeing you here,* but it's not a coincidence, is it?" Lucas said.

It was embarrassing to be this uncool, to be working this hard at something and basically be failing at it. There'd been so many girls who had chased him over the years, and a few guys too. He'd let a few catch him, at least for a little while, but it had never mattered what happened to those relationships. He didn't know how to play it cool when it *mattered*.

"No," Tony admitted.

"Ah," Lucas said. "Well, at least you got a spin class in?"

"It was . . . uh . . ." Tony rubbed his neck with the t-shirt, and wished he stank marginally less—both physically and also at flirting with this guy, who was so effortlessly cool he reminded Tony of *himself*, just a few years ago.

What had happened? Was he too old? Did he give too many shits? Had Wyatt and Ryan's beautiful "happily ever after" ruined him because now he craved it too?

"That bad, huh?" Lucas said, smiling again, his hazel eyes lighting up with amusement. Tony could only pray that he wasn't secretly laughing at him. Maybe *with* him. But it was hard to say, because Lucas was locked tight, letting so little through his tall, nearly impenetrable walls that Tony never quite knew where he stood.

Tony decided there was no point in pretending that it hadn't been hell. Maybe even admitting that he'd suffered through it would give him a little extra advantage. "It was fucking terrible," he said.

"Yeah, I don't usually do spin," Lucas said. "A little intense for me, but I like the yoga classes here. Ria does a good job. A little less bark and way less bite."

"Maybe I like a little bite," Tony said. Maybe he wasn't sweat-free, and he wasn't casually leaning against one of the weight machines, showing his height to his best advantage, and maybe he couldn't actually *walk*, but he wasn't going to give up without trying. That he could do, even with one foot in the grave.

Lucas stared at him. "Are you flirting with me?"

Abort, abort, abort, Tony's brain screamed. *Too far, way too far.* "Uh, yeah, I guess?" Tony said, totally mortified he'd been called out like that.

"I said I was single," Lucas said, and somehow, impossibly, his face had closed over even more, "not that I was looking for a boyfriend."

He'd seemed at least a little into the attraction brewing between them yesterday, which was why Tony had come down here in the first place—to try to jump-start something outside of the truck—but maybe he'd read it wrong the whole time. That *would* be a first, but then Lucas wasn't like anyone else, which was one of the reasons Tony liked him so much. Not necessarily because he liked the challenge, though he always had before, but because it felt like an accomplishment to see Lucas *really* smile.

He'd seen that smile yesterday. More than once. Today? It was totally MIA. *You* are *a creep,* Tony decided. *Coming here was a colossal mistake, and not only because you can't feel your fucking legs right now.*

"Is anybody?" Tony said, trying to recover.

"You are," Lucas said steadily.

"Oh," Tony said. "I am?"

"You want . . . all that crap that your brother has with Ryan Flores. The house and the happy marriage and the two point five kids probably on the way." Lucas waved his hands around, like he was trying to push away the fantasies brewing around Tony's head. But there weren't any. Did he want a boyfriend? Sure, he did. He wanted to find happiness, just as much as the next person. And he'd thought that maybe he could find it with Lucas.

"I don't think my brother is getting pregnant anytime soon," Tony said.

And there, just when Tony was about to give up, to walk away—despite the agony and impossible numbness in his legs—there it was. That real smile again, blooming across Lucas' features, brightening his eyes, and breaking down that wall, just a little bit more. Could anyone blame Tony for not giving up, when this was what success looked like?

"I'm . . ." Lucas stammered, and somehow that was even cuter, that Tony had finally figured out how to break up some of that unflappable composure.

"It's fine. But really, I'm not looking for that right now. Not what my brother has. We're busy, we're trying to start a food truck empire, right? And you're busy too," Tony said. He would have to figure out a different way to convince Lucas to date him. The direct, *would you like to go get a coffee with me?* approach was not going to work at all. Clearly that would send him running for the hills. But that was okay, because Tony had more than one weapon in his arsenal, and he could figure out just how to woo Lucas without it looking like wooing at all. "Honestly, I came down here to catch you so we could discuss how to catch our thief."

Lucas looked slightly dubious. "You suffered through that spin class so we could talk about catching the guy who stole less than a hundred bucks from you?"

"*And* my onion dip recipe," Tony added seriously. "You did offer, so I assumed that was still good, that we were still on?"

"Sure," Lucas said, and relief swamped Tony. Okay, he hadn't scared him away after all, by coming on too strong.

"Good," Tony said. "I just wanted to check, make sure my 'flirting' hadn't put you off."

"No, of course not," Lucas said, his chin jutting out, determination evident in his face. "I was just . . . worried we wanted two different things."

"Okay, 'cause it's just hard for me to turn off," Tony admitted with a grin. "Part of my completely natural charm. *And* I'm pretty damn sure we want the *same* thing."

Lucas rolled his eyes and smacked him in the shoulder despite his disgustingly sweaty shirt, and everything, it seemed, had returned to normal. If Lucas wanted a friend, Tony could be that. If Lucas wanted something more than just friends—some benefits, maybe—Tony could do that too. Lucas wouldn't even notice that he was falling for him until it was too late.

That was, if everything went according to plan.

"I've been thinking," Lucas said, "we could stake out the truck."

"What?"

"A stakeout," Lucas said impatiently. "Like, let people know, somehow, that there's something valuable inside and then lock up for the night, and watch to see if anyone tries to break in."

Tony thought that sounded like an incredibly dumb idea, except for one very important detail. Stakeouts meant that you had to sit in the same close, tight space with someone for an extended period of time. And this time, it would be him and Lucas, together. Tony mentally rubbed his hands together with glee. This hadn't even been *his* suggestion, and it was freaking perfect.

"Sure, we can do that," Tony said, making sure not to betray any of his excitement that Lucas was willing, for no real reason other than obligation and friendship and *feelings* that he might currently be denying, to be holed up with him somewhere for hours.

"Okay, where are we scheduled tomorrow?" Lucas asked.

"Lunch shift outside Studio City, and dinner down by the Hollywood Bowl. There's a big concert there tomorrow."

"Perfect," Lucas said. "There'll be other trucks there for the concert, right?"

"Yeah," Tony said. "Lots of them. Maybe even those fucking Basket bastards."

"Good. We'll make it clear there's more cash in the truck and then watch it after we lock up for the night."

Tony didn't really think this would work, but frankly, he'd lose a hundred bucks all day long if it meant he could be pressed up right next to Lucas for a few hours. That seemed a small enough price to pay for getting closer to him.

"Sounds good," Tony said. He was going to have to run this by Wyatt, but he couldn't see his brother thinking it was a bad idea; especially when he'd heard about how terrible *Tony's* idea had been.

"I'll see you tomorrow," Lucas said, "I've got a client showing up in a few, so I've got to get ready." He turned to go, and then turned back, a quicksilver grin on his face. "Make sure you ice and you know . . . Advil, stretch, all that good stuff."

"Why?" Tony said, which was stupid, but then Tony was stupid, at least over Lucas.

"Because," Lucas said, and he was smiling that real smile again, the one that made Tony want to kiss it right off of him, "you're not going to be able to walk tomorrow otherwise, boss."

CHAPTER SIX

MAYBE IT WASN'T EXACTLY the most romantic thing that any-one had ever done for him, but suffering through Charles' spin class just for an opportunity to see him? Lucas thought that was pretty fucking dedicated. Though, Lucas thought it might have meant more if Tony had realized just what he was getting into. It seemed he'd come in blind, and frankly, the fact that he hadn't run out immediately, after Charles started his obnoxious barking, Lucas had to give Tony a lot of fucking credit for that.

Lots of absolutely insane people came to Ria's Gym for Charles' spin classes, and most of them even came back, which Lucas had never understood. He always coached with positive reinforcement, so Charles' litany of insults had never made any sense to him.

"I saw you talking to the newbie," Ria said, coming up to him. "Tall, dark hair. He was cute. A little naïve, maybe."

Was Tony naïve? Or just determined? Lucas wasn't sure. He nod-ded absently, filling out the last bit of paperwork for his last client of the day, who'd just left. "I work at his food truck," Lucas told her, because eventually she'd weasel the truth out of him, anyway. She was alarmingly like Tony in that regard.

"Ooooh, *that* guy," Ria said, reaching over and pinching his cheek. She really was obnoxious; he didn't even know why he was friends with her.

Oh, maybe because she paid him solid wages and let him keep a flexible schedule. Also, because she was the one exception to his mostly solitary existence and made him feel a little less lonely.

"You don't even know about him," Lucas told her. He'd deliberately not told her anything about the new job he'd taken for the summer, only mentioning offhandedly—and vaguely, which was totally on purpose—that it would mean he could get free commercial kitchen space.

"No," Ria said with that obnoxious grin still on her face. "But the fact I don't means there's something there. You *like* him."

"Have you seen him? I'd like to climb him like a fucking tree," Lucas grumbled. "Unfortunately, I think he might want a boyfriend."

Ria shot him an unamused glare.

"Seriously," Lucas said. "I am not boyfriend material."

"Just because you've told yourself that you're not boyfriend material," Ria said. "Jasmine and I . . ."

"Are the most perfect couple in existence," Lucas said, rolling his eyes. "Trust me, I'm aware."

"No, I mean it," Ria said, smacking him in the shoulder. "She didn't think she wanted a partner, she was always just good with hookups, and now look at us."

"True love," Lucas retorted sarcastically, even though Ria and Jasmine *were* #couplegoals, even if you weren't into #couplegoals, which Lucas definitely wasn't.

"Yes, actually," Ria said, grinning. "I'm glad you recognize it when you see it, because I thought all those hookups fried that part of your heart into a cold, dead, desert."

He was definitely not going to tell her that Tony made him want to break all his rules. Just seeing him today, sweat-damp hair and sheepish grin at being caught, had tugged impossibly at that spot, the one he'd totally believed was long dead.

But if Ria even suspected for a second that Lucas was interested in Tony for more than just tree climbing, she'd never leave him alone.

"I think Tony's brother and his husband seriously give you and Jasmine strong competition for cutest couple. That's probably why he wants a boyfriend so bad," Lucas said. That was what he'd told himself anyway, hoping that it would help him reconcile the part of him that wanted to pursue Tony even though it was a terrible idea, even though they both wanted such different things. After all, if you were around all that "happily ever after" shit all the time, you'd probably become brainwashed into thinking it was totally awesome.

Tony was brainwashed, that was all. Lucas was doing him a charitable service by rewiring him back to the way he'd used to be, if his and his brother's comments were any indication. It was really too bad Lucas hadn't met him when he was still into hookups; the fun they could've had in bed would've been legendary.

As it was, he really should stay away from Tony Blake, even if Tony Blake couldn't stay away from him.

"Is that what he told you?" Ria wondered.

"He hasn't told me much," Lucas said defensively, even though the opposite was true. Tony was somewhat of an open book; the one who held things back was Lucas himself, plus he had denied it when Lucas had suggested he might want a relationship. And Ria knew it, because she shot him a soft, chiding look.

"I know that's not true. He had that open look about him," she said, waving around the front desk where Tony had probably stood to pay for his spin class. "You know I have instincts about people."

It was Ria's superpower. She could always tell who would be a problem, and who would end up becoming a regular. Who should really try her hot yoga seminars instead of tolerating Charles' nightmare spin classes. Who she should really send to Lucas because they could use a confidence boost. Who might be best off taking Brandon's aerobics classes. Ria always knew, and Lucas noticed that she'd avoided saying what her impression of Tony had been.

"Why did you even let him take the spin class?" Lucas asked, *not* because he was worried at all about Tony, and how painful his next day might be. *Nope, nada, not at all.*

Ria shrugged. "He could handle it. Might not be where he's best suited, but it wasn't the worst idea to try him out in the hardest class, and then throttle back to something he's more comfortable with."

"You dropped the hints, I assume." Lucas had watched and listened to Ria work enough times that he knew that she was absolutely fucking brilliant at gently, carefully prodding her regulars into classes that suited them.

"Of course," Ria said. "Why? Are you worried about him?"

"He's my boss, why would I be worried about him?" Lucas asked.

"The boss you'd like to climb like a tree," Ria reminded him.

Lucas shrugged. "That's just a chemical thing, it'll pass."

"He's really cute, though," Ria said. Clearly, she did not think it would pass. Lucas wasn't quite sure himself, and that was a situation he was not fucking prepared to deal with at all.

"You don't even *like* guys," Lucas pointed out.

"I can still objectively tell when they're cute, and he was," Ria said with an offended sniff. "I'm a lesbian, not fucking *blind*."

"Fine," Lucas said, shutting the folder shut with a decisive snap. "I'm done. Are you done lecturing me on how cute my boss is?"

"Bothered, huh?" Ria said slyly. "Just a quick little step away from *hot* and bothered."

"Stop it," Lucas said, smacking her shoulder with the folder. "Seriously, you are not good at matchmaking. It's not your strong suit."

Except it kind of was. Whether it was a long-term regular discovering they really loved yoga or trying to push Lucas at Tony, she had an unerring knack for it. Lucas knew it because he'd seen it in action so many times, and also because not once had she ever tried to push a patron or a guy at him. Not ever. Tony was the very first. And it just happened that Tony was the first guy in a very long time that made him wish, every once in a while, that he wasn't quite so preoccupied with his life plan. That he *might* have the time for a boyfriend, after all.

Lucas was not surprised at all to see Tony limping like he had a massive stick up his ass when he arrived at the storage lot the next afternoon.

"Hey," he said, pushing his sunglasses up. He was here just for the evening shift, but Tony and Jeremy had been at the truck since the morning, first taking care of the day's prep, and then doing the lunch shift over at Studio City. Tony had texted him to say to meet at the storage lot mid-afternoon, to do a final set of prep for the concert gig.

"Hey," Tony said, sounding just about as miserable as Lucas had expected. "I think your friend Charles is a sadist."

"Not my friend," Lucas said with a quick grin, "and I do remember warning you to ice up."

"I did," Tony said miserably. "And yet."

"Spin class is not for the faint of heart."

Jeremy walked around the corner of the food truck, a half-smoked cigarette dangling from one hand. He didn't acknowledge Lucas, which was also expected. He and Jeremy were never going to be friends, because they wanted the same thing: the man standing in front of them, grimacing as he dumped some ice out of a bin.

"I didn't even know you did spin," Jeremy said. Like he should know every single fucking thing Tony did. Lucas barely held himself back from making his own kind of grimace.

"It was a first-time kind of thing," Tony said with a groan as he carefully leaned against the side of the truck. "Never to be repeated."

"You really should have tried the aerobics," Lucas said. "Or Ria's yoga class is great."

"The only thing scheduled yesterday afternoon was the spin class," Tony said stubbornly, and Lucas' traitorous heart leapt. Even though he'd tried to shut Tony down by saying he wasn't looking for a boyfriend, he still couldn't stop himself from liking, a little too much, how Tony had come to Ria's just for him. Because he'd wanted to see him, even though Lucas wasn't working at the truck. It was cute. Maybe it should've been a little *Twilight* creepy, but despite that, he'd still enjoyed it. Liked it so much, in fact, that he'd volunteered to spend a whole evening crammed together with Tony, watching a food truck that nobody was going to break into.

Why? Because even though Tony refused to consider the possibility, Lucas was damn sure that the culprit—at least of taking the cash—was Jeremy. No other explanation made any sense.

Normally, that sort of blind loyalty would've also driven Lucas nuts. But with Tony? It just proved that he was a good person and an even better friend; the stupidity belonged entirely with Jeremy. Who had such a choice job and a great boss and friend and betrayed them by stealing? Lucas didn't fucking get it at all.

"I still don't get why you had to go work out yesterday," Jeremy said sullenly.

Instead of answering, Tony turned away, heading back into the truck. Which confirmed, once and for all, what Lucas had suspected the entire time—the only reason Tony had come to Ria's was for him.

And yeah, maybe it should've been creepy, maybe it should've sent Lucas running away screaming, maybe he shouldn't have believed him when he'd said he didn't want a boyfriend, but damnit, he *wanted* to take Tony's words at face value. He *wanted* to believe him, because if he didn't, nothing would ever happen between them and that seemed like the worst thing of all.

The dinner rush went by a lot easier, because having Jeremy there, while a total buzzkill, was also the third set of hands they needed to get orders done quickly. Lucas was not unhappy that Jeremy mainly took the orders, and he got to work directly with Tony. Tony was . . . as much as Lucas didn't want to admit it . . . really, really great. He was fantastic at his job, quick and efficient, with a delicate touch that belied how quickly he could prep dishes. And he always had a smile on his face, always happy to be feeding people his food, giving people an opportunity to try something different than what they might eat every day. It was what had originally prompted Lucas to offer to share his jackfruit pulled pork recipe. He'd felt differently at first, but now he was almost sure that Tony's reaction to Lucas questioning the lack of vegetarian options hadn't been because he didn't want to try something new, but because he'd been embarrassed at forgetting one entirely. He hadn't had time to prep the jackfruit yesterday—his shift had gone long and then there'd been Ria's interrogation—but he was going to make it a priority to bring to his next shift.

And the more Lucas watched Tony, the more he realized Tony watched *him*. Maybe he'd intended to impress Lucas with the menu, but instead of being impressed, Lucas had pointed out the most glaring issue with it.

"Hey," Tony said, leaning over the counter where Lucas was putting the final touches on a few plates of fish tacos. "Hey, I just thought of something."

"Hmmm?" Lucas gave the tacos a final sprinkle of chopped cilantro and slid them onto the window ledge. "Fish tacos for Marcy!"

"How are we going to stake out the truck?" Tony said softly. He was clearly trying to keep their investigation from Jeremy, which Lucas was happy about. Maybe he didn't think Jeremy was the problem, but it made sense to keep quiet about it.

"I don't know," Lucas said, sliding another serving of battered fish into the fryer for the next order. Fish tacos were a big hit tonight. "We stake it out?"

"*How?*" Tony hissed.

"What do you mean *how*?" Lucas asked. Tony was kind of weird, except it was in this endearing way that Lucas didn't think he'd tolerate in someone who had shittier hair or was slightly shorter or even worse, had less natural charm.

"Like, I drive a motorcycle," Tony said. "How are we supposed to stake out the truck on a motorcycle?"

Lucas glanced up. He didn't know if he loved or hated the frisson of heat that sparked through him when he thought of riding with Tony, plastered to his back, the engine roaring between their thighs. "I have my car," he said.

"Oh, I didn't know you had a car," Tony said.

"What do you think I do? Skateboard around town?" Lucas retorted. "Of course I have a fucking car."

"Okay," Tony said. "What about snacks?"

"Snacks?"

"Snacks and binoculars," Tony said. "We need both of those things for a stakeout."

Lucas actually didn't know what they needed—he hadn't thought this through any further than suggesting it. "Do you own a pair of binoculars?" he asked.

Tony appeared to be trying to figure out if he did. "Uh, no?" he finally admitted. "Do you think they're a requirement?"

We're not going to be catching anyone; only spending several hours pressed up together in my tiny-ass car, a situation which I am already regretting. "No," Lucas said. Because the chance of anyone *trying* to break into the truck was so slim that getting a pair of binoculars just for this seemed silly.

"I think we can just look really hard, you know," Tony said. "But the snacks, those are non-negotiable."

"I have some of my energy bars," Lucas said. "Is that snack-like enough for you, Mr. Stakeout?"

"I think so," Tony said, nodding enthusiastically. "I've been wanting to try them."

"Spin class and now energy bars. Give it a few more weeks, and you're going to actually be . . ." Lucas gave a faux shocked gasp. "*Healthy.*"

Tony smacked him on the back as he turned towards the window and an approaching customer. It wasn't quite low enough to be anywhere near his ass, but Lucas felt the sting, and *wanted*, even as he tried to push the temptation so far out of reach that it'd stop bothering him with everything he couldn't have. Because even as he acknowledged that he *shouldn't* have Tony, he slid further down the slippery slope of rationalization.

Maybe they were just fucking inevitable.

The crowd had slowed to a trickle, and Tony took the opportunity to go make small talk with some of the other truck owners. "I'll drop a few hints," Tony said, because apparently he really liked the idea that the Basket guys were behind the petty thefts. And that left Lucas and Jeremy alone in the truck.

Lucas was not surprised when Jeremy opened his mouth and asked, a pouty edge to his voice, "What were you two talking about over there, so quiet?"

"Like to listen to other people's conversations?" Lucas asked, dodging the question. "That's not really nice."

"I'm looking out for Tony," Jeremy said stubbornly. "He's too nice, too trusting." His glare told Lucas that not only did Jeremy see him as an interloper, he thought Lucas was going to take advantage.

Lucas swallowed his frustration and only said, "He sure is."

"And," Jeremy burst out, "I know he's pan, but he's fucking picky, just so you know."

It shouldn't have made him feel good that Tony didn't pursue just anyone, and he was pursuing Lucas. It should have put him off, it should have freaked him out, because he *didn't* want a boyfriend, and no matter what Tony said, he still might. But instead of making him want to run for the hills, Lucas slid a little more down that slippery slope.

What would it hurt if they hooked up a few times? They'd have fun. Tony was so tense about things, sometimes, and the exercise would help that, but so would a nice regular sexual outlet. And Lucas could definitely help with that. It would almost be a charitable exercise. Except that Lucas would be getting just as good as he was giving. Tony was that kind of guy. Lucas knew, because his attention was focused and specific. He'd want to take Lucas apart and put him together again.

It would be so damn good. Lucas already knew it, and the shiver that went up his spine when Tony returned to the truck, his gaze immediately falling on Lucas, was way more evidence than he'd ever needed.

"Let's pack up," Tony said. Lucas glanced at his watch. It was twenty minutes early, but they *had* sold out of most of their prepped food, and they hadn't had a customer in ten minutes. It wasn't *so* early, but it was early enough that Lucas knew Tony was eager to start the stakeout.

Eager to catch the thief in the act? Or eager to get Lucas alone?

Lucas was afraid he knew the answer, already.

Tony didn't think he was imagining things when Jeremy seemed to clean up even slower than usual. Maybe he was just extra eager, Tony rationalized. Because goddamnit, he wanted to get Lucas alone. He wanted to be crammed together in Lucas' hopefully tiny car, breathing the same air, only the console separating them.

Jeremy had definitely guessed that was the way the wind was blowing, because while he normally was somewhat slower than Tony liked, he usually didn't actually dawdle, but he was tonight.

"Come on," Tony said, finally losing his patience. "I can finish cleaning up when we get back to the lot."

"Fine," Jeremy grumbled. "You got a hot date or something?"

"Something like that," Tony said, even though Lucas was right there. Okay, Lucas didn't want a boyfriend—he'd made that abundantly clear—but that didn't mean that Tony wasn't going to work his ass off anyway, trying to convince him that what he thought having a boyfriend would be like wouldn't be anything like dating Tony.

It'd been over a year since Brody had dumped him, and that sting was long gone, but he'd not found anyone since then he was even passingly interested in. Until Lucas. And that was unusual enough that Tony wasn't going to let a commitment phobia derail his plans. And he had *plans*. Plans for Lucas' big meaty biceps and his chiseled abs and his careful, deft hands. And his dick, too.

Definitely his dick, Tony thought as he watched Lucas bend over to stow something on the bottom shelf of the storage fridge, *and even more definitely, that absolutely fucking perfect ass.*

Just looking at that ass, outlined in his loose shorts, made Tony nearly forget about the pain in his legs.

"I didn't think you were dating anyone," Jeremy said.

"I'm not," Tony retorted. Why the sudden incredible interest in his sex life? Did Jeremy *like* him? No, that was just not possible. They'd been friends forever, and casual work buddies before that. Jeremy hadn't appeared interested one single time since they'd met. Maybe he was just a big fat gossip.

"Maybe he *wants* to be," Lucas added slyly, and the amused glint in his hazel eyes was almost enough for Tony to order Jeremy to leave, and to proceed to press Lucas up against the nearest convenient horizontal surface and kiss him like he was dying to.

"Just tell me it's not your ex," Jeremy said.

Tony rolled his eyes. "Hell would freeze over first."

"Why?" Lucas asked casually, but there wasn't anything casual about the sudden laser focus of his gaze. He wanted to know about Tony's ex. Tony felt like doing a little celebratory dance, right here in the middle of the food truck.

"No offense, T, but he was a real jerk," Jeremy said, not sounding particularly sorry about this fact.

"It's hardly a state secret," Tony said, feeling warm all over because Lucas' eyes were still on him. Like he couldn't quite look away, even as he finished wrapping up the leftover salsas.

"Yeah, you deserve someone *loyal*, this time around," Jeremy said, and Tony wanted to roll his eyes at his self-important tone. Like only Jeremy was qualified to pick Tony's next romantic partner.

"I'll keep that in mind," Tony said dryly. "Okay, are we ready to go? Yes? Okay, let's blow this joint."

It took them a long-ass forty-five minutes to drive the truck back to the lot. It couldn't have possibly been the longest drive of Tony's life, but it sure felt like it. When he finally parked Belinda, he felt like he was going out of his mind a little. Jeremy had claimed the front seat next to Tony, by length of employment history at the truck, and Tony hadn't been able to argue with that. Unfortunately, that also meant that Jeremy peppered him with questions for nearly the entire forty-five minutes, because he obviously did not comprehend Tony's reluctance to talk about who he wanted to date.

After the third time Jeremy had insisted on meeting the person, so he could make sure they were "worthy," Tony had been mighty tempted to turn to him and say, "It's Lucas, you fucking idiot." But that would create so many problems, not only between Jeremy and Lucas, but with Tony's plan to woo Lucas slowly and carefully, that he kept his mouth shut.

"See you in a few days?" Jeremy said hopefully as he climbed down from the front seat. Tony was already out, unlocking the back door.

Lucas was lounging against the kitchen counter, eyes glued to his phone. When he looked up though, his eyes were full of laughter. Jeremy's voice was loud, and when he whined, it could really carry. Lucas must have heard their entire conversation, and he'd definitely found it funny.

Tony was going to extract a pound of flesh from him in retribution, one mind-blowing orgasm at a time.

"Yeah," Tony said distractedly. "I'll text you next week's schedule." How could he even *think* about schedules when Lucas was gazing at him with that knowing look in his eyes? Like he understood exactly how crazy he drove Tony and how crazy he wanted Tony to drive him in return.

"Okay, good," Jeremy said, finally, *finally* turning and walking away, back to his own car, leaving him and Lucas alone.

"You shouldn't egg him on," Tony said, but he was smiling and he couldn't even help it. Lucas brought that out in him.

"No, but it's fun," Lucas said.

"I didn't think you did 'fun,'" Tony retorted. With the amount of hours Lucas put into his various jobs, did he even have *time* for fun?

Lucas just smiled, like a cat with the canary, and sidled up to him, so casually, but with so much intent, Tony's heart rate doubled. "I like fun just fine," he murmured. "I could show you sometime."

Gah. Tony wanted to melt to the floor. He thought he was good at flirting and innuendo, and at making sure someone knew he wanted them, but this was a master at work. Having all that expertise focused just on him? Tony wasn't sure whether he wanted to cheer or die.

There was part of Tony who wanted to just say *fuck the stakeout,* but then he remembered what Lucas had said, just the day before. *I said I was single, not that I was looking for a boyfriend.*

Lucas would want it free and easy, quick and simple. Uncomplicated. He'd want to hook up without any strings. And it wasn't like Tony *didn't* want that, but he also wanted more. He wanted every single damn string, tying them together until Lucas didn't ever want to leave.

"You almost done here?" Tony said, like Lucas hadn't practically just offered to get naked.

"Yeah," Lucas said. Maybe surprised that Tony hadn't just dropped his pants then and there. *Good,* Tony thought, *make him work for it a little.* "Let me grab my stuff, and we can go to my car."

"Where'd you park?" Tony asked.

"Across the street." Lucas shot him a quicksilver grin. "We're staking the truck out, so *duh.*"

Tony couldn't help it, he tilted his head and turned it so he could see out the open doorway. And there was a very small little car over there. A Mini Cooper, in fact. A car that Tony had always complained was designed for small children and clowns.

He shot Lucas a look. "Am I even going to fit in that car?" He'd wanted small, but *Jesus.*

Lucas eyed him up and down once, gaze lingering, lighting up every single one of Tony's nerves until he felt luminous.

"I think we can make it work, boss," he finally said. "But let's get going. Lock up?"

Tony did, jiggling the handle of every door once, just to make sure they were locked. They hadn't set their trap with anything—only words—but he still felt protective of Belinda and didn't want anyone to *actually* break in. He just wanted to catch them in the act.

"Okay," Tony said, "let's do this thing."

CHAPTER SEVEN

LUCAS KNEW HE WAS playing with fire. But it was no longer an abstract idea in his mind that he and Tony might hook up—it was a blazing certainty, fired by knowledge that he wanted him so much that he couldn't push him away anymore. But if they were going to do this, they were going to do it on *his* terms. Quick and easy, an uncomplicated hookup that guaranteed that Tony couldn't tie him up with any unwanted strings. No, they would definitely keep things simple, and Lucas knew it wouldn't be hard to convince Tony to go along with it. The heat in his eyes was evidence that he wanted Lucas enough to not care how he got him.

Lucas unlocked his car, stashing his bag in the backseat, and then climbing in the front, just in time to watch as Tony gingerly folded himself into the passenger seat.

"Ouch," Tony said when he was finally seated and he'd shut the door behind himself. "Remind me to never do spin class ever again."

"I told you, you're perfect for aerobics or yoga," Lucas said, shaking his head. "But it was a little bit cute."

Tony grinned, and his smile lit a spot up inside Lucas that wasn't anywhere near his dick. *Playing with fire,* his mind screamed, but he ignored it, because Tony had been right. He didn't have fun often, and this was *fun.* He was going to enjoy this, even if everything ended up going straight to hell because of it.

"Me almost dying was only a little bit cute? I think it might've been even a . . . *medium* amount of cuteness," Tony claimed.

"You weren't almost dying," Lucas said. "Not even close. All you had to do was get off the damn bike."

Tony just shook his head, still smiling so brightly that it *hurt* to look at him. How did people encounter him every day and walk away? Lucas wished he could learn their secrets, because he'd discovered he was literally incapable of walking away from this guy. He kept trying to do it and kept failing spectacularly. "Ride or die, man," Tony said, *"ride or die."*

Lucas laughed despite how utterly pathetic he sounded. "You sound straight out of a Vin Diesel movie."

"Are you insulting Vin Diesel?" Tony said. "Because if you are, I'm not sure you're the right partner for a stakeout."

"Does Vin Diesel go on stakeouts a lot?" Lucas wondered.

"Of course he does. He's Vin Diesel. That's what he does. Looks intimidating with big biceps and says silly catch phrases in a very serious tone of voice. Fucks you up with just a look. *And* goes on stakeouts."

He laughed *again*. Goddamnit. "Have you ever seen a Vin Diesel movie?"

When Tony shook his head, the laughter came before he could even help himself. Tony was the kind of guy who charmed you even when you were absolutely determined *not* to be charmed. It was like a disease.

"Okay," Lucas said. "Noted. I think I'll drive around the block and then we'll park further back." They were right under a streetlight which he hadn't been thinking about this afternoon when he'd initially parked. Why? Because he hadn't been thinking of stealth. He'd been thinking of Tony. And thinking of Tony usually meant there was zero room to think about *anything* else.

"Why?" Tony asked, looking around, obviously missing the streetlight that was practically shining on top of them. It was adorable, and it shouldn't have been. But then Tony was quicksand, and Lucas was already in deep.

"Because we're right under a goddamned streetlight, you idiot," Lucas said, but instead of annoyed, he just sounded fond. "Don't you know anything about stakeouts?"

"Nope," Tony said cheerfully. "Do you?"

Lucas started the engine and pulled out onto the deserted street. It was after ten, and while this might be a busy industrial area during the day, it was always very quiet at night. "No, not really," Lucas admitted. "Which is why we're lacking even the most basic supplies for this. Like binoculars."

"It's okay," Tony said, pulling something out of his pocket. "I brought a disguise, just in case we have to sneak up on someone." He waved something dark around Lucas' face just as he pulled back to the curb, further behind the streetlight. With a quick grab, Lucas snatched the dark item and unrolled it. "This is a beanie," he said incredulously. "What are you going to do, pull this over your head so you can't see anything?"

"No, silly," Tony said, snatching the cap back. "It's meant to cover my hair."

"Your hair?"

"I mean," Tony said, tossing it like one of those Instagram models, "it's pretty memorable, don't you think?"

He wanted to laugh, but he couldn't, because it was too spot on. Lucas rolled his eyes, even though, frankly, he agreed with him. He wanted his hands in all that hair, to use it to pull Tony down closer to him so he wasn't so damn far away. It looked soft, and he had a feeling it'd feel even softer.

"You are incredibly fucking vain," he said.

"Does it count as vanity if it's true?" Tony wondered.

"Yes," Lucas said, exasperated. "It definitely counts."

"Well, I was thinking of doing something with it as a backup career, you know, in case the truck doesn't work out," Tony said. "So many people are always going on and on about my hair, I thought, why not become one of those Instagram influencers, you know, always tossing my hair around and shilling hair products."

"I don't see you selling gel and mousse for a living," Lucas said shortly, except that he *could*. He could totally see Tony doing it, and making a fortune at it, because surely some of that charisma would translate to a screen.

"It's just a backup," Tony said, shrugging. "I don't think I'll need it, but it's always good to have one. I mean, what's your backup? You know, other than part-time food truck guy, and personal trainer guy? You could totally go into porn."

Tony shot him a quick, knowing grin, and the air in the compact car, already feeling too close, wrenched even tighter. Or maybe that was just all the sexual tension. "You know I'm kidding, right?" he added, even though he hadn't had to say it. Lucas had already figured it out.

"I figured it out," Lucas said dryly.

Tony leaned back in the seat, stretching those long, endless legs in front of him. "This is actually surprisingly comfortable," he said.

"Thanks?"

"I was totally expecting it to be cramped, but it's fine. Plenty of room," Tony said, and just when Lucas thought he might be serious, he wiggled his dark eyebrows suggestively.

"Oh my god," Lucas said, trying not to laugh *again*. "Do you ever turn it off?"

"This is one hundred percent me, baby," Tony said.

There was nothing Lucas hated more than pet names. They drove him wild, and not usually in the enjoyable way. But there was something about the knowing way Tony said *baby* that made him want to climb over the console and convince him with only his mouth and his hands that everything he was doing wasn't sexy.

Yep, not even a little bit sexy.

To distract himself, he finally glanced away from Tony—it was harder than it looked, to be in the same small space as him and not glue his eyes to him. But the whole point of being here was to monitor the truck.

"So, who did you talk to about the cash that you're apparently keeping in your truck?" Lucas asked, resolutely staring at the shadowed outline of Belinda.

"Oh, the guys from Basket were there, of course." Tony rolled his eyes. "They are such assholes."

There was no way those guys had tracked down Belinda and picked the lock without a sign, all to steal less than a hundred bucks. "Who else?"

"Gabe and Sean were both there. I had to separate them, they kept yelling at each other," Tony said. "It's too bad."

"Why were they yelling?"

"Oh, they have the same truck name," Tony said sheepishly. "And I told Gabe it wasn't a big deal, because you know, LA is an enormous city, and it's just a name? But Sean is really intense about it, and I wish I hadn't told Gabe it was okay, because now every time they end up in the same area, shit happens."

"Shit happens? What kind of shit?" Lucas wondered. He didn't know much hot food truck gossip, even though he liked to try them out, because his budget for fine dining was basically zero. Even then, he didn't think two guys with the same truck name would break into Tony's truck, but you never knew what angry people would do.

"Oh, they just get into each other's face. Oh, and Gabe threw a meatball at Sean once."

Lucas gaped. "He threw a meatball at him?"

"It was hilarious. Sean has these pristine white aprons, with this cute little wrap logo embroidered on them, and Gabe nailed him *right* in the sternum with it. Got tomato sauce everywhere. It was fucking *priceless,*" Tony said with a wide grin.

"Okay, I think it's safe to say that meatball throwing is a far cry from stealing money out of your truck," Lucas admitted.

"Well, *yeah*, they don't dislike *me*, they dislike each other. Though," Tony said thoughtfully, "they really are pretty obsessed with each other."

Lucas raised an eyebrow. "Like that?"

"I don't know," Tony admitted, "but maybe."

"Well, it's definitely not them," Lucas said, even though he'd never really believed it could be. Jeremy was still the number one suspect on a very short list.

"No. Who else was there?" Tony pondered. "Um, I think Tate was too. He probably heard me. He's usually at these events. Ash too."

"But you don't think any of them would steal your money," Lucas said, because that much was clear enough.

"No, of course not, they're friends," Tony said. "But I thought maybe someone who works for them? I don't know. I don't know who would steal it."

Jeremy would steal it, you idiot, Lucas thought. And Jeremy had enough of a warning something was up that he probably wouldn't try tonight.

"Well," Lucas said, "that's why we're here. So we can catch them."

"Right," Tony said, except he sounded less than convinced. And frankly, Lucas didn't think they'd be catching anyone either. They were absolutely fucking terrible at stakeouts.

The one thing Tony was sure of was that they were *terrible* at this. The chance of someone coming and breaking into Belinda tonight, while they just happened to be watching, was basically *nil*, and yet he was here anyway. The reason for that was pretty fucking obvious, but they still hadn't really acknowledged it yet.

"So," Tony asked after a few silent minutes had passed, with their eyes glued to Belinda, sitting in the dark across the street, "I do have one stakeout-related question."

"Hmmm?" Lucas asked.

"How are we supposed to pee?"

Lucas laughed, and the sound lit Tony up from the inside. "I think that's obvious, though I'm not sure I'm prepared . . ." He broke off and suddenly was unbuckling his seat belt, twisting in his seat so he could stick his head into the backseat. "I just cleaned . . ." he said, his voice muffled. "But I think we might be lucky . . ."

Triumphantly, he returned to the front seat with an empty glass bottle in his hand. "Cheat day was yesterday," he said, "and I had a Mexican Coke. Hadn't had a chance to recycle it yet."

"You are something else," Tony said. "Cheat days. Recycling your bottles. What is wrong with you?"

Nothing's wrong with him, except that he's too fucking perfect.

"I'm beginning to figure you out, you know," Lucas said knowingly. "You keep trying to shock me but it's not working."

"It seems to be working pretty well from over here," Tony said. "*I like fun just fine; I could show you sometime.*"

Lucas smiled sheepishly. Like he'd just been caught. "Yeah, yeah, that was a weak moment." Except that it hadn't been, and they both knew it. The tension was stretched so tightly between them, Tony couldn't believe he hadn't given in yet and just leaned over and kissed Lucas the way they were both dying to. But the fact that he knew Lucas wanted it quick and easy and uncomplicated kept stopping him. He had to make Lucas understand that this wasn't just a quick fuck. It needed to be more than that.

"What's the bottle for?" Tony asked.

"For peeing, of course."

"You want me to pee in this bottle?" Tony said incredulously. "Really?"

Lucas grinned. "It's not a real stakeout unless someone whips a dick out."

"Oh, did Vin Diesel teach you that?" Tony wondered.

"He could, and I wouldn't complain." Lucas waved the bottle in Tony's face. "Just let me know when you get desperate, *baby*."

Tony knew that he'd been trying to make fun of him with the *baby*, but the moment it came out of his mouth, everything changed. Lucas knew it too, because Tony could see his breaths coming in short, desperate pants, and for a long moment the tension stretched so tightly between them, Tony was shocked it didn't just *snap*. But they both stayed in their respective seats, eying each other. It was only a matter of *when*, not *if*. And Tony desperately needed to outlast him, because if Tony broke, he knew he'd give Lucas exactly what he wanted. It'd be fierce, and it'd be hot, and then it would be over.

Suddenly, something caught his attention out of the corner of his eye. "Shit," Tony exclaimed. He'd been so fucking distracted by trying not to kiss Lucas, he'd missed the movement across the street. "I think someone's out there."

Lucas peered through the windshield. "You think so?"

"I swear I saw something," Tony insisted. He'd definitely seen *something* move, but he couldn't see anything now. It had just faded into the shadows, melted away like he'd never seen it at all. "Grrrrr," he whined. "This stakeout stuff kind of sucks."

"Yeah," Lucas agreed. "Except . . ."

Tony really didn't want him to finish that sentence. If Lucas acknowledged the tension between them, he wasn't sure he'd be responsible for his actions.

"Hey," Tony said, changing the subject, "where are those famous energy bars? I want to try one."

Lucas chuckled, like he knew exactly what Tony was up to. "Fine, fine, I'll grab one. Do you want blueberry cobbler or white chocolate apricot?"

"White chocolate apricot, *duh*," Tony said.

"I thought chefs were supposed to hate white chocolate," Lucas teased as he handed him the bar, wrapped in simple packaging. Tony looked over the wrapper carefully, and wasn't surprised to see the letters of the brand, SoYou Energy Bars, stamped in a simple, strong black font against a plain white background. It matched the aesthetic of Lucas' Instagram, which he nearly mentioned as he finally tore it open, but he was trying *not* to look like a stalking creep, and admitting that he'd been all over Lucas' Instagram multiple times, without ever actually *following him*, might not help his case.

He took a bite of the white chocolate-studded bar and, to his surprise, didn't immediately want to spit it out. He'd had zero expectations, because frankly most energy bars tasted like over-processed garbage, with no distinctive flavor at all. But this was sweet and crunchy. He could taste the nuts and the white chocolate and the apricots, all layered into a bar that must contain the "energy" the label had boasted about. Really, he shouldn't have been surprised, because he'd worked next to Lucas in the truck for nearly two weeks now, and he was an excellent cook, with an innate attention to detail, and a flair that Tony had always prided himself on. Instead of going into the energy bar business, he could've worked his way up the line at so many California restaurants, and done really well for himself. But even though he was good at cooking, that clearly wasn't where his heart lay.

"It's good," Tony said, finishing his bite and swallowing it. "It's *really* good."

"I know," Lucas said, and if he was a little smug, Tony couldn't blame him. The bar was really not very high in energy bars, and he'd way exceeded it.

"The flavor combo is also really fantastic, and the nuts add just the right amount of salty crunch."

"That's what he said," Lucas teased again. "Or maybe it's what Vin Diesel said?"

Tony couldn't stop the laugh that escaped him. "Is that your type, then, the cage fighter, 'beat you half-to-death with a wrench if you looked at him wrong' type?"

"Maybe I just like a shaved head," Lucas said lightly, and the irony was not lost on Tony, who'd *just* said he wanted to start an Instagram to advertise his hair.

But they'd come too far now for Tony to believe that Lucas wasn't attracted to him, even if he claimed Vin Diesel—practically the opposite of Tony in every way—was his type.

"Sure you do," Tony said. And then, just as he was finishing another big bite of energy bar, kind of wishing he had some of that Mexican Coke to wash it down with, he saw another flash across the street, but he didn't think it was tall enough to be a person—unless that person was weirder than he'd ever imagined and was *crawling* towards the truck.

"Hey," Lucas said as Tony automatically reached for his door. "What are you doing?"

Tony threw him a challenging look. "Defending Belinda's honor," he insisted, even though he was sure that whatever was creeping around the truck wasn't actually in any danger of stealing anything.

He climbed out of the car and Lucas, after making an exasperated sigh, followed suit. "You know we're probably going to die," Lucas hissed.

"You're strong," Tony said, pointing across the street. "Maybe you could just go punch out whoever's over there." Except he knew that they wouldn't be punching *anyone,* not tonight.

"And you're tall," Lucas retorted. "What are you going to do? Hold them still while I punch their brains out?"

"Sure," Tony said, pulling his ski cap over his hair, even though he was almost sure it would be unnecessary.

They crossed the street, Lucas doing a really cute kind of walk-run type of thing. Tony realized he was trying to be stealthy, and somehow, impossibly, it got even cuter. When they finally made it over to where Belinda sat in the quiet parking lot, Tony looked around for the figure he'd sworn he'd seen creeping around.

"So?" Lucas whispered harshly. "Where are they?"

"I think . . ." Tony said, and just as he started to say what he thought, an orange and white cat darted from between the two front tires and came to a stop, just out of reach of Tony's hands. "I think we've found our culprit."

Lucas eyed the cat dubiously. "You think this cat broke into a locked food truck and stole a hundred bucks in cash, and also your onion dip recipe?"

Tony didn't know much about cats, but he'd always assumed cats on the street that weren't cared for looked starving and straggly, but this one looked anything but. If he could pinpoint its expression, he would guess it was more . . . *smug* than desperate. "Maybe? You see the way he's eying us? I think this cat could do anything he wanted."

Lucas rolled his eyes and dropped to eye level with the cat. "Hey," he cooed at it, "you wanna tell us where you hid the money? Huh? That's a good kitty." He reached out a hand, but the cat just looked unimpressed and uninterested in being coaxed anywhere near him.

"Maybe we should leave it something to eat?" Tony wondered aloud. "Maybe some water? Some milk? One of your energy bars? What do cats even eat?"

Like it had heard and understood his words, the cat gave a hearty meow of denial and turned and, its tail flicking behind it, trotted off.

"Well," Tony said, "I don't think he wanted anything to eat. Definitely not one of your energy bars."

"Like I'd waste one on him," Lucas grumbled. "Though I feel better because I definitely feel that was a *fuck you* to any help."

"He's doing fine," Tony said, a little wistfully. He wouldn't have minded a cute, fuzzy kitten to cuddle up to at night, when his bed felt especially empty. But maybe he'd get even luckier and Lucas would end up there, someday.

"Yeah," Lucas agreed. "But maybe we should try to trap him? Make sure he's neutered or spayed?"

"Really?" Tony didn't know how they'd ever capture such a street-savvy cat; they couldn't even manage a simple stakeout.

"My mom does it," Lucas said. It was the first thing that he'd ever said about either parent, and Tony had begun to wonder if he wasn't on good terms with them. But when he opened his mouth to ask more details, Lucas gave a sharp shake of his head. "Don't bother," he said. "We haven't talked in years. Apparently stray cats need a lot more care than gay sons." His voice only contained a hint of bitterness; mostly he just sounded resigned to the situation.

But that didn't make it okay. Tony reached for him without even thinking about it, pulling him into a tight hug. "I'm sorry," he said.

"You didn't make them choose the cats," Lucas said, voice muffled by Tony's shoulder.

"Doesn't mean I'm not sorry," Tony said and then realized he was still holding him, their bodies pressed together, and they fit just as fantastically as he'd ever imagined, late at night and early in the morning when he was lying in that lonely bed.

For a split second, he considered tipping his head down, and brushing his lips against Lucas' but he wasn't going to take advantage of his shitty familial situation to push their relationship. Reluctantly, he released him, and Lucas went, taking a few steps back, his expression blank under the bright light of the streetlight above them.

"We should at least name it," Lucas said.

"The cat?"

"Of course the cat," Lucas retorted. "How about we call it Vin?"

"What if it's a girl?" Tony wondered, and Lucas shot him a disbelieving look.

"I think you actually *care* about the cat," he said.

Tony raised his hands in defeat. "Yeah, of course I do. But I'm not the one who wanted to *name* it."

"Okay, that's fair," Lucas said, chuckling. "How about Dom?" he suggested, naming Vin Diesel's most famous character from the *Fast and Furious* franchise. "It could either be Dominic or Dominique."

"I like it," Tony said, and then raised his voice. "Bye, kitty Dom!"

Lucas rolled his eyes. "You don't know *anything* about cats, do you?"

"Actually, no," Tony said. "Just about as much as I know about stakeouts."

"First lesson. If you want to trap it someday," he said, "don't raise your voice. Just stay calm and relaxed, even if you're excited."

"How do you know I'm excited?" Tony wondered. But he *was.* The sexual tension between them hadn't lessened with the discovery of Dom, and it definitely hadn't evaporated since Tony had hugged him. Want was still flowing thick and easy through his veins, making it hard to concentrate.

"Oh, I can tell," Lucas said knowingly, and Tony nearly groaned in frustration. He was trying to put things in Lucas' court and not rush anything, but the man was making it goddamned difficult—and even worse, Tony was sure he *knew* it, too.

"Well, I'll keep that in mind," Tony said shortly. "You have the schedule for the rest of the week?"

"Yeah," Lucas said, nodding and scuffing a chunk of weeds growing in between a crack in the asphalt with one rainbow-doodled toe. "I've got it."

"It's too bad the stakeout didn't work out," Tony said, even though he'd never expected it to. Still, he'd gotten an hour or two alone with Lucas, and that was what he'd *really* wanted.

"Yeah," Lucas said, and then after hesitating, continued. "We should do it again sometime."

It was exactly what Tony had wanted to say, but he hadn't wanted to push his good fortune. "Really?"

"We didn't catch him, did we?" Lucas said. "Just Dom, and I don't think he's been breaking into Belinda."

"Yeah, yeah, right," Tony said, grinning. Unfortunately, he couldn't think of another excuse to stick around. He reached for his keys to unlock the truck and grab his stuff. "I'll see you tomorrow morning?"

"Yeah," Lucas said, and he started to turn away. But then he was back, and he was suddenly right in Tony's space, crowding him against Belinda's door. Their bodies were pressed together like they had been only a few minutes ago, but this wasn't just a comfort, it was a match to gasoline. Tony stared down at him.

"One more thing," Lucas said, his casual tone the complete opposite of the sudden galloping of Tony's heart. Then, like it was nothing, Lucas reached up and pressed his lips to Tony's.

It wasn't a short or sweet or polite kiss; it was ravenous almost immediately, Tony's hands reaching up to cup Lucas' cheeks, to angle him perfectly so he could just dive into his mouth, his tongue stroking against Lucas'.

Tony had had a lot of kisses in his thirty-one years. He'd had some great ones, quite a few mediocre ones, and even a handful of terrible kisses that he'd tried to block out. But nothing quite reached the level of this one. Even the first kiss he'd ever had with a man—with *Brody*—hadn't felt like this. Like he'd been searching for something, and he'd finally found it in the way his mouth and his hands and his body fit so fucking flawlessly against Lucas'.

Lucas groaned into his mouth, clearly enjoying the kiss as much as Tony was. He was still pressing Tony against the door, and then his hands drifted down his chest, leaving trails of electric wake in their path, and before Tony could wrap his head around what was happening, Lucas was tugging at his belt.

He broke off the kiss with a muttered oath. He hadn't wanted to stop. He'd wanted to keep going until they were both red-faced and sweaty and uncontrollable. He'd wanted to let Lucas do whatever he wanted to him against this door. But . . . then there was a distinctive difference in how he and Lucas wanted to approach this thing brewing between them. Lucas wanted it fast and easy and simple, no strings, nothing to hold him to Tony. Probably so he could disappear in a few weeks, or if Tony was especially lucky, a few months. He'd just fade away, and all Tony would have would be the memory. And Tony wanted so much more than just a memory.

He wanted it enough that he could even sacrifice the sweet, easy pleasure of *right now.*

"Hey," Tony said, stepping to the side, Lucas' hands falling from his waist. "*Hey,*" he repeated when Lucas gave him a confused, wild-eyed look. Like the last thing he'd expected was for Tony to stop him from going for his dick.

"Is there something wrong?" Lucas asked before Tony could reassure him.

"Nothing's wrong," Tony soothed, reaching for Lucas again and pulling him close, even as he slightly resisted. Was he embarrassed?

Annoyed? Tony wasn't sure, but the words came to him anyway. "Hey," he repeated, leaning down, giving Lucas' ear a quick nibble before dropping his voice down to a mere rumble. "Hey, you know when you really, desperately want something? Want it so bad you think about it all the time? Like you're fucking *craving* it? Like you'll die without it?" Lucas' breath was coming in short, choppy pants, and Tony felt his cock grow even harder. God, he wanted this man, and not just for a few nights. He had to fucking get this right, or else that would never happen. "When you want it and you wait for it, it's even better," he murmured into Lucas' ear, giving it another quick nibble, and feeling him shudder under his hands. "By the time we hook up, you're going to be crying for it, but it's gonna be so damn good, you won't care."

Lucas huffed out something that might have either been a laugh or a moan. But he didn't move an inch. "You're kinda a sadist, you know?"

"Yeah," Tony said, sucking an unbroken chain of kisses up his neck as Lucas' fingers tightened into sharp points against his shoulders. "But you love it."

Lucas gave a long, shuddering sigh, and then finally turned his head, capturing Tony's mouth in another long, hot kiss. But this time he was the one who pulled away, just as Tony was beginning to think this was a terrible idea, and they should just go at it right against Belinda.

"Yeah, I thought so," Lucas said, his voice low and gravelly with desire. "I thought so. You want it just as much as I do."

"More," Tony said, scrubbing a hand over his face. His lips felt swollen and hot. "A whole lot fucking more."

"Good," Lucas said and then turned and this time vanished back into the night. A second later, Tony saw his car lights flip on and then he was driving off, leaving Tony with a pretty serious case of blue balls and the satisfaction that he'd gotten Lucas exactly where he wanted him.

CHAPTER EIGHT

"You're all sparkly and smiley." Wyatt's voice emerged from the gloom of the kitchen. Tony jumped, because he hadn't even thought anyone was still up. But Wyatt was, sitting by himself in the dark cave of the kitchen, and as Tony walked closer, he could see that he had a beer bottle at his elbow, the label shredded into a pile next to it.

"Wow, you're not creepy at all," Tony said, grabbing his own. He *felt* sparkly, even though he had no intention of telling his brother why. But he could use a beer to try to calm all the sexual adrenaline he'd felt at playing cat and mouse with Lucas.

He sat down on the barstool next to Wyatt. "You gonna tell me what you're doing up so late, hiding out here?"

Wyatt's gaze swung his direction. He was just wearing a pair of athletic shorts, his tanned chest exposed in the dim moonlight. "You gonna tell me what's got you all smiles?"

"No," Tony grumbled.

Wyatt sighed. "The new next-door neighbors came over tonight." He gestured to the back counter of the kitchen, and now that Tony's eyes had adjusted to the darkness, he could see the white bakery box Wyatt had used to bring the coffee cake over. The lid was open, and a fork had been unceremoniously stuck in the half-eaten side of the cake. "Apparently they're gluten-free or whatever. And the parrot's staying. It's part of their brand, or whatever."

"Their brand?"

"I guess they post about it to their Instagram or something. It's some kind of rare albino parrot, I guess. 'Fits their aesthetic.'"

"Weird," Tony said, taking a gulp of his beer. "Who has a freaking aesthetic?"

Lucas does; maybe he could invite him over to meet the white parrot that would coordinate with all his black and white pictures.

"It's terrible," Wyatt said morosely. "What are we going to do?"

"Plant some trees? Get a sound system and try to drown it out? Live with it? I don't know."

"Ryan is freaking out," Wyatt said, which explained why he was out here in the dark kitchen, and not in bed with his husband.

"You could always move."

"Hell no," Wyatt said stubbornly. "This is our home." *We met here. We fell in love here.* Tony could hear the words even though Wyatt didn't say them. He had never been particularly romantic, but meeting Ryan—who'd been even *less* of a romantic, if that were possible—had changed everything. And even though Tony wanted that soul-deep connection they'd found, he'd be lying if he said that kind of pressure didn't freak him out sometimes. The key with

Lucas was it was a *long* game. Nothing was written in stone yet. Right now, they were just having fun; playing around. Even though Tony knew he wanted more, there was a kind of comfort in knowing that it didn't have to happen *right now*.

"Well, trees and a sound system and *dealing with it* are your choices, then."

"Maybe," Wyatt said. And Tony knew that voice. Knew it was the one goody-two-shoes voice Wyatt had always used when he knew something was a terrible idea, but he was going to do it anyway. And now that voice also applied to when *Ryan* was committed to a terrible idea and Wyatt had decided not to stop him.

"What," Tony retorted flatly. "What is Ryan going to do?"

Wyatt looked up in surprise, like he hadn't expected Tony to guess his late-night ponderings were over his husband.

"It's like you think I haven't lived here for almost three years, and I wasn't your brother for twenty-plus years before that," Tony said wryly. "I know you really well, and Ryan almost as well. What are you going to do?"

"Ryan wants to call our lawyer," Wyatt said.

"And you think it's an awful idea, but you're going to let him do it anyway."

"It's annoying, like . . . incredibly fucking annoying," Wyatt claimed, which *was* true.

"Do you actually think your lawyer can physically muzzle a bird?" Tony wondered out loud.

"No," Wyatt said despondently. "No."

"Then . . . why?" Tony asked, even though he already knew the truth.

Wyatt just sighed.

"Don't you dare say it's a marriage thing," Tony said. But that was exactly what it was. A marriage thing, and a *love* thing.

It made him a little grateful that the thing with Lucas was still only fun and easy and full of that electric kind of anticipation that preceded really, really good sex.

"Okay, I won't," Wyatt said.

"But," Tony added, "you should really talk to him about it. Figure out what you both want."

"For the parrot to shut the fuck up," Wyatt said in an amused, bitter voice.

"What else?"

"I don't know," Wyatt said, and that was really the root of the problem. "But yeah, I think we do. Need to get on the same page, that is."

"Then do that." Tony was grateful he'd been able to distract Wyatt from the "sparkly" comment he'd started out with. Because suddenly it felt like a little too much; wanting and hoping and praying that something might work out. It'd be a lot easier to just settle for "fun."

"Yeah," Wyatt said, and then suddenly he was eying Tony in that knowing way that made him want to squirm. "You gonna tell me what's up with you? Why you're all sparkly tonight? Did you have sex with Lucas?"

Damnit. "No," Tony said firmly. "No, I didn't."

"You did *something*," Wyatt said. "Seriously, you're fucking glowing."

"Maybe I got a sunburn," Tony muttered.

"You're really not going to tell me?"

Tony didn't *want* to tell him. But he also sort of did. Maybe this was the thing brothers did. He and Wyatt hadn't talked much about Brody, because by the time they'd grown closer, the thing with Brody had ended and the last thing Tony had ever wanted to do was talk about that asshole. He didn't even want to *think* about him.

"We kissed, okay?" Tony confessed. "And it was maybe even better than sex."

"See?" Wyatt said, gloating as he finished his beer and stood up. "You *do* know why I'm going to let Ryan call the lawyer."

"No, I don't," Tony protested.

Except he was secretly terrified that Wyatt was totally right; he was falling, hard and fast, and there wasn't going to be much to slow him down. Lucas made him want to go higher and faster until they both burned up, together.

Wyatt patted him on the back. "It's gonna be okay," he said. "Just take it easy, okay? We don't need another Brody."

But that wasn't even a question; Lucas was as far from Brody as you could get. Maybe that's why even though it was semi-terrifying to be feeling this way, like he was so buoyant he could just float off, he wasn't freaking out. Because Lucas was *good*. Lucas was *right*.

"Yeah," Tony said. "I'm not worried about that. At all, actually."

"I know," Wyatt said knowingly. "See you in the morning?"

"Yeah," Tony said. He'd already pulled his phone out, flipping first to Lucas' Instagram—no recent updates, damnit—and then to the text conversation that, prior to now, had been strictly about scheduling Lucas' shifts at the truck.

After Wyatt left, Tony's fingers hesitated over the keyboard. There was so much he wanted to say, but instead he just settled for: **Hey, wanted to make sure you got home okay.**

He finished his own beer, rinsed out the bottle, threw it in the recycling bin, and was halfway out to his little cottage when his phone dinged.

Do you ask all your employees if they got home safe? the text from Lucas read.

Tony had to resist the urge to text back immediately, before he even typed in the code to unlock the door, but he didn't want Lucas to think he was *that* desperate. He'd been desperate to keep talking to him, to keep kissing him, to give in and let Lucas go for his dick, even, but he was still trying to play it cool.

He typed in the door code, let himself in, and flipped on the corner lamp in the small living room, before sitting down on the couch and pulling his phone out. It'd still been only a minute or two, but that was long enough, right? Tony hated all these unspoken rules.

He wanted to tell Lucas everything; lay out every single confusing feeling that he was experiencing—but there was no fucking way that wouldn't send the guy running.

Just the hot ones, Tony typed back.

Oh, you think I'm hot? Lucas immediately texted back, which made Tony's heart leap in his chest.

I'm not fucking blind. Tony hesitated and then sent a second text. **Though I think I'd need to see you naked to verify my hypothesis.**

Lucas' reply was nearly instantaneous again. **In case you missed it, that was on offer tonight.**

I didn't miss it. Tony took a deep breath as he stared at the screen as he typed. **I got the message, loud and clear.**

Lucas texted back again, so fast that Tony didn't even get a chance to put his phone down. **If you'd listened to reason (and sanity), you'd be here right now, and you'd be full of this.**

Tony held his breath, waiting for the picture to come through. The picture that *had* to be of Lucas' dick. And *god*, he wanted to see it. Frankly, he'd have rather seen it in person, but there was only so much teasing even *he* could take, and if Lucas wanted to pay him back for pulling away, then Tony would take whatever he wanted to give him.

Finally, the picture came through. It was so slow that Tony actually briefly considered marching back into the house and demanding Ryan get better internet. He was willing to hire his lawyer to fight the parrot; surely he was willing to pay for faster download speeds. But he didn't, because he was already half hard in his shorts, thinking about Lucas' dick, fantasizing about what he was going to do with it, imagining the feel of it in his hands, in his mouth, buried so deep inside of him he was seeing stars.

Except, the problem was, unless Lucas' dick was cut up in little chunks and simmering in a pan of some kind of red sauce, the picture was definitely not of Lucas' dick.

Tony moaned out loud—and it wasn't the moaning he'd had in mind. God, that little tease. He was going to take him apart and put him back together again, all in retribution for that last stunt.

I can tell that you're sitting there, jaw dropped, just desperate to put it in your mouth, Lucas' follow-up text read. **Can't even wait til I bring it in, all hot and ready for you.**

OMG, you are a menace. A fucking insane menace . . . Tony got half his sentence typed and was thinking of what else Lucas was—delightful, funny, smart, insanely hot—when another picture came through.

This time it wasn't food.

It was undoubtedly a dick, hard and pressed against a pair of loose shorts, and it was definitely Lucas' because those were the shorts he'd worn today. There was just a sliver of tanned, toned stomach showing and Tony couldn't help it any longer, he reached down and palmed his own hardening cock, groaning out loud again at how good it felt, and how much he wished that the hand currently stroking it wasn't his own.

With one hand, he clumsily deleted what he'd already written and typed out something else. **A little desperate, huh?** Because he wasn't going to be the first one to break—no way, no how. Except then, instead of texting back, Tony's phone vibrated, and it wasn't a text coming through, it was a phone call.

"Fuck," Tony swore and fumbled to answer it and switch it to speakerphone.

"Just about as desperate as you," Lucas said, not even bothering to wait for Tony to speak. His voice was low and gritty, and goddamnit, Tony was ninety-nine point nine percent sure that he was doing exactly the same thing right now, his hand wrapped around his own dick, slowly jacking himself off as they talked to each other.

Who said phone sex was overrated and outdated? Tony was willing to throw down and challenge anyone that this wasn't the hottest thing he'd ever done, hands down.

"Who said I was desperate?" Tony said, but his own voice was high and whiny and he knew just how turned on he sounded. Like Lucas could come over and wring him out like a limp fucking rag and Tony would love every second.

"You did," Lucas said. Maybe that wasn't technically accurate, but it *was* true. He was really fucking desperate and growing more frantic by the moment. His dick was hard and leaking just a little at the tip, and he swiped a thumb over it, moaning a little as he spread the moisture down the shaft.

"It could've been me doing that," Lucas said, soft and low and intimate. "And it would've been fucking good."

"Yeah," Tony ground out. And yes, maybe he regretted that decision a little, but he couldn't entirely regret it because they were doing this instead and it was incandescently, melting-on-the-surface-of-the-sun hot.

"Feels good, huh," Lucas crooned again, and Tony was past words, past anything, and just groaned. "Feels so good but you're not gonna come. Not yet."

"Not yet?" Tony croaked, because they'd had over a week of foreplay and he was already right there, balanced on the edge, and then Lucas' words stopped him cold, mid-stroke.

"Yeah, not yet," Lucas murmured. "I wanna get a little pleasure out of you first."

"Trust me," Tony mumbled, "it feels pretty damn good."

"Could feel better." Lucas' words were punctuated by a tiny gasp that made it clear Tony wasn't the only one feeling good.

"Such a tease," Tony said, stilling his hand in an attempt to stave off his orgasm for at least a minute or two—at least long enough to make it good for Lucas. "I bet you didn't know I saw that picture and the first thing I thought of was your stomach."

"Really?" Lucas sounded surprised. And it *was* surprising, because his cock had been *right there*, obviously hard and desperate to be touched. But Tony had seen enough tiny glimpses of the glory that was Lucas' chest and abs, teasing glances as Lucas had worked, whenever he'd reached above his head, whenever he'd lifted his shirt to wipe his face at the end of a shift.

"I want my mouth on your skin," Tony said, his brain-to-mouth filter completely destroyed. He didn't even care if he sounded dumb. He burned with what he wanted to do to Lucas, his cock hot and throbbing in his hand as he dreamt about nibbling along his lower abs, pulling down his shorts with only his teeth. "I'd tease you a little, of course, enough that you'd beg for me to move lower, to put my mouth on your dick, and I would, *eventually*."

Lucas was panting now, his breaths short and loud through the speaker. "You'd make me beg for it?" he moaned, like that was the hottest fucking thing he could imagine.

"I'd make you *scream* for it," Tony said, because there was nothing else he wanted more than to destroy Lucas for any other guy. He wanted to turn him inside out until he only had to *see* Tony and his cock would get hard.

"Fuck," Lucas ground out. "Fuck, fuck, *fuck*."

"Don't come," Tony said, beginning to twist his hand again, his cock jumping at the sudden pleasure that shot through him. "Don't fucking come, not until I do."

"Fucking *hurry*, then," Lucas yelped. "I'm so fucking close."

"Yeah, yeah," Tony mumbled, and then he was right there—teetering right on the brink and then Lucas pushed him right over as he abruptly groaned, on the same edge as Tony was.

"Shit," Tony moaned as he stroked himself through his orgasm. He'd come so hard that a few droplets had even fallen on the couch, which he'd be more upset about if he wasn't sure that Wyatt and Ryan hadn't already fucked on this couch at least half a dozen times already.

"Oh my god," Lucas said in a rush, and the hiccupping gasp he let out might have gotten Tony hard if he hadn't *just* come.

Now he knew what Lucas sounded like when he was wrung out from pleasure. He would be hearing that sound in his dreams, for the next thousand years.

"That was . . ." Tony wasn't even sure what it had been. He sure hadn't intended for them to have phone sex when he'd texted Lucas to ask if he'd gotten home okay. But he'd let Lucas push him, and frankly, it wasn't like he hadn't been willing the entire way.

"Yeah," Lucas said, his voice all gravelly and satisfied at the edges, and not for the first time, Tony wished he'd taken him up on his offer. If he had, they'd be together right now, and not only would he have had his hands and his mouth all over Lucas' glorious body, he'd have gotten to see Lucas when he was all sleepy and sated. *Someday soon*, he promised himself.

"I'm not sure I'm even disappointed," Tony admitted with a laugh. "That was crazy hot."

"Might've been even hotter if you hadn't been so far away," Lucas said, and yeah, that was *hope* in his voice. He wanted to do it again. Well, scratch that. He wanted to do it again *together*.

"Next time," Tony said, because while he might have some self-control where Lucas was concerned, he'd burned most of it away tonight.

"Next time," Lucas agreed. "Shit," he added, urgency leaking into his voice. "Shit, I think I burned the jackfruit."

"Whoops?" Tony said. "I'd apologize, but I'm not really sorry."

"Me either." He heard some pans banging around through the speakerphone as Lucas dealt with the burned jackfruit. "But I gotta clean this up and start again, so I'll let you go. See you tomorrow?"

"Tomorrow," Tony said, and knew it sounded just like the promise it was.

The next morning, Lucas packed up the jackfruit. He'd stayed up way too late making a second batch, and then lying awake, unable to sleep. Would he have felt this conflicted if Tony had come back here last night and they'd had sex instead of delaying the inevitable? Lucas didn't know. But the truth was he felt like he'd already fallen in deeper and was more committed to this friends-with-benefits thing than he'd expected. Maybe if he'd just pulled Tony's pants down and got a mouthful of that cock, it wouldn't have meant anything—but even then, Lucas kind of thought he might be lying to himself.

The reason why? After he finally fell asleep, it was Tony's face floating through his dreams, and his laugh echoing in Lucas' ears, and the first thought he had when he woke up way too early, the alarm blaring, was that he didn't mind so much because he'd be seeing Tony.

You are kinda fucked, Lucas told himself as he got out of his Mini and, grabbing his bag and the plastic container, headed across the street to where Belinda was sitting in the lot. Lucas knew he was early—he was more than a little embarrassingly eager, especially after that hot-as-fuck phone call last night—he didn't see Tony's bike parked anywhere, and even Jeremy wasn't skulking around the shade of Belinda's canopy.

It was only then, after noticing that he was the only one here so far, that Lucas looked a little closer at Belinda and realized that the door, which Tony had securely shut and locked last night, was open.

"Shit," Lucas exclaimed, and pulled out his phone. He dialed Tony and waited impatiently for him to answer. But when it flipped over to voicemail, Lucas realized he must already be on the road, and couldn't pick up. His heart jumped at the sound of Tony's recorded voice, and normally he might have enjoyed the feeling of heightened anticipation, but now all he worried about was that Tony would get here, see the open door, and worse-case scenario think Lucas had broken in.

For a split second, he considered going into the truck himself and seeing what—if anything—had been taken, but then he decided it would be better if he didn't touch anything. Maybe Tony would want to call the cops after all. Something more than just a few twenties might have been taken.

A minute later, Tony pulled up on his motorcycle. Lucas knew he should've been totally occupied by the possible theft, but it was impossible to see Tony swing a long, jean-clad leg over the seat and pull his helmet off, shaking his hair out, and *not* be infinitely distracted by the mouth-watering sight.

"I guess that answers that question," Lucas muttered to himself as Tony walked up. Obviously he wasn't getting over this anytime soon; not when he wanted Tony even more than he'd wanted him last night.

"Hey," Tony said, and he was grinning from ear to ear, like he'd just won the fucking lottery, and Lucas' heart stuttered in his chest. *Fuck, danger, danger, get it together.*

"Hey," Lucas said. He pointed to the door. "I just got here and . . ."

He knew the moment Tony saw that the door was slightly ajar. "Oh fuck," Tony said and clamored up the steps, carefully using the corner of his t-shirt to nudge Belinda's door the rest of the way open.

Lucas followed him, because he was concerned too—even though he kept telling himself this was just a temporary job and he didn't really give a shit. But that ship had sailed, and he didn't know what he was trying to do by still pretending like he didn't care.

Maybe he was just putting up a front for Tony, so he wouldn't know that whenever those dark blue eyes swung his direction, he set every nerve in Lucas' body alight.

"Fuck," Tony repeated, staring at the empty spot on the back counter, right next to the grill and on the other side of the fryer where the really nice, heavy-duty professional sandwich press had stood. Now all that was left were a handful of stray crumbs they'd missed in their cleanup the night before and a faint line on the stainless steel from where it had once stood.

"They took the sandwich press," Lucas said, gaping. He couldn't quite believe it. That was *not* a hundred bucks of petty cash or a recipe. That was an expensive—and unfortunately for Tony—fairly portable piece of equipment. They'd just have to close it, lock the lid and cart it off.

"Fuck," Tony said a third time. He pushed his hair back, frustration etched on his handsome features. "I can't believe they fucking took my sandwich press. Probably right after we left."

"This is a dumb question, but you locked the door, right? I mean, I know you locked it before we went to my car, but you know . . . *after* . . . I wasn't sure if you had come back to get anything in Belinda." Usually Lucas was not even remotely prudish but the idea of saying "after we kissed" to Tony, who was standing there looking brighter than the sun, felt like a step too far. A step that might lead him to doing it again. As soon as possible.

"Yeah," Tony said, shaking his head. "I didn't go back in after we got back here, after we . . . after we saw the cat." He cleared his throat. Obviously he too was having some difficulty in vocalizing what they'd done last night. It made Lucas feel a little less like he was alone in going out of his fucking skin.

"Right, the cat," Lucas said, and then grinned. "At least it was a really cute cat?"

Tony sighed. "If Dom had broken in here, it'd make a fuckton more sense, that's for sure."

"Well, it definitely wasn't Dom," Lucas said. But then another thought occurred to him. "Maybe it was someone who knew what to look for, like they waited until we left, right? So they must have known my car, at least. And knew your bike was still parked here, and you were hanging around, maybe even waiting to catch them."

It was fucking Jeremy, Lucas wanted to add with exasperation, but then the man himself showed up in the doorway, and had either a stupid or innocent expression on his face. *Probably both,* Lucas thought.

"Hey, guys, what's up?" Jeremy's greeting sounded like it was for both Tony *and* Lucas, but the way his gaze immediately latched on to Tony made it painfully clear who it was really for.

"Someone broke in and stole the goddamned sandwich press," Tony growled.

"Oh, shit," Jeremy said. And really, Lucas thought he had it just about right; Jeremy was either stupid or innocent, and he definitely wasn't the latter. At least as far as Lucas knew.

"I know," Tony said. "We can get a new one, but I'm getting sick of this shit."

"Why would someone steal the sandwich press?" Lucas asked, because that was a legitimate question, and he figured he might as well ask in the presence of the person who'd probably taken it.

"God, I don't know," Tony answered instead. Jeremy suspiciously stayed silent, his expression blank. "Maybe they knew our new special was using it? Maybe they wanted it for themselves? It wasn't fucking cheap, that's for damn sure."

Lucas hadn't thought about *that* yet—that the artichoke spinach jalapeno grilled cheese was one of the few things on the menu that used it currently. And without it, today's work just got a whole lot tougher. They *could* cook the sandwiches on the grill, but it was a lot quicker and more efficient to just build the thing and brush the sides with butter and let the press do the bulk of the work. On the grill, the sandwiches would need to be watched and babied and then turned.

It wasn't the end of the world, but it was an extra step and an extra annoyance.

"Hey," Lucas said, pulling out the plastic container of jackfruit he'd packed up this morning. "We could add this too, as a special, just so we don't have to do so many grilled sandwiches."

Tony peered into the container. "Is that the pulled pork jack-fruit?" he asked. Lucas flushed, because the last time he'd mentioned it, he'd still had come all over his chest and he'd still been mentally fried from the incredible orgasm Tony had given him *over the fucking phone.*

"Yeah," Lucas said. "We could whip up a quick vinegar slaw and serve it warm."

"It *looks* gross," Jeremy said, also looking into the container. But Tony had already grabbed a plastic fork and was sampling it. Lucas didn't even have a chance to be nervous, even though he knew it was delicious, because Tony was already moaning with pleasure around the bite in his mouth. The only issue with that was Lucas wanted him to moan like that around his *dick.*

"This is fucking amazing," Tony said. "I'm in awe."

Jeremy made a disgruntled noise. "You're easily impressed," he said. "It looks weird to me."

"Your face is weird," Lucas retorted, because the only one allowed to malign his jackfruit was Tony himself, and from the way he was going in for another bite, that wasn't happening anytime soon.

"Let's make this the special. How many plates do you think we can make out of this?" Tony asked, waving his fork at the container. "And get it away from me, so I don't eat any more of it."

"Twenty maybe? I can stretch it to twenty-five if we include a side."

"Okay, perfect, we'll put it on the special board," Tony said, shooting him a look of immense gratitude and admiration. Maybe that shouldn't have been a turn-on, but Lucas could acknowledge at this point that just about everything Tony did and said was a huge fucking turn-on.

"Also," Tony added, "back to the stupid press. I still think we're looking at someone who runs their own truck. Because I bet you that any normal person wouldn't guess that the sandwich press was worth so much money. They'd probably think it was a little bigger version of a George fucking Foreman." He exhaled with frustration. "Okay, let's get prepping. We have a long day, and it's just gotten longer. Jeremy, you're on salsas and sauces, and, Lucas, you can help me with prepping the fish and the meat for the day."

Jeremy shot Lucas a glare, which he totally expected. Maybe Lucas might have been wary of being promoted over Jeremy, and wondered if it was because Tony liked him, but he'd seen just how ineffective Jeremy was and he *knew* he was damn good in a kitchen, so Tony's partiality *probably* had nothing to do with the fact that he wanted his mouth on Lucas' dick.

Except then when Lucas walked over to the cutting board where they filleted and portioned the fish and Tony, watching for when Jeremy's back was turned, leaned down and gave him a quick, brief kiss. "Sorry," he murmured under his breath so Jeremy couldn't hear. "I just couldn't get started without doing that."

Lucas knew he was smiling like crazy, but he couldn't quite get his face under control and tone it down. He'd just been thinking the exact same thing, and it felt so damn good to be on the same page.

"Seriously, though," Tony continued, "I think our culprit is another food truck owner. We should go out tonight to the Funky Cup, I know a few of the other guys will be there. We can do some undercover reconnaissance."

Tony looked very proud of himself that he'd come up with that phrase all on his own. And probably also because he'd come up with an excuse to get Lucas alone. It was pretty fucking adorable.

"I think we could do that," Lucas said, "but I was sort of hoping to go somewhere completely, totally alone."

"End of the night," Tony promised, his eyes promising even more, "after we do our very important, totally effective investigative work."

Lucas rolled his eyes. They might be a lot of things—desperate to fuck, maybe—but effective investigators? Not even fucking close. "I'm gonna hold you to that. No more teasing."

"Awwww," Tony said with a wide smile, "just a little teasing? Please?"

"I think a little teasing might be allowed, if I can tease a little back," Lucas murmured.

"Like I could stop you," Tony said and Lucas couldn't help it then, he just laughed. Free and easy like it was the simplest thing in the entire world even though sometimes it felt like the most complicated.

CHAPTER NINE

THEY SOLD OUT OF the jackfruit pulled pork sandwiches by noon, and Jeremy sulked about it all day. Lucas might have been annoyed, mostly because *he* was so annoying, but it was one of those days, even though he hadn't gotten enough sleep, even though the potential distributor of his energy bars hadn't emailed him back yet, even though they no longer had a sandwich press, that just felt *perfect*.

Was it the way Tony kept smiling at him? Like he just couldn't help it? Every single time Lucas caught him, he'd get this sheepish expression on his face, and then, before it could even *think* about turning into embarrassment, it'd fade away into sheer, unadulterated cockiness. As if he knew he had Lucas right where he wanted him.

And goddamnit, he *did*.

Because while Tony might have been smart enough to cloak going to the bar as an "investigation," Lucas thought he might know differently—and he wasn't even really against it. He wanted to meet Tony's friends, and the other food truck guys. They seemed cool, especially the one who had nailed the copycat with a freaking meatball. That guy sounded awesome.

They'd parked downtown by a lot of the bigger office buildings. When the lunch rush finally died down, Lucas grabbed one of his energy bars—dark chocolate cherry pistachio was the newest flavor he was experimenting with—and as he opened it up, leaned against one of the prep counters.

"What are you doing tonight?" Jeremy asked Tony as he inventoried the fish they had remaining. They were parking by a popular microbrewery tonight, and Lucas knew that the fish tacos would be a big seller. He hoped they had enough to satisfy demand. Tony seemed to agree, as he ticked off what they'd already portioned off.

"What?" Tony glanced up, distracted by his counting. And maybe, Lucas thought wickedly, by the idea of what he *wanted* to do tonight.

"What are you doing tonight?" Jeremy asked again. "We haven't hung out in forever."

"Last week, right?" Tony said absently, returning to the contents of the fridge.

"No." Jeremy impatiently drummed his fingers against the side of the fryer. "You said you were busy."

"Oh," Tony said. Still not answering the question. If Jeremy was actually paying attention to the words coming out of his mouth instead of continuing to check out his ass, he'd notice that Tony was avoiding it. But Lucas had a feeling that Jeremy just wasn't that smart.

Though Lucas couldn't really blame him for getting distract-ed by Tony, because he was hot and funny and charming. God knew Lucas had gotten distracted by him once or twice or fifty times. At least.

"Tonight," Jeremy continued, and Lucas had to at least give him full props for continuing to try. "I thought we'd go to the Funky Cup. Grab a couple beers."

"Uh." Tony hesitated, and he glanced up, meeting Lucas' amused stare. "I'm actually kinda busy tonight, Jeremy. Sorry."

"*Again*?" Jeremy asked, sounding rather annoyed now. "Come on. Tell me. Are you dating someone?"

"No," Tony said firmly, rising to his feet. "We'll stop on the way to the brewery and grab some more fish. I don't want to run out tonight. Also," he continued, turning towards Lucas, like Jeremy wasn't even there, and it was impossible to miss the disgruntled expression on Jeremy's face as a result, "if you had more ingredients, could you make more pulled pork jackfruit? How long does it take?"

"Not as long as regular pulled pork," Lucas said. "An hour, maybe? We'll need to stop by an Asian market for the jackfruit; I can't use a ripe one, the texture and the flavor won't be right. But most Asian markets will carry canned green jackfruit."

"Okay," Tony said. "There's a good one off Spring near Chi-natown, I think. And the fish market isn't that far from there, either. What else do you need?"

"Are we really going to get more of that weird vegan crap?" Jeremy inserted, and Lucas *almost* felt sorry for him, even though he kept insulting his jackfruit.

"We *sold out* of that weird vegan crap," Tony retorted, "so *yes*. And either you're with us, Jeremy, or you're off the truck."

"You need me," Jeremy said in a sulky tone, and yes, that was mostly correct, but they'd managed without him before.

"You could always call in sick again," Lucas added.

"I was *throwing up*," Jeremy retorted. "And not from your nasty-ass jackfruit, either."

"Guys," Tony said, and he seemed surprised at how calm he was. Lucas had a feeling he hadn't always been the calming influence in the room, and it was shocking to him he was now. But building and maintaining something like this food truck would mature a guy, and Tony had definitely come into his own. "Let's calm down and focus. We're going to be feeding a ton of people tonight and we need to be ready."

"We're gonna be," Jeremy said, and he sounded more than a little bitter. Probably because he *knew* he'd been replaced—if he'd ever even had a fraction of what Lucas already did. The thing was, Lucas didn't know what it was like to pine after a guy who didn't seem to notice you were alive, but he had to imagine it sucked bad. And then to watch as another guy waltzed in, and without even trying, got everything you'd ever wanted? That had to be hard. Lucas discovered as he took his break, finding a nearby coffee shop to grab a cold brew, that he actually felt sorry for Jeremy.

He resolved, as he walked back, slowly sipping his coffee, that he would try to be more understanding.

But that was before he got back to the truck and discovered that while he'd been gone, Jeremy had decided this was the best time to confront Tony about Lucas' employment.

"He's a *jerk*," Jeremy said, his voice echoing loudly out the open door. "He doesn't really respect you, and he doesn't respect me at all. He thinks he's hot shit, and while you're too busy panting after his *supposedly* hot ass, he's going to rob you blind."

Lucas stopped in his tracks, still a few feet away from Belinda. He couldn't believe that during his break he'd been thinking about ways to forgive Jeremy, to make working together easier, and Jeremy had decided that this was his opportunity to spout off about his "supposedly hot ass" and accuse him of stealing. Lucas clamped his lips together around his straw and sucked his cold brew down. He was *pissed*.

"You are seriously overreacting," Tony said. "He's not stealing from me. And I'm not *panting*, thank you very much."

"Do you think I'm blind?" Jeremy retorted angrily. "You're not exactly subtle about it, you know. I'd just think our friendship would mean more to you than this egotistical asshole who thinks the sun shines out of his dick."

"It doesn't, and I keep telling you, I wouldn't know anything about his dick," Tony said firmly. "You need to figure out how to get along with Lucas, or I can't have you on the truck. I'm sorry to be that harsh about it, but, dude, Belinda is just not that big, and I think Lucas would destroy her *and* you if you tried to fight him."

Lucas decided this was the ideal moment to make his appearance. He climbed up the stairs, just as Jeremy was staring at Tony incredulously, and said, "Hey, guys," all casual-like, as if Jeremy hadn't just maligned both his dick *and* his ass, never mind his loyalty.

"Hey," Jeremy muttered after a long, pained silence. A silence during which he'd probably decided that staying around Tony and keeping this job was worth the bare minimum of effort.

"And for the record," Lucas said silkily, "the sun shines out of my ass, not my dick. Just so we're clear."

Tony groaned and Jeremy muttered something that Lucas couldn't quite hear; which was probably better for everyone. Definitely for Tony's sanity and for Belinda's continued existence. Because Tony was right; Lucas *could* annihilate Jeremy if he ever chose to waste his precious time and energy on that worm.

"Seriously, I don't want to have to say this twice," Tony said, giving both of them a reprimanding glance. Maybe Lucas would be more affronted that he was grouping him with Jeremy, except that the boss-man look on Tony was hot as fuck. "You will get along, or you'll be off this truck. Okay?"

"Sure, boss," Lucas said. Jeremy didn't bother responding, just nodded his head jerkily, his eyes still shooting daggers in Lucas' general direction.

"Good. Now let's go restock and then we can head to the brewery." Tony's voice made it abundantly clear that he was in charge, and he was not going to tolerate any more shit today. Either from Jeremy or from Lucas.

But Lucas knew better. He knew as soon as he got Tony alone, he could work him up, turn him inside out, make him moan, make him beg, and they'd both love every minute.

It was the longest fucking day that Tony could ever remember.

First off, Jeremy was being a major douchecanoe over Lucas. He remembered what Lucas had thought at the beginning—that he and Jeremy were hooking up—and he wondered if somehow he'd missed some of the signs that Jeremy was laying down, but he didn't think so because they'd only ever be friends, and he'd only ever been interested in Jeremy as a friend and as an employee. *Though*, frankly, he was a hell of a lot less interested in having an employee who thought it was okay to insult his co-workers, undermine Tony's management of the truck, and generally be an asshole to everyone.

Maybe he should've listened to Wyatt after all.

"Hey," Lucas said, leaning right over into his space, and improving his day just by being in it. "We're out of the pulled pork jackfruit again. I just used the last of it."

"Fuck, really?" Tony glanced at his watch. It was only just past seven. Still another hour plus to go before they could reasonably pack up. "Well, I guess I just found myself a new menu item, and you've got another prep job each shift," he said.

"That's awesome," Lucas said, sounding like he really meant it. "Would you be interested in some more ideas I have? Not for a menu item, but maybe a special?"

"Hell yes," Tony said and didn't miss how his own enthusiasm made Jeremy's glower deepen. He was really going to have to do something about Jeremy, and a frank talk might not be enough. Not when Jeremy would infect and destroy the joy of running this truck with his jealousy. The problem was, Tony just wasn't sure what he should do about fixing it.

"Well," Lucas said, still grinning. "I'll let you know what I come up with."

"Maybe later tonight," Tony said, dropping his voice and turning slightly so that hopefully Jeremy couldn't eavesdrop.

"Maybe." Lucas was still grinning, his smile infectious and so much brighter than Tony had ever seen it before. Even Jeremy being his storm cloud of a self hadn't seemed to dampen Lucas' mood. Tony hoped that it had something to do with last night and a whole lot to do with what they were planning for tonight.

"We have orders," Jeremy said, his tone making it abundantly clear just how much he hated being left out.

"On top of it," Lucas said, reaching for the tickets.

"I'll cross the pulled jackfruit off the special board," Tony said, and went out the door, rubbing out the words he'd scribbled this morning with an elbow until they were mostly faded from view.

"Already running out of your special?" a voice behind him asked. When Tony turned, Ross from Basket was standing there, a smug look on his annoying face.

"Yeah, actually," Tony said. "I've got a genius back there. He turned some kind of mushy canned thing into the best vegan pulled pork sandwich. It was fucking brilliant."

"I didn't know you'd hired anyone new," Ross said, walking closer.

"Yeah," Tony said, which was all he intended to tell him about Lucas. Ross wouldn't blink twice over at least *attempting* to poach Lucas away from Tony. "What are you doing here anyway?" He glanced around. "Your truck isn't even here?"

Ross laughed. "Do you only ever go out with your truck? That must make for a pretty fucking boring life."

Do not engage, Tony reminded himself, *he's also a douchecanoe, but you can't fire him the way you could fire Jeremy*. Not that he was actually planning on firing Jeremy; he'd promised him the job for the entire summer, and right now, he was better than the empty gaping hole they'd be left with if he got rid of him. Of course, there was also their friendship to consider; Tony wasn't stupid enough to think if he fired Jeremy that they'd *stay* friends.

"It's great, actually. Zero complaints," Tony insisted.

"Well, I'm going to go grab a beer and *relax*. Too bad I've already eaten," Ross said, very obviously *not* sorry that he couldn't get something from Tony's truck. He turned and walked away, leaving Tony clenching his fists at his sides, wishing that he could've come up with a convincing excuse to punch the bastard in the face.

"Hey," Lucas said, emerging out of Belinda's doorway. "Everything okay?"

"I ran into Ross from Basket," Tony muttered as he turned back to his truck. "What a jerkoff."

"He seems to be," Lucas said. "Why was he even here?"

"Getting a beer or so he claims. My thought?" Tony said darkly. "He was scoping out the competition. *Us.*"

"He must be desperate, then," Lucas said with a chuckle. "He didn't even order anything."

"Maybe he doesn't have to. Maybe he'll stop by later, when we're parked in the lot, and try to steal something else," Tony said. Because that had to be it, didn't it? It was Ross and Aaron from Basket, and they were trying to sabotage his success. It was annoying, but it would also feel damn good when he finally caught them in the act.

"You think it's them?" Lucas did not sound convinced as they climbed into Belinda.

"I think it has to be," Tony said. It had to be, didn't it? Who else was always lurking around, being a general jackass? It was always Ross and Aaron.

"I guess we can do some reconnaissance tonight, when we go to the bar," Lucas said under his breath. "Will they be there?"

Tony sighed. "Yeah, maybe? But maybe just Aaron, since Ross was here tonight. But then, who knows what they'll do? I don't exactly think like a super villain."

"A super villain, huh?" Lucas asked, chuckling. "I'll have to remember that."

"We've got to put our best detective hats on," Tony teased. Except he already knew they didn't have *best* anything. They both sucked as detectives, probably because they kept getting distracted by flirting and kissing and all this fucking teasing.

"Do we have those?" Lucas wondered as he pulled some tater tots out of the fryer and deftly tossed them into a basket, using his other hand to gently shake seasoning onto the just-fried food before passing them over to Tony.

"No, because if you did, they wouldn't keep stealing shit," Jeremy groused.

"Probably true," Lucas agreed, but didn't seem particularly upset about it.

"It's the effort that counts," Tony announced. Except that he really wasn't looking forward to telling Wyatt that they needed to buy another sandwich press.

Still, if by some miracle he and Lucas ended up together and as happy as he knew they could be, it would be worth it.

"Finally," Tony said as Jeremy banged Belinda's front door shut on his way out.

"You're going to need to do something about him," Lucas said, without accusation. "He's really pissed about me."

"Yeah," Tony agreed. "But what?"

In Lucas' defense, he didn't immediately say that Tony needed to fire him. "God, I wish I knew," he said instead. "I wish there was an easy solution, because I know you're friends and you trust him. And that makes it hard."

It was more sympathetic than Tony had been expecting, and the hug that Lucas wrapped him in after he spoke made Tony feel so warm and fuzzy inside—and also like he was smart and strong enough to figure out the solution, even to a hard problem like the one with Jeremy.

"You look surprised," Lucas said, pulling back and grinning. "Did you think I would tell you to fire his ass?"

"Yeah, sort of," Tony admitted. "And maybe I should, but you're right; we're friends. That makes it tough."

"Well, maybe we can figure out a solution to at least *one* problem tonight," Lucas said. "Come on, let's get to this bar. I could use a drink after having Jeremy glare at me for three-quarters of the day."

"I'm sorry," Tony said with a sigh, and *meant it.* "I'll talk to him again."

"Nah," Lucas said, with a quick headshake. "It wouldn't do anything anyway. He's never gonna like me."

It would've been tough admitting this to anyone but admitting it to Lucas, whose respect he craved? "I think I'm not good at this," Tony confessed. "Before, it was easy, because Wyatt was here every day and I didn't have to really *manage* anyone. And when we needed the extra set of hands, it wasn't like Jeremy was going to get pissed off at either of us. He couldn't." He hesitated. "And don't say it's because Wyatt wouldn't have tolerated it. He wouldn't have, yeah, but Jeremy's turned different since you showed up."

"I get it, and I know," Lucas said softly and reaching up, brushed a kiss across Tony's mouth. "You don't have to apologize or explain. I really do get it."

And he really seemed to. Because he *hadn't* suggested Tony fire Jeremy. Probably because he was right—firing Jeremy wouldn't be easy or simple or even painless. It would suck, and he would lose a friend out of it. A friend he wasn't sure he *wanted* to keep around, because of the way he was acting, but what kind of friend would *he* be if he bailed at the first sign of trouble?

"Thanks for understanding," Tony said and sighed again. "Sorry I'm being such a downer, today."

"You're not," Lucas promised. "But let's go get a beer and get our detective on. I'm ready to leave Jeremy behind, at least for the day."

"Yeah, yeah, me too." Tony shook off the frustrating thoughts of how much it sucked to be the boss and refocused on the man next to him. "Hey," he said as Lucas went down the stairs and he followed, reaching for the lock. "Thank you for pulling me out right there."

Lucas smiled. "Of course. This managing thing is fucking hard, isn't it?"

"Yeah, it is," Tony agreed. He double-checked the lock on Belinda's door—he didn't need to lose another piece of equipment, not after they'd already lost the sandwich press. "How do you know, other than, obviously, watching me suck at it?"

"My friend Ria. You went to her gym and about died, remember?" Lucas teased. "Anyway, she had to learn the hard way on a lot of things. But watching her and being her friend taught me a lot. Enough that maybe I'll be able to do it myself, when the time comes."

"Your energy bars," Tony said, realizing that part of Lucas' intense focus was ambition. He wanted to make his business a success.

"Yeah. I mean, I don't have a real distributor yet. I'm just selling to some local stores. But if I could sign a contract to distribute, I could afford to find some permanent space and maybe get an employee or two."

"You're going to kick ass, you know that?" Tony said, nudging him with his shoulder. "Hey, have you seen Dom around today?"

"Nope," Lucas said, and sounded a little disappointed. "But maybe we will soon?"

"I hope so," Tony said. He hesitated outside of the gate to the parking lot. "Do you want to follow me to the bar, or we could take my bike?"

Lucas' smile was mischievous. "Like I'd miss a chance to ride your crotch rocket, baby."

There was nothing sexier than a man climbing on a motorcycle, and when the man had insanely long hot legs, and he was shrugging on a leather jacket? Lucas felt his blood thrumming through his body at the thought of climbing on behind Tony and wrapping his arms around his waist, feeling the vibration of the engine underneath them.

"You ready?" Tony said, handing him the helmet in his hands. "You should probably wear this."

Lucas eyed the helmet. "Really?"

But Tony just shrugged. "I know what I'm doing, but I wouldn't forgive myself if something ever happened to you."

"Maybe," Lucas said flippantly, before he could even think through his words, "maybe we could get a second helmet, if we do this often enough."

Tony stared at him, like he couldn't believe he'd said that. And frankly, Lucas couldn't fucking believe he'd said it either. "Okay," he finally said. "Okay."

Before he could say anything else, Lucas slipped the helmet on. It smelled like Tony, and desire surged through him as he swung his leg over the seat. He settled down, reaching inside Tony's jacket, his fingers digging into the fabric of his t-shirt.

Without warning, Tony kick-started the engine, and it roared to life underneath their legs. Lucas tried not to shudder, feeling the vibrations surge through him. He was already right on the edge, because Tony seemed to pull him there effortlessly, without ever trying. Just by fucking existing.

Tony tilted his head, and that was all the warning Lucas got, because suddenly they were pulling away from the curb, and Tony was confidently steering them through the spotty late evening traffic. He'd already looked up the Funky Cup—and told himself it had nothing in common with Tony finding Ria's Gym, even as he knew that wasn't true—and it wasn't very far from this lot. Only about a five-minute drive. But it was an exhilarating five minutes, Lucas nestled right up against Tony, torn between watching his hair whip in the wind, and the neon lights flash by as they sped past. He'd ridden bikes before—both by himself and with other guys—and it had never ever felt like this before, like Lucas could *live* this way, pushed up against Tony's broad back, fingertips dug into his sides.

Too soon they pulled over near a squat brick building with a flashing neon sign that advertised "The Funky Cup."

Lucas' legs were shaky when he dismounted, and he told himself it was because it was his first ride in a while, but the truth was it had nothing to do with the ride and everything to do with Tony.

"Hey, you good?" Tony asked, grinning as Lucas pulled the helmet off and handed it to him.

"I'm good, yeah," Lucas said. *So fucking good, you don't even know.*

Tony strapped the helmet to the seat and turned to head into the bar, but before he could, Lucas reached out and grabbed his arm, pulling him down into a hot, searing kiss. Maybe he wasn't great at using his words to tell Tony how desperately he wanted him, but he could *show* him. Tony made a muffled groan against Lucas' mouth and suddenly they were stumbling back, Lucas' back hitting what must have been the brick wall of the bar, and his hands were in Tony's hair, and Tony's fingers were digging into his waist. It was so perfect, all lips and teeth and tongue, a mad, wild, furious kiss that spun out and out until Lucas was gasping helplessly, trying to get his leg between Tony's so he could try to alleviate some of the pressure that was building in his cock, fizzing along all his limbs.

He thought he heard some kind of sound, but everything at the forefront of his mind was *Tony*, and how goddamn much he wanted—no, he *needed* him. Fuck this stupid investigation. They didn't need an excuse to go back to Lucas' apartment and finally fuck out all the feelings that had been building from the first moment they'd seen each other.

But then Tony tore his mouth off Lucas' and he was left reeling for a split second. Had it ended? It'd felt like the kiss would never, ever end. It would spin out forever, grasping and frantic, pulling them right along with it.

"Shit," Tony muttered. His lips were red and wet, and for a single sluggish second, Lucas seriously considered wrapping a hand around his neck and pulling him right back to where he belonged.

The thing that stopped him was that noise again. He refocused and actually *listened*, and he realized that they'd drawn a crowd, and the crowd (of two), were clapping and wolf-whistling.

"Hey," Tony said, wrapping an arm around his lower back, which again, might have pissed Lucas off in another life, but in this one, just comforted him, "Hey, Lucas, this is Gabe, and this is Ash. They own two of the best food trucks in LA."

"Hey," Lucas said and extended a hand, shaking both of theirs in succession. Gabe had dark hair, darker even than Tony's, and a pair of dark intense eyes. Ash was shorter, even shorter than he was, with lighter brown hair and a pair of blue eyes sparkling with mischievousness. "So which one of you is the meatball-thrower?"

CHAPTER TEN

"That was me," Gabriel admitted with a chuckle, as they walked through the door, and approached the enormous expanse of polished wood bar. "Totally me. I shouldn't be proud . . ."

"But you totally are," Ash inserted wryly. "And I kinda think Sean deserved it."

"No way," Tony said. "Sean's a good guy, he's just trying to make it. Same as you."

Gabriel groaned as he waved at the bartender. "Hey, Shaw," he said, "how's it going?"

"Can't complain," the bartender said, giving their group a slow, lazy grin. "At least not when y'all come in."

"We're here way too much. But then, that must be good for business, right?" Ash teased and Shaw shot him a commiserating grin back.

Lucas was more than a little glad he'd distracted everyone from his and Tony's show by bringing up the meatball-throwing incident, because it seemed to have worked. Gabriel and Ash hadn't asked who he was, and Shaw hadn't either, even though he must've been very familiar with the group.

"Your usual?" Shaw asked, pulling back lids on the giant under-counter fridge units and pulling out bottles of beer. "Except you," he said, tilting his head towards Lucas. He popped the tops off with an expert flick of the wrist. "You're new here."

"Yeah," Lucas said. So much for not bringing any attention to himself. "I'll take a Corona."

"Lime, yeah?" Shaw asked, and when Lucas nodded, he slid one into the neck of the bottle after popping the cap off.

"I've got this round," Tony said, pulling his wallet out before Lucas could protest. He had cash. He could buy his own beer. But it'd sound rude now, if he made an issue of it, because Tony wasn't just covering him, he was covering Gabriel and Ash too, who both nodded absently, like this was something they did all the time.

It was definitely ridiculous that Lucas was angsting about this, but it was one of his primary rules for keeping things light and casual. Meeting up at a bar was fine, but Lucas always insisted on buying his own drinks. It just happened that Tony had gotten around that rule without even knowing about it.

"Come on," Gabriel said, his eyes crinkling with amusement. "I wanna show you the fire pit out back. It's sick."

"It's really why we come to the Funky Cup," Ash added, and Lucas let the drink thing go, and as Tony finished paying, he followed the two of them through the bar and out the back door. They'd built a fire pit in the center of a massive concrete patio, and it was ringed by comfortable-looking benches, strewn with colorful pillows. Brightly colored string lights crisscrossed the trees overhead, giving the entire area a fun, happy vibe.

"This is great," Lucas admitted. He hadn't known what he was expecting, but it wasn't this.

"Yeah, it's our favorite hangout, hands down," Ash said as he took a seat on one of the benches opposite the fire. "Hey, isn't that Aaron over there?"

"Ugh, it is," Tony said, sitting down. Lucas hesitated for a moment, knowing it was weird that he was overthinking this. Would they all think he and Tony were dating if they sat next to each other? Of course, they'd caught them making out five minutes ago, so it wasn't like sitting next to him was even a big deal. Finally, Tony just reached up and tugged him down by the hem of his t-shirt. "I'm pretty sure," Tony added quietly, under his breath so Gabriel and Ash wouldn't hear, "your head was about to explode from all the overthinking you were doing there."

"Yeah," Lucas admitted. "Yeah, it kinda was."

"Don't worry about it," Tony said, and Lucas *was* kind of worried, because he kept *not* worrying. It was unnerving that he kept breaking all his rules for Tony and then *not caring* that he'd broken them.

"Okay," Lucas said. Because it *was* easier.

"So," Ash said, turning towards Lucas. "Is this new?"

Tony groaned before Lucas could react. "Guys, really? Do we have to gossip like little old ladies?"

"You *live* to gossip like a little old lady," Gabriel retorted. "How else does Lucas already know about the meatball incident?"

"Speaking of the meatball incident," Tony said smoothly, "isn't that Sean over there?"

"Ugh, don't ask him over," Gabriel said, just as both Tony and Ash waved at the guy who'd paused at the patio doorway. "You guys *suck*," he hissed as Sean made his way over to where they were sitting.

"Hi, guys. Tony, Ash, *Gabe*," Sean said. "And you're new," he added, pointing to Lucas.

"Lucas Barnes," Lucas said, shifting his beer to his other hand and extending his free one to shake. "I work with Tony."

"I'm Sean. And I'd heard you finally got some new staff," Sean said, sitting down next to Gabriel, even though he'd stiffened considerably. "Must be doing good."

"I can't complain," Tony said casually, but Lucas knew enough about the way food trucks worked and their schedules to know that What a Catch was actually booked pretty consistently—which was not always the case. There were a lot of food trucks in the LA area, and the competition for choice bookings was fierce.

"Yeah, must be nice to have a rich brother," Ash teased.

"Brother-*in-law*," Tony corrected, but he was grinning. "And yeah, we got a leg up at the very beginning, maybe, but I also think we've got a strong menu this summer. Lucas even added a few vegetarian specials that I think are gonna kill it."

"Well, I'm impressed," Gabriel said, reaching around to slap Tony on the back. "I never thought I'd see the day you'd focus on anything that wasn't meat."

"Hey," Tony exclaimed, but Lucas was more than happy to take credit for the change of approach—even if it was because Tony had been trying to win him over.

For a split second, Lucas nearly thought, *because Tony had been trying to* woo *him,* but that wasn't right, was it? Tony knew he wasn't interested in a boyfriend or a relationship. They were just having fun.

"Maybe you could give me some pointers," Ash said. "I do mainly chopped salads, but I'm wanting to branch into more vegan protein options."

"Yeah, sure, of course," Lucas said, taking a sip of his beer. "What's your truck?" he said, turning to Sean and making sure he knew he was talking to him. It took courage to come over here and hang out with these guys, when they were close to his mortal enemy—or at least the guy who'd chucked a meatball at him.

"Wraps," Sean said. Unlike the rest of them, he wasn't holding a beer bottle but a short, squat glass with an inch of clear liquid in it. "And I'd love to hear some more feedback on my vegetarian options." He shot a snooty glare at Gabriel, who just laughed in response. "Unlike some people, I give a shit about alternative lifestyles."

"I'm hardly an expert," Lucas admitted. "I just went vegan for a while, and I eat meat sometimes now, but not frequently. I just like learning the alternatives, you know? Plus, my best friend still is, and if I ever want to feed her, I've got to know my shit."

"Ria?" Tony asked.

He shouldn't continually be surprised that Tony was so observant, but he was. Every single damn time.

"Yeah," Lucas said. "Ria. She runs this gym I work at part-time, and god knows if I didn't feed her sometimes, she'd forget to eat."

"She was nice," Tony said wryly. "She even tried to convince me the spin class of death was an awful idea."

Lucas laughed.

"What," Gabriel stated incredulously. "You went to a *spin class*? You have vegetarian specials on your menu? Who are you and what have you done with Tony Blake?"

"I'm branching out, guys, it's a good thing, really. I'm trying to make better choices, smarter choices," Tony said, his tone a trifle self-conscious. But Lucas *knew* the real reason Tony's palate was more adventurous these days—and it was all because of him. Maybe that should've freaked him out and sent him running for the hills, but he *liked* being a good influence on Tony. Enjoyed opening his eyes to new foods and getting him to try things he wouldn't normally. Even if that was spin class with Charles the Sadist.

"Let me guess," Ash teased, "you went to spin class because Lucas happened to be there. Stalking him at work, you sly dog."

Lucas could see Tony's flush even though the fire pit didn't throw much light. It was seriously adorable. He'd known that was why Tony was really there, but it was unexpectedly nice to have Tony confirm it for him.

"Yeah," Gabe added, "don't think we didn't notice that you changed the subject."

"Did I?" Tony said. He finished his beer in one long gulp, his throat working as he swallowed. There was nothing Lucas wanted more than to lean over and just take a bite out of it, right there, in that vulnerable pale skin he'd just exposed.

"You totally did," Sean agreed solemnly.

"You hadn't even showed up yet!" Tony said, throwing up his hands in mock outrage. "I'm done with this and I'm getting another beer. Does anyone need a refill? Lucas?"

For a moment, Lucas hesitated. Tony was going to leave him here with these friends of his, and the second he was gone, they would pounce, wanting to know all the stuff that Tony wouldn't tell them. What would he even say?

"I'll come with you," Lucas said, standing. "It's my turn to buy this round."

Tony rolled his eyes, but he looked pleased. "If you insist," he said.

As they walked back into the bar, Tony turned to him. "I hope they aren't making you feel . . . uncomfortable or anything," he said.

"No, no, never," Lucas said, and meant it. "They're cool guys. I'm glad you brought me."

"They really are," Tony said. "I keep thinking . . . Wyatt wants to expand, create more trucks, find a more permanent home, and it'd be great to have them there with us, you know?"

Us, like Lucas wasn't just helping out for the summer. Or maybe Tony was talking about him and his brother. He was almost tempted to ask which *us* Tony was referring to, but then they approached the bar, and Shaw was wiping it down with a towel, glancing over at them expectantly.

"Thirsty tonight?" Shaw asked, mouth twitching into a grin.

"Yeah," Lucas said, pulling out his wallet. "Another round."

As Shaw grabbed their beers, Tony leaned back against the bar, eying Lucas. "I am sorry if they got weird, I didn't . . ."

"You didn't expect me to grab you and kiss you again?"

Tony grinned bashfully. "I'm not exactly complaining. I'd *wanted* you to."

He'd known it; that much hadn't been exactly a secret. But Lucas hadn't kissed him because of that; he'd done it because he couldn't wait another single second.

"I'm even tempted to just say, let's get out of here," Tony continued, "but we're supposed to be gathering information."

"By watching Sean and Gabriel pretend they hate each other?" Lucas asked, as he slid Tony's beer on the bar towards his hand. "What kind of foreplay is a meatball, anyway?"

"Weird foreplay," Tony agreed with that quicksilver grin of his that always made Lucas' heart beat just a tiny bit faster. "Promise you won't be bringing any to bed tonight."

"I promise," Lucas said, his voice low. He was already thinking about what he would bring to bed, and meatballs definitely weren't on the list.

"Good." Tony's voice had gone low too, gravelly at the edges, and as he lifted his beer to his lips, Lucas remembered exactly what those lips had felt like against his own. Hot and wild and desperate. "Seriously, though," he added, "you've gotta stop looking at me like that."

Lucas swallowed hard as he picked up his own beer. His throat felt dry, parched, but no liquid on earth was going to quench his thirst. "Like what?"

For a moment, Tony just stared at him, his gaze pinning Lucas to the spot. "Like you want me to finish what you started."

He leaned in and nipped right where he'd imagined earlier, and loved how Tony didn't jerk back but trembled instead, leaning right into his teeth. "Maybe I do," Lucas said. He'd never been more grateful for his loose shorts than he was now, because he was hard as a rock and the last thing they needed was to give the gossip mill more material. It wasn't like all the guys back at the fire pit didn't know what they'd probably get up to in the bar, despite the handful of people scattered across the tables, but they didn't need to confirm their suspicions.

"I'd tell you to stop teasing," Tony said, his voice guttural. The light in his eyes was dark with promise. "But I like it. A lot."

"You'd better," Lucas said, and he tossed a couple dollar bills on the bar to tip Shaw.

When they returned to the back patio, Sean yelped in a terrible approximation of a catcall. "You guys were gone *forever*," he said as they sat down.

"Don't listen to him," Gabriel retorted. "That tequila shit he likes always makes him mouthy."

"Oh, come on," Ash said. "You like it *better* when he's mouthy."

Gabriel spluttered, but Lucas noticed that he didn't disagree. *Yeah*, they really hated each other. Meatballs definitely were the weirdest kind of foreplay.

"We haven't seen Wyatt in a while," Sean said, and Lucas totally understood his reasons for wanting to change the subject. Lusting after your mortal enemy was tough; almost as tough as lusting after your "boss."

"Yeah, he's got that cookbook thing he's working on," Tony said. "We knew he wouldn't be working much this summer. But we've got big plans."

"More trucks?" Gabriel asked.

"Yeah, and we're really wanting a spot where we can just . . . park a lot of the time. Maybe a lot where we get some picnic tables, have some live music in the summers, you know?"

"That'd be great," Ash said. "I actually know someone who's interested in selling some property, over by the Coliseum. It'd be lit there, on USC game days, in the fall. And it's in a mix of residential and industrial area, so we'd have a decent lunch crowd there, I think."

"It'd sure be nice to park and just *stay* there," Sean said.

"Send me the info," Tony said. "I have one requirement."

"No Basket?" Gabriel asked with a chuckle.

"Ugh, I hate those guys. They're assholes," Tony complained. "They just bring down the mood whenever they're around."

"You're just bitter they copycatted your onion dip," Ash teased.

"Hell yes I am," Tony said.

"Do you know if they've stolen any other recipes?" Lucas inserted casually. They were here to gather information, and they'd gathered exactly zero. Of course, this was just like the stakeout—had he really expected to learn anything tonight? He knew Jeremy was at fault, he just didn't know how to convince Tony that was the case, even if they caught Jeremy with his hand in the cookie jar.

"The Basket guys?" Ash exchanged a glance with Gabriel. "Not that I know of. Honestly, don't listen to this one." He jabbed an elbow into Tony's side and Tony yelped. "They're not the evil villains in anyone's story."

"Does *anyone* have an evil villain in their story?" Lucas wondered. Even though he had a feeling he was the inadvertent evil villain in Jeremy's story.

"Gabe sure thinks so," Sean said slyly, and everyone laughed at how Gabriel spluttered in annoyance.

"Seriously though," Ash said. "Aaron and Ross are decent guys."

"Betrayer," Tony muttered.

"I'm not saying, let's invite them to the lot if we get it, but they're not all bad. I swear."

"You should've seen Ross lurking around the microbrewery we were at tonight," Tony claimed. "There was no way he was up to anything good."

"Maybe he's dating someone, you know, *secretly,*" Ash teased. "You wouldn't know anything about that."

"I wouldn't," Tony claimed. "I'm not dating anyone."

"Yeah, just swallowing Lucas' tongue outside the Funky Cup," Gabriel added.

"That's just some fun," Tony protested. Lucas found himself both relieved at Tony's insistence this wasn't a date, and also weirdly annoyed that he was working so hard to convince his friends.

"Looked like a lot of fun from where I was standing," Ash said.

"Okay, that's it," Tony said, standing abruptly. "We're good, right? I'm going to go have some fun, without you losers."

"Yeah, *get it,*" Gabriel added as Lucas stood amid all the catcalling and encouragement.

Tony glanced over at him, and his gaze was supportive and encouraging and *eager.* It was the eagerness that fucked Lucas up every time. Like Tony, who turned heads wherever he fucking went, was blown away by the fact that Lucas couldn't keep his hands off him. "You ready to go?" he asked.

Lucas hadn't drunk more than half of his second beer, but suddenly that was just a beer, and Tony was there, holding out a hand, and asking—practically *begging*—to get him alone. What else could he do but nod?

"Good," Tony said. He turned back to the other guys, who were all watching. "Don't do anything I wouldn't. Catch you later."

"Yeah, stay safe," Sean yelled as they headed towards the gate that opened right onto the street. "Use a condom!"

"I'm not sure we got anywhere with the investigation," Lucas said semi-apologetically as they reached Tony's bike. This time he didn't argue when Tony handed him the helmet.

Tony shrugged on his leather jacket. "Me either. But apparently we should eliminate the Basket guys, even though I think they're shady as hell."

"Do you trust Ash?" Lucas asked.

"I've known him about as long as I've been in LA," Tony admitted. "He's a great guy. His heart's in the right spot. And he knows his shit with the truck and with food. He's been around this scene a long time, even though he kinda looks like a kid."

Ash *might* look young, but he also struck Lucas as someone who was damn determined. Which was something he not only admired, he understood.

"Hey," Tony said, reaching out for Lucas' arm and giving it a quick squeeze. Not possessive, but reassuring. "We're gonna figure this out."

As Lucas climbed onto the bike behind Tony again, he knew he was right, but he was afraid at the cost it would extract from Tony when he discovered that the guy he'd defended all along turned out to be the guilty one. *That's on Tony, not on you; you're not really involved*, Lucas reminded himself, and pushed away his worries. He wasn't going to let the situation eat him up, especially not tonight, not when the night held so much promise.

Tony took them back to the food truck. He realized as he pulled away from the curb at the Funky Cup that he hadn't asked Lucas where he wanted to go—to Tony's place or to his own—so he decided they could talk about it when they reached the lot where the truck was parked.

The ride back was just as arousing as the first had been; feeling Lucas' body pressed close to his, the way his fingertips dug into his t-shirt under his jacket, like they could brand him, mark him as *his*. It felt like they were playing with fire; one wrong move and they were both going to get burned, but right now? The risk was exhilarating.

He parked in his usual spot, and when Lucas dismounted and pulled off his helmet, his expression was hard to read. The thing was, Tony couldn't stop thinking about that kiss back at the Funky Cup, how Lucas had grabbed him and kissed him like he'd die if he didn't do it, but now, somehow, things had grown awkward.

Tony turned to him, ready to ask him what he wanted, when he caught a flash of heat in Lucas' eyes. That was all the warning he had before Lucas reached out and hauled him close, pressing their bodies together. "God," Lucas muttered before he reached up, pressing their mouths together again.

That was all it took to light the fire that had already been smoldering for days. It roared to life, and Tony was suddenly unbelievably desperate. He wanted Lucas a hundred different ways, a thousand, and as his back hit the side of Belinda, he had the brief fleeting thought that he still didn't quite know what Lucas wanted.

This time when Lucas reached for his belt, he didn't stop him. Instead, Tony lifted his mouth and managed to get his brain functioning just long enough to murmur, "Not here." He fumbled for his keys, just as Lucas was fumbling for his belt, and despite that all the blood in his body was headed towards his rapidly hardening dick—Lucas' hands kept brushing against it and sending sparks of pleasure shooting through him and it was unbelievably distracting—he got the door unlocked and they stumbled up the stairs and into the truck. Not a lot of privacy, but enough.

Enough that they wouldn't get arrested, anyway.

That was the last coherent thought Tony had, because Lucas was furiously removing Tony's clothes, like they fucking offended him. First his shirt, then his belt, then his jeans were down, and finally his boxer briefs, his cock bobbing as Lucas glanced up at him, already partially on his knees.

I guess, Tony thought semi-hysterically, *this answers the question of what Lucas wants. It's me.*

"You've been driving me crazy," Lucas muttered darkly as he reached out and stroked the sensitive skin on Tony's hip with his fingertips before grasping hard and pushing Tony back against the edge of the stainless steel countertop. "I think you know you have."

"Driving myself crazy too," Tony murmured. He was right on the edge, waiting for the moment when Lucas would lean in and he'd finally get to know what that smart-ass mouth felt like on his cock. He couldn't wait, but at the same time, he was kinda enjoying that Lucas wanted to give back as good as he got.

"Hope you're in for a little more," Lucas said, a mischievous glint to his eyes as he glanced up at Tony. "I want you to *beg* for it."

Tony was perfectly happy to beg *now*, but that seemed to defeat the game that Lucas wanted to play. "Okay," he said.

When Lucas leaned in, the touch of his hands and finally, achingly, his mouth wasn't necessarily hesitant, but it was light and fleeting, just pinpricks of intense pleasure, fading away slowly like starbursts of sensation as Lucas worked him up into a nearly unbearable frenzy. First, it was just the brush of his tongue along the bottom ridge of his cock. Then his fingers circling the head, just the bare edges of them smoothing down the moisture leaking out of it. Finally, Tony couldn't look any more because he might actually just *come* from the way Lucas was reverently nipping and sucking along his dick, and he *knew* that wasn't the game. The game was to drive him past endurance, past caring, past sanity, right into bliss. He squeezed his eyes shut and let himself just *feel*.

"You like this." Lucas' voice had gone dark and guttural, and Tony hoped, with the one bit of his brain still working, that Lucas liked it just as much as he did.

"I do, god I do," Tony ground out, "you're making me insane."

"You can take a little more," Lucas said thoughtfully and then suddenly, his fingers were a tight ring around the base of his cock, and his mouth was all the way on it, hot and wet and perfect sliding down, and if he hadn't been gripping him so damn hard, Tony would've just come, but he couldn't, not yet, and he cried out.

Someone was muttering *fuck, fuck, fuck,* over and over again, and for a split second, Tony wasn't sure who it was. It couldn't be Lucas, because his mouth was full of Tony's cock, and *god*, right there, *right there*. His own brain was so fucking fuzzy, with pleasure and the pain of not overloading on all that glorious pleasure.

It was only when Lucas backed off, and wrapped his tongue around the head, giving it one last suck, before resuming his horrific teasing, that Tony realized it was him. He was the one chanting mindlessly.

Was that begging? God, Tony hoped so.

"Please," he finally ground out, hoping that finding a new word that he could actually say would convince Lucas to show him a little mercy.

But the wicked twist to Lucas' mouth as he dove in again, pulling himself closer and closer to Tony, until he felt like he was fucking buried in his throat, made it clear that there'd be no mercy here.

Lucas held him there for a moment, and as he swallowed hard, his throat working, Tony had to concentrate every ounce of will not to just lose it then. It felt so goddamn good, so fucking perfect, and he'd never wanted to come so badly in his entire life.

"Please," he murmured brokenly as Lucas pulled back a little, his spit-slick dick just teasing at his mouth. "God, please."

"You wanna come?" Lucas asked, and Tony nodded, maybe even past speech as Lucas reached up, cupping his balls in his fingers. Then he leaned in, and without a word, sucked him down hard again, and this time it was an unstoppable force that Tony couldn't hope to contain. It roared through him, with teeth, with claws, as the orgasm finally hit him. It ricocheted through him with a devastating intensity, and through it all, Tony was sure Lucas was there for the entire thing, coaxing every bit of heart-stopping pleasure out of him until it was finally over and he felt emptied out, *spent*.

The first thing Tony realized when the pleasure finally ended, was that his hands were aching, almost unbearably. And that's when he glanced down and realized that he'd clamped his fists around the edge of the stainless steel counter, so tightly that he wasn't even sure he could actually unclench them now that it was over.

"You liked that," Lucas stated, rising to his feet as he wiped his mouth with the back of his hand. He looked almost as wrecked as Tony felt; his eyes dilated in the dim light of the truck, his own cock a hard line in his shorts, his hands shaking just a little as he reached out and splayed his fingers on Tony's chest.

"Uh, yeah," Tony said, finally managing to remove his own hands from the edge of the counter. He flexed them once and then twice, trying to get the feeling back. He was going to need them for everything he wanted to do. "What gave it away?"

Lucas grinned. "Maybe your constant yelling? I think we woke up the entire neighborhood."

Tony leaned down and kissed him. Tasted himself on Lucas' tongue. "I think we should take this back to my place, and see if we can keep that entire neighborhood up, too."

"What about . . ." Lucas swayed closer, pressing his cock against Tony's thigh. "I could just get off right here, right now."

"That easy?" Tony scoffed. "I don't know if you deserve that, after what you just put me through."

Lucas grinned cockily. "You mean the best goddamn orgasm you've ever had?"

"Exactly," Tony said, nodding. "Exactly my fucking point."

Lucas still seemed to hesitate, so Tony kissed him again, more insistently, and this time, Lucas just melted against him, and that was all the motivation that Tony needed to take him by the hand, lead him out of the truck and to the bike.

"What about my car?" Lucas asked.

"I'll drive you back here in the morning. You've got an early shift, anyway."

"Yeah, I do," Lucas said, and there was something worried in his eyes. Like staying the night might mean something he didn't want it to.

"Don't you want to have some more fun?" Tony challenged, and that seemed to be the final push that Lucas needed because without a single word, he put on the helmet and climbed on right behind Tony.

CHAPTER ELEVEN

By the time they pulled into the driveway of the big house that Wyatt and his husband shared, Tony driving into the garage and parking next to another pair of sleek black Ducatis, and several other expensive-looking cars, Lucas felt like he'd already been on the edge for hours.

Days. Weeks. Probably from the first moment he'd ever fucking seen Tony's gorgeous face. And maybe that should have terrified him, but instead all he felt was the rush of adrenaline through his veins. He'd known he would enjoy taking Tony apart, but he hadn't expected that it would feel like this. Like he could do it a hundred times, a *thousand*, and it would never, ever get old to hear him beg like that.

"Hey, it's just through here," Tony said, and suddenly their hands were intertwined and he was leading him through the backyard, to a tiny cottage set back from the main house.

He punched in the code to the door lock, and it swung open, revealing a simple living room and a small kitchenette, with fridge, microwave and even a small sink. There was a doorway to another room on the far side and that's where Tony led him, flipping on a light in the corner and revealing the large bed.

Lucas didn't think he'd ever been this hard for this long in his entire life; it felt like a fucking eternity. Surely at some point he'd grow soft or get some much-needed release, but then Tony leaned down and kissed him, and his cock twitched again, only the taste of Tony's mouth, the lazy, fiery sweep of his tongue making him burn all over again.

"Hey," Lucas said, panting hard as Tony's lips sucked a bruise on his neck, the momentary pain flashing through him and fading into acute pleasure. "Hey, I want you to do something for me."

Tony glanced up, his eyes hot and reassuring. "Anything."

"I want you to fuck me."

Lucas hadn't always enjoyed penetration, but he'd learned to like it, especially if it was with someone he trusted. And, it turned out, he trusted Tony, because he wasn't just vaguely interested in it as a way to get off, but he wanted Tony buried inside of him, so far in he didn't know where Tony stopped and he began.

"I think we can manage something like that," Tony said, and there was a firm edge to his voice that made Lucas wonder what *something like that* meant, but he didn't ask because Tony was pulling his t-shirt over his head, and his fingers were at his waist, tugging his shorts off and all his arguments evaporated when Tony circled his hard, straining dick with those clever, talented fingers and began to slowly jack him off.

"Get on the bed," Tony said, moving his own hand away, and Lucas wanted to cry or whine that the pleasure had stopped, but that edge of steel was still there. Just enough of a hint that for once in his life, Lucas didn't argue, didn't overthink, just *went* with it. He climbed onto the bed and arched his back, making Tony mutter something under his breath. Yeah, he *would* like that, wouldn't he? But Lucas only wanted to tempt him into moving this along, so maybe he wouldn't drag it out like he'd done for Tony. Someday, he might like that, but he'd been right there for so long now, that he felt like he was already going crazy with it.

He heard Tony rummaging around and he tensed, so ready for the first touch, but instead, he felt Tony's lips against his spine, brushing a string of sweet kisses along it, and then he moved to his hips, sprinkling kisses along his skin like he was seasoning and Lucas was a delicious dish that he couldn't wait to devour.

"I want you to tell me how you're feeling," Tony said, his voice a deep rumble against his back, "and I want you to touch yourself."

Lucas felt a frisson of panic race through him. "If I do that . . . if I touch myself . . ."

"You're not going to come," Tony said, and that hardness was back again, and it wasn't intimidating or scary, it was hot as hell.

"I'm . . . I'm . . . not?" Lucas stuttered as he wrapped a hand around his own cock. It jerked in his hand, desperate for some friction as he slowly slid his fingers up and down. Carefully, so he wouldn't give himself too much and lose control.

"You're not," Tony said, and then Lucas nearly erupted anyway when instead of the cool, damp fingertip he expected, he felt something hotter and wetter circle his hole.

He pitched forward into the covers, his fingers flexing helplessly around his dick as Tony's tongue burrowed deeper, his fingertips digging into his ass, the pain and pleasure mingling together until all he could do was pant helplessly into Tony's comforter.

This was nothing like what he'd expected, and not quite what he'd asked for, but suddenly, it was all he wanted. For Tony to hold him like this, right on the precipice, until he allowed him to fall over it.

"Don't come," Tony said, his warm breath washing over where he was open and sensitive and nearly making him cry with it. "Don't fucking come."

His fingers were already barely touching his cock, sliding in the precome that kept leaking from the head. "I can't, I won't," Lucas practically wailed, but when Tony slipped a finger alongside his tongue, he nearly did, undone by the realization that this was Tony—he was smart and funny and a little bit cocky and totally, unbelievably loyal, and he wanted Lucas *this* much.

"I can't, I can't," Lucas moaned, not even caring if anyone heard him anymore.

"You can," Tony said inexorably, as he slid another finger in. He wiggled them and it lit Lucas up from the inside out. He felt shiny and new and invincible, teetering right there and then Tony turned and crooked them both and he was babbling incoherently as he fell right into the longest, hardest orgasm of his life. He almost wished he could've lasted longer, but when he finally stopped shuddering, his cock striping up his chest with come, he found he couldn't regret a goddamn thing. Not when Tony's gentle hand was on his back, soothing him through it, and when he turned Lucas around finally and gave him a warm and slightly smug smile, and then asked, "You okay?"

Lucas let out a shuddering breath. "I've never been better."

"It wasn't quite what you wanted, but . . ." Tony flushed. "I wanted to do that. So it was selfish, I guess."

"Hey, you know," Lucas said as he took the tissues Tony handed him, "anytime you want to selfishly stick your tongue in my ass, I'm down for that."

Tony laughed. "I'll remember that for next time."

Next time. Lucas had known there would be one, but he'd not thought of it in such definite, concrete terms before. And yes, now that Tony mentioned it, there would have to be a next time. There'd need to be a hundredth time. Probably a thousandth time.

"You should," Lucas said. Mostly clean, he leaned back on the bed. It was unsurprisingly comfortable, and suddenly, with the force of his orgasm emptying him out, he realized just how tired he was. It'd been a long day, and he hadn't gotten much sleep the night before. He yawned hard and deep.

"Yeah," Tony said. "I'm worn out too. There's a spare toothbrush here and you can always shower here in the morning and borrow some clothes."

Lucas was surprised. Tony had just sort of insisted on bringing him back here for the night, but now he was giving him an option. An out. If he wanted to take it.

Every other time, he'd have jumped at it without a single thought.

But now he hesitated. He was tired, but he also *wanted* to stay. Even with what that might mean.

"Okay," he said, watching as Tony's face relaxed into a smile.

"Good, I'm going to use the bathroom," he said. "You need anything?"

"Sleep," Lucas said, pulling back the covers and climbing underneath them. They smelled like Tony, and it lulled him even further into believing this was right.

"Good, me too," Tony said, and flipped the light off. A few minutes later, Lucas felt rather than saw Tony slide into bed, and then suddenly Tony was right there, hair falling all around that incredible face. "I'm glad you stayed," he whispered, and pressed a kiss to Lucas' cheek before everything went soft and black and he fell backwards into an exhausted sleep.

Lucas definitely didn't make it a habit of sleeping in beds other than his own, so when the sun crept over LA the next morning, shining into his eyes in a way that it never would have at his apartment, where he'd hung dark blackout curtains, he knew something wasn't right.

For a split second, he wasn't even sure whose bed he was in. Then it hit him. He'd had sex with Tony. He'd had *fantastic* sex with Tony. Such good sex that he hadn't even argued about staying over, even though in any other circumstance, he would have dragged himself back to his own apartment afterwards.

It hadn't even been how much Tony wanted him there that had convinced him; it was how much *he* wanted to be there.

Lucas rolled over, cracking open one eye. Tony was sprawled out next to him, one leg under the covers, the other hooked over them. His hair was a wild mess, and he had the most peaceful expression on his face as he slept.

He didn't want to wake him, but he reached out anyway, smoothing back some of the unruly strands that kept threatening to fall into his eyes.

For the first time in a very long time, he didn't know what time it was, when he needed to get up, or what he needed to do when he did, besides follow Tony to the food truck whenever he dragged himself out of bed. Would he want to do this every day? No, he had way too many things he wanted to accomplish to just sit around every morning, lazing in bed. But sometimes? Once in a while? He could see it. And he also knew it was Tony he'd want to do it with.

An unsettling realization. He turned onto his back and stared at the ceiling for what could've been five minutes or five hours. He wasn't sure; he was just aware of a gradually spreading realization that something had changed, fundamentally. And he wasn't sure if he wanted to go back or if he was ready to move forward.

"I can hear you thinkin' from over here," Tony groaned out, startling him. He hadn't realized that Tony was awake, but when he glanced over, one bleary eye was open and he was grinning.

"Hey," Lucas said, shifting so he could face Tony again.

"Good morning," Tony said, stretching out his big frame. "You sleep okay?"

"Actually," Lucas said, considering the question, "yeah, I did."

Tony was still grinning madly, like he'd just woken up to his favorite thing ever. Lucas' heart accelerated at the thought that could be *him*. "You sound surprised."

"Well, I don't usually sleep in beds that aren't mine," he admitted.

Tony's smile impossibly grew even brighter. "I should be flattered, then," he said, ducking his head a bit, like he couldn't quite believe his own luck.

"Yeah," Lucas said, and he was grinning now too. Embarrassingly, but he couldn't stop even if he'd wanted to.

"Hey," Tony said, scooting closer, his hands drifting down to where Lucas was naked under the sheets. "Maybe we should . . ."

A blaring noise suddenly echoed through the room, startling both of them and making Tony grimace. "Shit," he said.

"What the fuck is that?" Lucas said, yanking the covers up to his chin. He *was* naked, thank you very much, a situation he'd hoped Tony would take advantage of. There was nothing better than hot, sleepy, lazy, morning sex.

"Ugh," Tony said, flopping onto his back. "My stupid brother."

"Your brother has an alarm in *your* house?" Lucas asked incredulously.

"Well, technically, it's a walkie-talkie," Tony said, reaching over and grabbing a small black device just as it squawked again. "We just don't use the talkie part, because the couple times he used it, a disembodied voice waking me up from a deep sleep scared the ever-loving shit out of me."

"So what's he trying to say, then?" Lucas wondered, trying to mentally reconcile the fact that Wyatt talking was worse than that loud-as-fuck noise.

"That sound means breakfast is ready," Tony said. "Come on."

"Breakfast?" Lucas was not totally *okay* with spending the night with Tony—he was a work in progress, thank you very much—but breakfast? With Tony's brother and his husband? That might be a step further than he was completely comfortable with.

Tony must have sensed his apprehension, because instead of climbing out of bed, he rolled back to where Lucas was lying. "Hey," he added, "we'd love you to join us, but if you want me to drive you back to your place, instead, or back to your car, I can do that."

Tony made it sound simple, and maybe it was, but it would also be a huge inconvenience. The easiest thing for Lucas to do would be to have breakfast, take a shower like Tony had suggested, and go with him to the food truck after they were done. It wasn't a marriage proposal; it wasn't a white picket fence; it wasn't any kind of commitment except just food in the morning and a ride. That was it. Lucas took a deep breath and shook his head. "Yeah, no, it's fine. Breakfast sounds good, actually. I'm starving."

He followed Tony out of bed and into the bathroom, which was just big enough for the two of them. Tony appeared to have zero qualms about the situation because he immediately headed towards the toilet and started peeing, as he gestured towards the toothbrush, still in its packaging, on the counter next to the sink. "That's for you," he said.

There was part of Lucas that desperately wanted to ask if he kept these around for situations like this—if these sorts of situations happened to him often enough that he needed to keep a stash of spare toothbrushes around. But he didn't, because deep down, he wasn't sure he wanted to know, and also because they'd both made it clear that this was just some fun they were having.

Maybe Tony might be amenable to more, but Lucas wasn't sure, and he wasn't going to rock the boat. Not this morning, anyway.

"Thanks," he said, and after shucking the toothbrush's packaging and digging out the toothpaste, brushed his teeth. It felt so domestic, hip to hip with Tony in the bathroom as he finished finger-combing through the worst of the tangles in his hair and pulled it back up into one of his buns. They switched places then, Tony brushing his teeth, and Lucas using the toilet, and then there was nothing to do but get dressed. "We'll shower after breakfast," Tony explained. "Wyatt gets tetchy if his food gets cold."

Lucas had never had a brother who cooked for him—he didn't have a brother at all—and so he just nodded. Hopefully Tony knew just how lucky he was.

When they emerged out of the cottage into the backyard, there was already a table set on the back patio, and Ryan was lounging there, wearing only a pair of athletic shorts, as he scrolled through his phone.

He glanced up as they walked closer to the patio, not looking even the tiniest bit surprised that it wasn't just Tony coming in for breakfast. And when Lucas looked at the table, he could see that it'd already been set with four plates. They'd known he was here, which he couldn't decide was creepy or not.

"I told them we might have a fourth for breakfast," Tony said with a flush creeping up his cheeks.

Ryan smiled. "It's only weird if you make it weird," he said, extending his hand. "It's great to see you again, man. Tony can't shut up about what great work you're doing on the truck."

"Thanks," Lucas said, giving Ryan's hand a brief shake. "Is there anything I can do to help?"

"No," both Ryan and Tony said at the same time. They exchanged a rueful smile. "I'll go see if Wyatt needs any help, but if I know him, he'll smack me with a spatula and tell me to get out," Tony added.

Lucas watched as Tony disappeared into the house.

"So," Ryan said, lazily indicating one of the empty chairs. "Sit down and tell me how it's going."

"How it's going?" Lucas asked. There was already a pot of coffee on the table, and he reached for it, pouring a mug full and stirring some sugar into the hot liquid.

Ryan shot him a knowing look. "How it's going," he repeated firmly.

"I enjoy working with Tony," he said, carefully. He wanted to be honest because Ryan was a decent, friendly guy and didn't deserve to be lied to, but at the same time, Lucas didn't know him either. He was just Tony's brother-in-law, still, and the one thing Lucas was never sure how to trust was family. "He's great. And I really appreciate him giving me the opportunity to create more specials."

"The way Tony tells it, you're revolutionizing the truck," Ryan said warmly. And it made Lucas like him a little more—not necessarily *trust* him yet, but definitely like him more—that he hadn't wanted Lucas to dish on their personal relationship, or why he'd stayed over. He'd been asking about work, and Lucas could appreciate that. As far as he knew, the truck was self-sustaining, but he had a feeling that Ryan would be the financial backer for a lot of Wyatt and Tony's other big plans they had in the works.

It was fair of him to want to know how things were going, especially when Lucas had walked in and started changing stuff.

"How is Jeremy?" Ryan asked.

That was one question that Lucas wasn't sure how to answer. *He's creepy? He doesn't like me because he feels like he has some kind of possessive grip on Tony? I'm nearly sure he's stealing from Tony and Wyatt?*

"Uh." Lucas hesitated. "I guess he's fine . . . we're . . ."

"He's awful, isn't he?" Ryan said conspiratorially. "Just *terrible*. I think Wyatt will go nuts if Tony doesn't get rid of him soon. We all hoped with you on board, he'd see what a shitty job Jeremy was doing and fire him, but I guess not yet."

Lucas breathed out a sigh of relief. At least he wasn't alone in thinking that guy was a total waste of space. "I think . . . I think . . ." He hesitated, wanting to choose his words carefully. "I think Tony is super loyal to people he trusts," he said. "And Jeremy's not given him any real reason not to trust him yet."

Yet. Lucas knew that someday, hopefully sooner rather than later, Jeremy would expose himself for the thief he was, and it would force Tony to confront that he'd given his trust to someone who didn't deserve it. And as much as Lucas wanted him gone, he was also kind of dreading that day because Tony didn't deserve to second-guess himself, and Lucas knew that he inevitably would.

Ryan shot him a level stare. "You are not what I expected," he said, and Lucas wasn't sure if that was a good or a bad thing. Was it one of those compliments that was really an insult? Instead of answering, he just sipped his coffee.

"I think you really have Tony's best interests at heart," Ryan continued after a lengthy silence. "I think you really care about him. About the truck."

"Why?" Lucas wondered. "Because I didn't immediately go spouting off about how Jeremy sucks, and he's slow and works at a snail's pace, and is probably stealing, and should've been fired yesterday?"

Ryan cracked a smile. "Yeah, that," he said. "Exactly that."

Lucas shrugged. "You know, anyway."

"But you get it. Tony isn't dumb or blind. He's just . . . he wants to see the best in people. Wyatt can be the same way too, sometimes. I have to . . . remind him periodically that people sometimes want to fuck us over." Ryan's smile morphed into something a lot more killer. The kind of smile you wouldn't want to fuck with. Lucas thought anyone who tried was really stupid.

"Does he listen?" Lucas wondered. He'd been thinking about trying again to convince Tony to get rid of Jeremy, but the timing hadn't been right yet, and he also wasn't sure he wanted to stick his neck out that way. Not when things were going so good, their lack of sandwich press notwithstanding.

"Sometimes," Ryan said wryly. "They can be a stubborn bunch, those Blakes."

"Tony mentioned there was a younger brother."

"Yeah, that's Marco, who's still up in Napa. Wyatt and Tony don't talk to him much, mostly because unlike how they might suspect Jeremy, they know that Marco's into some shady shit." Ryan sounded regretful. "If Tony hasn't mentioned him much, it's because he doesn't know how. I think he's embarrassed that he couldn't pull him out of all that crap that he's tied up in."

Giving up on his brother was something that would kill Tony; Lucas wasn't surprised that he hadn't mentioned it. It wasn't like Lucas was desperately wanting to tell him about his shitty parents, either. He'd mentioned them, but only because of the cat they'd seen the other night.

"Anyway," Ryan continued, "I'm glad you're on board. Really, really glad, if I'm being honest."

"Even glad I stayed over last night?" Lucas asked, raising an eyebrow and breaking all of his own damn rules. *Again.*

But Ryan just shrugged. "I don't like to interfere in Tony's personal life. But he's happy, and that's all that matters."

I'm happy too, Lucas thought, feeling his heart swell, even as he tried to tamp it back down again.

Just then the back door to the house swung open and Tony walked out, carrying a big platter of French toast, and another of sausages and eggs, still sizzling on the plate. Wyatt was right behind him, carrying his own coffee mug in one hand and an enormous bowl of fruit in the other.

"Hey," Wyatt said, nudging Lucas with his elbow as he walked by. "It's good to see you again."

"That's what I thought too," Ryan said, smiling impudently.

"Can we not, please?" Tony complained as he sat down, reaching for the coffee. "I haven't ingested enough caffeine yet to witness you two dissect my personal life."

"I'm not sure there's enough caffeine in the universe for that," Lucas added.

"Amen," Tony said, clinking his mug with Lucas'. "Now let's eat before it gets cold."

The food, unsurprisingly, was incredible. Lucas hadn't expected anything else, but the French toast was crisp and perfectly cooked, the eggs creamy and well-seasoned, and the sausages browned and delicious.

He'd just reached for seconds, when another otherworldly noise stopped his hand on the serving spoon of the fruit bowl. "What the fuck is that?" he demanded, as the squawking continued.

"Ugh," Wyatt said, "that fucking parrot."

"It was so quiet earlier I kind of hoped it died. Or they finally got rid of it," Ryan complained.

"That's a bird?" Lucas asked.

Tony was laughing, because of course he was. "Ryan thinks he can get his lawyer to shut it up."

Lucas eyed him skeptically. "Really?"

"No," Ryan said. "I was hoping my lawyer would find some kind of noise ordinance or loophole in the HOA document to make them stop bringing the parrot outside."

"Let me guess," Tony said, "that isn't working out for you."

"He's still figuring it out," Ryan said stubbornly.

"You could just . . . get used to it?" Lucas suggested, but even as he spoke, the bird made another horrible noise, followed by about ten more, and then a loud, insistent, "Shiver me timbers."

"It's also a pirate bird, did I mention that?" Wyatt said dryly.

"You didn't, but *wow*," Lucas said. It was funny to realize that even with all their money and this gorgeous house, Wyatt and Ryan's lives weren't quite perfect.

"I try to ignore it," Wyatt added, but frankly, it was a lot to ignore. "So, Lucas," he asked, turning his direction. "How are the energy bars doing?"

"I'm actually still waiting to hear back from a distributor who said they were interested in carrying them throughout the western US," Lucas said. Every time he thought about how he hadn't heard back yet, his stomach got a little tighter. But it was okay. Financially he wasn't in a bad spot. He could always take more shifts at Ria's, or even work more with Tony. Neither of those would be a hardship.

He'd been through worse, and he knew he'd make it out all right. He'd just thought, so stupidly, that this was it, and maybe he'd finally made it.

"That's exciting," Ryan said. "I'd love to try some. Maybe distribute them in the clubhouse for some of the other guys to try? I'm assuming they're low sugar?"

"Yeah, of course, I can email you the nutritional info, and send Tony with a box in a few days," Lucas said, genuinely grateful. Ryan seemed like a super nice guy—not at all the egotistical baseball player he'd kind of assumed he must be. "I appreciate it a lot, thank you."

Ryan shrugged. "Don't thank me yet. But Tony said they were really good."

"Tony is possibly slightly prejudiced," Lucas admitted.

"Not *that* prejudiced," Tony retorted. "I told you those veggie specials were great, and they sold out, didn't they?"

They had, and even Lucas had been a little surprised. Tony and Wyatt's food truck wasn't exactly known for their alternative menu options. "I've got more ideas too," Lucas added.

"We're looking to diversify a bit," Wyatt said casually. "Have you ever thought about starting your own vegetarian or vegan food truck?"

He hadn't, because he'd been so sure that his energy bars would be the thing that pulled him out of his current frustratingly circular life, where he worked too many part-time jobs and never got enough sleep. "No," he said, shaking his head. "But I'd be willing to think about it." He'd have to be a fool to tell Wyatt that he wasn't interested. And not just because he had the money to make things happen—but because Lucas had discovered just how much he enjoyed the work.

He'd worked in kitchens before, but he'd gotten bored easily, every day feeling way too much like the days that had preceded it. But on the food truck? They went to so many different places, met so many different kinds of people, and instead of being locked away in the back of a restaurant, they were right there, *part of the action*.

"It's a brilliant idea," Tony said, seemingly very enthusiastic.

"I'd have to figure out how it might work with the energy bar business," Lucas said. He'd dumped way too much money and energy into developing recipes and finding the following he'd developed, one hard-won customer at a time.

"You could sell them at the truck," Wyatt said.

"Really?" That was something Lucas hadn't considered, but it wasn't a half-bad idea, especially if they focused the food truck on a healthier, cleaner lifestyle. His energy bars would fit right in.

"I love that," Tony said, and even though Lucas had initially felt unsure, he did too.

"Something to think about," Wyatt said, and Lucas nodded.

"What are you guys up to today?" Ryan asked.

Tony pulled out his phone. "Big tequila festival. God, I hope those fuckers from Basket won't decide to crash it."

"Do they do that?" Lucas wondered, forking a piece of pineapple and popping it in his mouth.

"Well, *no*, but tequila and picnic food? Not a great combination," Tony said with a grimace. "I'm sure they'll try to make it work. Probably with your onion dip recipe."

"Oh, are you *still* going on about that?" Wyatt said, rolling his eyes.

"Hell yes I am. That was a great recipe." Lucas wasn't sure which Tony was more affronted by: that the Basket guys had stolen his recipe or that his brother wanted him to let it go.

"It wasn't exactly *mine*. It came from a lot of different places," Wyatt said.

Tony crossed his arms over his chest. "It *was* ours," he retorted. "It absolutely fucking was."

"Okay, the Basket guys are copycat assholes," Ryan piped up. "Anything else new?"

"No," Tony said with a sulk. "We'll be at the tequila festival all day. Probably pack up when we sell out, or about nine-ish, whichever comes first."

"Maybe someday I'll have time to work in the truck again," Wyatt said mournfully. "This cookbook is kicking my ass."

"How far along are you?" Lucas asked, curious, because he didn't know what it took to develop enough recipes to fill a cookbook, but at least knowing it wasn't easy, because even developing the handful of energy bar recipes he'd used had taken him forever.

"Not far enough," Wyatt said, sighing. "It's a good thing the Dodgers don't mind me sending botched recipes to the clubhouse."

"They're not botched," Ryan said. "Just because they don't meet your ridiculously high standards, babe, doesn't mean they aren't delicious. Also, the guys are basically all enormous fans at this point. They even requested you make that brisket again, soon."

"Good, because the recipe still isn't right," Wyatt said, frustration etched on his face.

"You'll get there," Lucas said, encouragingly. To his surprise, he actually believed that Wyatt would, and he'd gone out of his way to say so. That wasn't something he normally did.

Frankly, this whole fucking thing wasn't something he *normally* did. He never spent the night, he rarely even went over to someone else's place, far preferring his own, and he'd never, ever dream of staying for breakfast, especially not with the hookup's brother and his husband.

But then, Lucas realized slowly, Tony wasn't just a hookup. And even more insanely, Lucas wasn't even horrified by the realization; it was almost *expected*. Like he'd known from that first meeting that if he let Tony in, if he gave him an inch, he'd take a mile, and Lucas wouldn't even resent it. He'd *welcome* it.

"Thanks," Wyatt said warmly. "That means a lot."

"We've got to get going," Tony said, rising to his feet. "Sorry about the cleanup, bro."

But Ryan was the one who waved lazily. "I'll take care of it," he said. "Our game's not til late tonight, so I don't have to be at the stadium for another couple hours."

"You're the best," Wyatt said gratefully. "But I'll do it. I'll be messing it up again right after, because I want to get this brisket recipe right. If all goes well, maybe we can even put it on the menu. What do you think, Tony?"

Tony nodded as he rested a hand on Lucas' back. It didn't feel possessive; it felt *right*. And yeah, maybe that *was* fucking Lucas up a little. He'd never had a boyfriend before, but he had a feeling it wasn't much different from what he and Tony were already doing.

Had they segued into this so seamlessly, so easily, that it was stupid to even put up a fight anymore?

"Yeah, that sounds good. Keep me posted," Tony said. "But seriously, we've got to run."

Lucas stood then, pushing his chair out, and Tony's hand fell naturally down his back, just above his butt, and stayed there as they said goodbye and then walked back to the cottage.

"Are we really running late?" Lucas wondered as Tony typed in his door code.

"Naw," Tony said with a mischievous grin, "but I was kinda hoping I might get another helping of sausage this morning."

"You're the worst," Lucas said, but he was already letting Tony pull him inside, and the moment their lips met, he already knew that was a lie.

Tony wasn't the worst. Not even close. Not even at all.

CHAPTER TWELVE

TONY DIDN'T THINK HE'D ever had a better morning, or a better evening preceding it. He felt loose and relaxed, not just from the fun he'd had with Lucas the night before, the soul-draining orgasm he'd given him, or the intense one he'd jerked out of him this morning, but from the way he felt around the guy. It wasn't just sexual, and he hoped, more than he had any right to, that they would somehow end up on the same page, if they weren't already.

Tony drove them over on the bike to Lucas' apartment building. He was a little disappointed when Lucas said after dismounting, "I'll just be a second, just gotta grab some clean clothes." He'd hoped that Lucas would invite him up, even though they were running *almost* on time and the last thing they needed was another distraction to make them actually late. Tony had been really stoked to win the bid to go to this particular festival because he had a feeling their food would be just the kind of thing that people drinking tequila all day would want. So he'd ordered extra fish, and there was all that to prep for the day, as well as additional salsas to chop and mix.

Still, he'd wanted to see Lucas' apartment.

You will, he told himself, *you just have to be a little more patient.*

Lucas was back downstairs quicker than Tony thought possible. He'd changed into another one of his punk rock t-shirts, this one with the sleeves cut off, and a pair of loose shorts. Perfect for a long, sweltering day working on the truck.

Also, it happened to expose just enough of Lucas' skin that Tony was already craving the taste of it again.

The problem with really good sex was that you always wanted more of it.

"Let's go," Lucas said, straddling the bike again, his arms wrapping around Tony's middle, pulling them close together.

A few minutes later, they were parking at the truck lot. Tony was glad to see that the delivery truck had just pulled up behind them, and he could check all the fish as it came off, carefully verifying that each container looked and smelled fresh.

"That's a lot of fish," Lucas commented, leaning over to pick up a few of the cases of fruit. "I'm assuming you're hoping the tacos are a big hit today."

"Tequila? Tacos? Seems like a solid combo to me," Tony said. Just as they approached the truck, the door swung open and Jeremy was standing on the bottom step, an accusatory glare on his face.

"Hey," Tony said, apparently unconcerned by the doom and gloom currently decorating Jeremy's expression. "Come help us get this inside. We've got lots to get done before we have to leave for the festival."

But Jeremy didn't budge. Just stared. And not at Tony, at Lucas.

God, please don't cause a scene today, Tony prayed. He knew he would have to do something about Jeremy—at the very least have a talk with him that Lucas was sticking around, and that he needed to find a way to get along with his new co-worker—but he really did not want to have to take a break from this already insane day and do it now.

"We had another theft," Jeremy said dramatically. "You're gonna wanna come see this."

Tony's heart raced. It wasn't that they couldn't afford to replace equipment—though it was incredibly frustrating to have to keep doing it—but he was annoyed, more than anything else, that he might have to do without something important today. He'd already put a new sandwich press on order, but he just hoped that the frustrating thief hadn't stolen something he couldn't live without.

Tony followed Jeremy into the truck, Lucas close at his heels. The first thing he noticed, immediately, was that their cheap food processor was missing. It wasn't even a professional grade one, merely one he'd grabbed from Wyatt and Ryan's kitchen when he'd needed one last minute. It had been hard-used, and he'd been thinking of replacing it with a tougher, bigger version anyway.

"It has to be him," Jeremy said, pointing at Lucas, who'd just set the boxes of pineapple down by the prep station. "He's the only one who's new. Ever since he started, things have started disappearing."

Lucas didn't look upset by this accusation, merely annoyed. Which was exactly what Tony felt—accompanied by a profound sense of exhaustion and pity.

"It's not him, J," Tony said firmly. "I know it's not."

"No, you don't. He's just got you wrapped around his finger, so you trust him, but he's not done anything trustworthy!" Jeremy's voice grew high and nearly hysterical. Tony barely restrained an eye roll.

"No," Tony repeated. "It's not him. He couldn't have taken it." He already had his phone out, texting his brother. Could they manage without a food processor today? *Maybe?* But it would just be easier if Wyatt stopped by the kitchen supply store and bought them a new one.

"Why do you keep defending him?" Jeremy demanded.

"It's probably because he knows I'm not guilty," Lucas inserted casually, like he hadn't been accused of being a backstabbing thief.

And honestly, Tony had kind of hoped Lucas would stay out of this, because Jeremy's face was growing redder and angrier, but could he really ask Lucas to stand by and let his character be dragged through the mud without defending himself?

Tony sighed inwardly, frustrated and annoyed that this day, which had started out *so* well, had totally turned to shit.

"It's because I know he didn't take it," Tony said more firmly this time around. "Because he was with me the whole night, and I definitely would have noticed if we came back to the truck and he stole a food processor."

Jeremy's jaw dropped, and he looked, impossibly, even more pissed off. "*What*," he said on a sharp exhale. "You guys were *together?*"

Like being together was some kind of crime.

Like Jeremy couldn't believe that Tony would stoop that far, when the reality was Tony couldn't believe how lucky he was that Lucas was willing to give him the time of day, never mind sleep with him. *And* stay the night, because he'd known that probably wasn't something Lucas usually did. But he'd done it last night, and he'd even stayed for breakfast.

Tony mourned the fantastic fucking start to his day *again*.

"Yes, we were together," Lucas said, because Tony was too busy throwing a mini-wake and hadn't replied fast enough. "Is that a problem for you? Two guys together?"

Tony gave him at least a little credit, because even though Lucas' tone had risen and was slightly more confrontational, he'd only let his temper slip when it appeared Jeremy might be disgusted by something that might be queer. Not because Jeremy had accused him of stealing.

How could Tony be pissed about that even though he knew that Jeremy's anger wasn't homophobic but probably based entirely in jealousy?

Jeremy reared back, like Lucas had just shot him. "No, you fucking idiot," he snarled. "I'm gay, why would I have a fucking problem with two guys being together? I have a problem with *him* being with *you*." He pointed at Lucas like he was unclean or something, and Tony knew in that moment he had to put a stop to this.

"Jeremy," he barked out. "Outside, *now*."

As he passed by Lucas, he pressed a reassuring hand on his shoulder. "Hey, I'm sorry," he said. "I'm really fucking sorry."

But Lucas just smiled, a little sadly, but not appearing to be overly concerned about Jeremy's rude behavior. "It's okay. He sucks, but I'll be fine."

"Start the salsas, please?" Tony asked softly. "We've got a lot to do, and we're probably going to lose him over this."

Lucas did *not* look disappointed at that turn of events. In fact, he was already pulling a knife out. "I'm on it, boss," he promised.

When Tony got outside, Jeremy was waiting for him, sulking against the side of the truck, a cigarette dangling from his hand.

"This has got to stop," Tony said. "You can't fucking do this anymore. I've made excuses for you and I've forgiven you for shit you've said that you shouldn't, but you were way out of line today, when you attacked Lucas. I'm sorry if you're pissed we're together, but *one*, it's none of your fucking business, and *two*, I want you to be a goddamn professional. That's what I hired you to be, not some kind of an amateur investigator with an ax to grind."

"I don't know what you mean," Jeremy said sullenly.

"Yes, you fucking do," Tony said. He really didn't want to fire him, but he would, because he'd burnt the last bridge today. If he didn't apologize to Lucas, then this was done. He was perfectly willing to let him walk away, and not because Jeremy had insulted the guy who Tony desperately wanted to be his boyfriend, but because he'd insulted a co-worker who'd done nothing but work his ass off and earn Tony's respect. Just like he should've earned Jeremy's.

"I just thought . . ." Jeremy huffed. "I just thought this summer it'd be *my* turn."

"Your turn?" Tony was afraid he understood exactly what he meant, and that would make this already hard conversation even tougher.

"You know what I mean," Jeremy muttered.

"Jeremy, I hate to say this so bluntly, but I'm just not interested in you that way. I see you as a friend, and only a friend," Tony said, trying to be as kind as he could, which was probably not as kind as he should have been. The problem was his temper was still flaring, because as far as he was concerned, even good old-fashioned jealousy was not a good enough reason to accuse someone of stealing, and then continue to insult them.

Jeremy didn't look sad or resigned at Tony's words—just more determined. Which was really an enormous problem.

"You never gave it a shot," Jeremy said. "You were still mooning after that asshole who dumped you, and then Lucas showed up."

Tony reined in his temper even though it was difficult. "I got over Brody awhile ago," he said. "If it was going to happen for us, it would've already happened."

"You don't know that," Jeremy challenged, dropping his cigarette and smearing it with his sneaker-clad foot. Then suddenly he was in Tony's space and Tony was forced to suddenly duck as Jeremy tried to press an unwanted kiss to his lips.

"Hey, hey," Tony said, putting a hand on Jeremy's chest and gently pushing him back, out of his space. "I told you, we're just friends."

Jeremy pouted. "But you didn't even *try* it."

"I don't have to try it to know that it's not going to work out," Tony said, barely holding on to the ragged edges of his temper. "I just don't feel that way about you, I'm sorry. *But* I do want to be friends, and I do want you to work on the truck, but this has got to stop. You've got to stop shitting on Lucas constantly, you need to find your fucking professionalism, *and* you've got to apologize."

"Why should I?" Jeremy's voice had turned from sullen to just plain belligerent.

This is it, Tony thought, *this is where I have to fire him, and it'll suck, but it's probably the right thing in the end.*

"You need to because you've been a crappy employee lately and a shitty friend, and I should really fire you, but instead I'm giving you the chance to apologize for it, and make it right," Tony snapped.

But instead of Jeremy snapping right back, he visibly wilted.

"I really don't want to leave," Jeremy said. "Please don't fire me."

Then please don't act like an asshole, Tony fumed internally.

"Apologize," Tony repeated firmly, "and start acting like an employee I want to keep around."

"Okay, I'm sorry," Jeremy said. It was a little trite, but he seemed to mean it. Tony's fears weren't entirely put to rest, but at least it was a start. And at least they wouldn't have to figure out how to pull off the tequila festival with only two sets of hands on deck.

"Not to me. To Lucas," Tony reminded him. But frankly, he probably deserved an apology too, at least for the shitty work he'd put in lately, and definitely for the unasked for kiss.

"Ugh, really?"

"This is a deal-breaker," Tony said. "And it's also a warning. No more slacking. No more glares and eye rolls and nasty comments. I'm *done* with that shit, okay?"

Jeremy looked like he wanted to argue that he'd done any of that stuff at all, but then he must have reconsidered because he gave Tony a sharp nod. "Okay," he said, and turned and went back into the truck.

Tony lingered outside for a moment, giving himself an extra moment to calm down and re-center himself for the day, and also giving Jeremy a chance to apologize to Lucas.

When he finally headed towards the stairs, he heard the tail end of it.

"Really, I *am* sorry," Jeremy said, sounding mostly contrite. "I didn't mean it."

"You did," Lucas said steadily. "Don't say you didn't mean it, because you did. You're jealous of me and Tony. But being an asshole isn't going to get you what you want."

There was a long silence, and Tony rolled his eyes. These two might actually kill him with their sucky apologies and inability to just fucking accept them. Why had he wanted to do this again? Running the food truck with Wyatt had been fun; a real test of their work ethic and their skills. But managing employees? That *sucked*. Or maybe it wasn't that it sucked, maybe it was that Tony just sucked *at it*.

"Fine." Jeremy's voice was still stiff and unfriendly, but it wasn't nasty anymore which Tony *had* to take as a win. "Fine. I'm sorry, okay? I'll cut it out. You win."

"It's not winning," Lucas said, but Tony decided this would be the best time to emerge into the truck, and cut this whole conversation off before it got out of hand again, no prep got done, and they ended up showing up at the tequila festival with nothing fucking ready.

"Hey, guys, let's get moving, okay?" Tony said, and yes, maybe there was a hint of a sulk still on Jeremy's face, and Lucas didn't look exactly pleased with the apology he'd just been given, but given today's schedule, that would have to do.

"Sure thing, T," Jeremy said, and bent his head and got down to work.

Tony let out the breath he was holding. Maybe this would all work out after all.

They were just about done with prep when Wyatt showed up with the new food processor.

"Everything okay?" he asked, leaning down to where Tony was just finishing up portioning out the fish after setting the box on the counter where the old processor had sat.

"It's fine," Tony said shortly. He really didn't want to get into any of this with his brother, at least not right now. Definitely not with Jeremy and Lucas listening to every word he was saying.

"Are you sure?" Wyatt sounded concerned. "I can take the day off, if you need me to."

"Four people in this tiny truck? I don't think so." Tony hoped that Wyatt would just take his words at face value and *leave*, before he brought up any more of the difficulties they kept trying to leave behind.

"Okay." Wyatt seemed at least convinced that he didn't want to discuss it right now. "But let me know if anything changes."

"You'll be my first text," Tony said, setting down his filleting knife and stretching out his neck and back muscles. "I promise."

"Sure thing," Wyatt said, and after a friendly pat on the back, he was gone.

Lucas walked over, and Tony gave him a look before he could even speak. "If you ask me if I'm okay too . . ." He warned with an easy smile.

"No way, *boss*," Lucas said with a grin of his own. "I just wanted to see if you needed help with the fish, 'cause I'm already done with the salsas."

"That was quick," Tony said, though he didn't know why he was continually surprised by how efficiently Lucas worked. "Even with doubling it?"

Lucas nodded.

"Okay, since we've got the food processor here, you want to start on the filling for the spinach artichoke grilled cheese? We've got to get that done before we take off for the festival."

"Sure thing," Lucas said.

Tony turned so he could check on Jeremy, and to his surprise, he was actually almost done with his tasks too. He'd *known* Jeremy could work harder and faster, and maybe he should've been gratified that he was finally living up to his potential, but he was frankly a little pissed that he'd had to go through all that shit to get him to actually deliver.

"One more round of prep and then we're festival-bound," Tony said.

Lucas stretched his tired back muscles as he leaned against one of the picnic tables the festival had provided. It had been a long fucking day, and he was glad it was almost over. Still, it was just past eight, and they'd already sold out of just about everything. Tony had set both him and Jeremy loose, closed up the truck and had gone off to see the festival organizers, hoping they could duck out early.

He wasn't sure where Jeremy had gone, but frankly, even though he'd apologized—because Tony had *made* him—Lucas knew they weren't ever going to be friendly. Maybe less openly hostile, but friendly? No way. Jeremy would always see him as the guy who had caught Tony's attention, even as he'd hoped he might finally win him over.

It didn't matter that Jeremy would never be the guy Tony wanted—Jeremy couldn't see that and *wasn't* going to see that.

But maybe, just maybe, he'd do a decent job now, and maybe, just maybe, Lucas thought darkly, now he would stop stealing shit from the truck.

But that remained to be seen, because even though Lucas was more convinced than ever that he was guilty, he still didn't know *why* Jeremy had done it. Did he need the cash? Tony paid fairly, but this was LA, and shit was expensive here. Maybe he'd done it to get Tony's attention, and he could finally quit that now. Or maybe he'd done it to frame Lucas. Hopefully, if it was the second or the third theory, Jeremy could finally fucking stop doing it.

"You look worn out." Lucas glanced up and Tony was standing there, a glimmer of a smile on his face, his hair finally falling free around his face after being up in a bun for nearly the entire day.

"I feel worn out," Lucas admitted, stretching his legs next. "It was a busy day."

"Yeah," Tony agreed. "And the fireworks this morning didn't help." He settled down on the picnic table next to Lucas, stretching out his much-longer legs.

Lucas leaned in, resting his head on Tony's shoulder, which felt awesome. Like coming home. "Which fireworks?" he teased. "The ones in the shower? Or when we showed up at the truck?"

"Oh, *those* fireworks are what got me through this shitty-ass day," Tony said, voice lowering to a sexy growl. His fingers reached up, tugging on Lucas' chin, pulling him closer, and then Tony's mouth closed over his in a hot, lazy, possessive kiss.

Lucas had been trying to keep it professional between them, at least when they were at the truck, but they were technically closed, right? And Jeremy had wandered off god knew where, so he couldn't even get jealous and offended that Lucas had succeeded where he'd failed.

The kiss spun out, leaving Lucas breathless and more excited than someone who'd worked as hard as he had today had any right to be.

Tony finally lifted his lips, his eyes sparkling. He was so gorgeous sometimes, the only thing Lucas wanted to see, that it was almost impossible to look away. Maybe he felt a little sorry for Jeremy after all. It'd be hard to be around all *this* all the time and know it wasn't ever going to be yours.

"Hey," he murmured, "I brought you something."

"A gift?" Lucas wondered.

"Yeah, kinda?" Tony reached behind him and Lucas saw two of those little plastic shot glasses in his hands, the ones they were giving out at the festival to try all the different kinds of tequila.

"You brought me tequila?" Lucas was amused.

"I was walking back to the truck and saw the stand. It's a new brand, but the biggest deal is that it's the Rock that's sponsoring it. So like . . . maybe not Vin Diesel, but Vin Diesel-adjacent?" Tony grinned bashfully. Like he should be ashamed for remembering the conversation they'd had on their stakeout.

Lucas reached out and plucked one of the shot glasses from his hand. "I love it," he said. "I can't wait to try it. Even if it's not Vin Diesel's brand of tequila."

"I can only work with what I've got, babe," Tony teased.

Lucas lifted the plastic to his lips. "What do you have, then?" he wondered. His heart pounded in hard, rhythmic beats, and he threw back the tequila, feeling the burn as it trickled down his throat, hoping that it might calm his racing pulse. But of course it didn't work, because Tony was like a flamethrower and he set him on fire with one look.

Tony's gaze on his face didn't waver, even for a moment. "You, I hope," he said.

And *god*, they weren't together, not like that, but the way Tony was looking at him? Made him want to break every single goddamn dating rule he'd ever made. Would it even be so bad, dating a guy like Tony? Having him around all the time? Seeing him smile? Making him laugh? Making him gasp like he was actually dying for it while Lucas was working him over?

It wouldn't be bad. It wouldn't be bad at all.

Lucas felt a twinge of regret that just the night before when confronted with the B word, Tony had insisted they were just having fun. And they were, but Lucas knew, and he hoped Tony did too, that fun wasn't all they could have together.

Tony's expression morphed from serious to playful in an instant. "I'd much rather take this shot off your abs, but I don't think they'd allow that here, in public."

"Why wouldn't they?" Lucas wondered, feeling Tony's muscles tense as his hand gripped his thigh. He glanced around. Half of the guys at the festival had shed their shirts.

"The real problem would definitely be me if you're shirtless," Tony said with a chuckle. "I can't guarantee I'd keep my hands to myself."

"You wouldn't," Lucas agreed, a shiver going up his spine at the thought of Tony laying him back on this picnic table, with all these people watching. Tony sliding his mouth and his teeth and his tongue over his chest and his abs, making him cry with how much he wanted him to drift lower, to suck his cock. Not giving a single fuck that he'd be doing it in front of an audience. He'd never been particularly into exhibitionism, but maybe with the right guy? And the right scenario? Lucas felt like he'd do just about anything to get Tony on top of him *right now*.

Lifting the cup to his lips, Tony tossed his own tequila back. "You ready to go?"

Lucas had never been more ready to go in his whole fucking life. He thought he'd been horny before—all those teenage years when all it took was the right guy to look at him the right way, and even the other night, when they'd been in the food truck and he'd practically *died* at the way Tony had melted down into mush at how Lucas had edged him—but every nerve ending felt sensitive, like they were all attuned to the guy who was sitting pressed up against him.

"I've never been readier," Lucas said, and hoped the way his fingertips dug into Tony's thigh made it perfectly clear just what he was ready for. His cock throbbed in his shorts and probably when they stood up at least half the festival would get a very good idea of just how much he wanted Tony. But shame? That felt like a remnant of a past that Lucas just didn't give a fuck about anymore.

Tony stood up, but instead of walking back towards the truck, he tucked himself right before Lucas' outstretched legs and leaned in, taking Lucas' mouth in such a hot, heavy kiss his head tilted back.

Just when Lucas thought he was going to scream from the way Tony's mouth moved so confidently, so perfectly over his own, it was over, and Tony was standing back, smirking. "I think I'm ready to go too," Tony said.

On anyone else, that cockiness might have been a total turnoff, but the truth was, he *had* Lucas, and Lucas couldn't exactly complain because it felt too good.

It felt too right.

Tony knew he was an impatient mess by the time they got back to the lot to park the truck. He'd thought he wanted Lucas a lot the night before, and he *had*, but somehow that desire had multiplied and grown claws, and now it tore at him, distracting him from even the simplest tasks.

As they finished the last bit of cleanup and got ready to lock up, Jeremy couldn't stop glowering, probably because Tony couldn't stop staring at Lucas. At least three times as he'd de-greased the grill top, he'd gotten distracted by the way Lucas' t-shirt pulled across his shoulders and hugged his waist. And his ass? He couldn't even *look* at it because the urge was so strong to just say *fuck the consequences*.

"Do I need to leave you two alone?" Jeremy asked sullenly. "I feel like I'm interrupting something."

"No." Tony took a deep breath and tried to get himself back under control. But the memories of Lucas begging to be fucked, of his tongue sliding right where his cock desperately *needed* to be, were way too fucking strong.

"Well, it sure seems like it," Jeremy bit off.

Tony had always prided himself on being a professional—at least since he'd come to own the truck with Wyatt. He'd never fucked around, not when shit needed to be done, and he wasn't about to start now, except . . .

"Actually," Tony said, decided that Wyatt had done enough stupid shit with Ryan that this could at least be partially forgiven, "you can take off. I think we're just about done here."

They weren't, not really, and Lucas shot him a questioning look. "We're not booked tomorrow," Tony said by explanation. "I was thinking I could come give the truck a real deep clean."

"If you say so," Jeremy bit off. Tony couldn't even blame him for his annoyance, because even though they weren't exactly trying to, he and Lucas were totally rubbing his nose in the "we're gonna hook up the moment you're gone" vibes.

"Yeah, yeah, get out of here," Tony said, giving him a friendly nudge. "I'll take care of the rest tomorrow."

Jeremy shot him a disbelieving look, and yeah, maybe he was transparent as fuck, but had Jeremy *seen* Lucas? It was all Tony could do not to fall to his knees right here in the middle of the goddamned truck and just beg to suck him off.

Jeremy let the door slam behind him, the sound punctuating his bad mood, but hardly puncturing Tony's good one—or the heady arousal flowing through him.

"I thought he'd never *leave*," Tony said, dropping the rag on the cooktop and meeting Lucas in the middle of the tiny kitchen, his hands gripping the other man's hips, pulling him flush against his own, so he could feel just how crazy Lucas had been making him.

"You're incorrigible," Lucas teased, but his eyes were hot and then they were kissing, and it was clear from the abandoned way Lucas gave himself to the passion flaring between them he'd been thinking the exact same damn thing.

Tony's hands drifted down Lucas' abs, tucking themselves under his shirt, tracing the lines of the muscles. His cock throbbed as Lucas' stomach quivered, both way too ready for what might come next.

But then Lucas pulled away. "Hey, you wanna not do this here?" he asked. His breath was coming in hard, short pants, and Tony squeezed his eyes shut. He desperately wanted to follow through on what Lucas had asked for last night, and while a pair of hand jobs might feel fucking amazing right now, he could think of a few things that might feel even better. Things that might need a bed.

That was it; this was a really fucking small kitchen, but he'd find a way to install a bed. That was the only thing it was missing—a comfortable horizontal surface where he could fuck Lucas comfortably and hopefully let him fuck him in return.

Tony opened his eyes and nodded. "Yeah, yeah, we could do that."

"Here's the thing," Lucas said, "I get up early. I need to get up early. I have a ton of bars to make tomorrow. I was gonna use the kitchen here, if that was okay."

"The truck kitchen?" Tony's brain was foggy with lust, and he wasn't quite following.

"Yeah. You said you wanted to clean tomorrow, and I could help with that too, if you help me with the bars. You down for that?"

"If that means I can come over tonight, I'd do a hell of a lot harder shit," Tony admitted. "But only if you want me to."

Lucas pressed a quick, deep kiss to his lips. "I want you to. I'm asking, aren't I?"

For almost the whole time they'd known each other, Tony had been the one slightly nudging them along, hoping that one morning, Lucas would wake up, hopefully with Tony in bed next to him, and realize that he liked things just as they were, maybe even loved them, and had no intention of changing them. But this was Lucas being the one to push, to grab Tony's hand and say, "Let's go." Feelings crashed through Tony's chest, making him feel sweet and hot and a thousand other things in between.

"Yeah, then let's do it," Tony said.

"We can take my car," Lucas said. "You good leaving your bike here?"

Even if he wasn't, there was no way Tony was going to get on it right now, not with the hard-on he was currently sporting and the haze of lust his brain was suffering from. He'd crash, for sure.

And right now? The only thing he wanted to crash into was Lucas.

CHAPTER THIRTEEN

Tony had been so distracted that morning by how *good* he felt that he hadn't really noticed what Lucas' apartment building was like. Now that Lucas was pulling up to the building, parking in an adjacent lot, Tony had more time to take it in. It was one of the very standard squat brick apartment buildings all over LA, a little run-down and nothing fancy.

"So this is it," Lucas said, as they got out of the car. Suddenly, in the last minute or so, awkwardness had crept in, and Tony wondered how often Lucas took people back to his place. Maybe he never did? But he'd offered tonight, and Tony wasn't stupid enough to turn that down.

"A lot nicer than the place I lived in when I was in Napa," Tony confessed. Because maybe that was why Lucas could barely meet his eyes as they walked into the foyer, with the dirty, old linoleum and the run-down elevator.

Lucas pressed the button and glanced over at him, disbelief written all over his face. "Seriously?" he said.

"This place is a fucking palace compared to that one," Tony said, and it wasn't even a lie. That place had been a shithole. His friends had wondered why he'd ditched Napa and come to LA to live with Wyatt, but *duh*, it was not that complicated. Wyatt wanted him to help him start a food truck, *and* he'd offered that cute little cottage. Technically was he living with his brother? Yeah, but as long as he didn't have to listen to Wyatt and Ryan hook up, he could give a shit.

"You're just trying to make me feel better." They stepped into the elevator, and Lucas hit the sixth-floor button, probably with a lot more force than was really required.

"Actually, there was this slumlord guy in Napa, *god*, he ran our lives with his fucking rules and his rents always skyrocketed. Anyway, it was not a nice place. I think I could've busted through the door without even trying. People were getting their shit stolen all the time."

"Did you?" Lucas wondered. He'd relaxed a little, Tony thought, as the numbers climbed.

"I didn't have anything worth stealing," Tony admitted.

The elevator doors dinged open. "Hey," Tony said, "top floor. That's nice."

Lucas rolled his eyes. "Save your praise. It's really not much. But it's mine, and I don't have to share it."

"Hey," Tony said, reaching out and wrapping an arm around Lucas as he stopped in front of a plain wood door. One it didn't look like you could break through with a prayer and a bit of beer-induced force. "Hey, that's something. I feel like everyone's got a roommate. It's fucking LA."

A small smile crept over Lucas' face. "Yeah. Yeah, it is."

Tony leaned down and brushed a kiss across his mouth. Softer, and then a little deeper, the heat igniting between them like they'd experienced no awkwardness at all.

That was the other thing, Tony marveled as Lucas unlocked the door, every single relationship, no matter how good or how promising, always felt awkward at some point, but other than assuming that Wyatt had invited Lucas over for a surprise date, they'd never had a single moment of it. It had always seemed *right*, like this fated, "happily ever after" thing that Tony had never really believed in until he'd fallen in love, and suddenly, he'd hoped he was wrong about it.

Obviously it hadn't worked out with Brody, but Tony had gotten a taste of it, and wanted it. And now, he wanted it with Lucas.

They walked into the apartment. It was a glorified studio, a bed on one side of the large loft-style space, a tiny kitchenette on the other, and a mismatched sofa and loveseat occupying the middle, with a flat-screen TV against the outside wall. A doorway near the bed led, Tony assumed, to the bathroom. A single lamp was on in the corner, shining light in so that Lucas wouldn't come back to a dark, empty apartment.

"It's great," Tony said. "I can't believe you've got so much space."

Lucas chuckled and reached down, taking his hand. "You really don't have to be nice about it."

Not for the first time, Tony wondered what kind of guys Lucas had been with—and if they thought since it was just a hookup and they wouldn't see Lucas again, they hadn't bothered with even the basic social niceties.

There'd been a time when Tony had thought that way too—when he hadn't given a shit about other people, when he'd waltzed through life, feeling like he was blessed with enough charm that he could make sure things never got complicated—but he'd learned. He'd changed.

Why wouldn't you be nice if you could, if it didn't cost you a damn thing?

Lucas tugged his hand, trying to pull him towards the bed. And *yes*, they were definitely here to have sex, but maybe Tony wanted more than that.

He leaned down and kissed Lucas again, soft and slow, pouring into the kiss all the words he wasn't sure Lucas was ready to hear yet. *I'm here, I want to make you happy and treat you right, if you'd let me. I want to make you smile all the damn time. I want so much, and I'm afraid you won't give it to me. But I'm here anyway, because how could I be anywhere else? I care about you so much; I think I'm falling for you . . . God, I hope you're falling for me too.*

Lucas broke the kiss, his breath coming a little faster. Tony wondered if he put a hand on his chest, if his heart would be beating hard. If it would be beating as hard as his own was.

"Let's go to bed," Lucas said, the hazel of his eyes barely visible as the pupils swallowed it. "God, I want you so much."

Tony wanted him too; wanted him enough that he couldn't pretend any longer.

"Yeah, yeah," Tony said, and let Lucas pull him towards the bed. The coverlet was a dark mossy green, but after Lucas tugged them back, the revealed sheets were a pristine ivory. When Lucas pushed him down onto the bed, Tony's head falling back, he let out an agonized groan.

"I've fucking wanted to see you like this forever," Lucas said, as he tugged his shirt over his head.

"You haven't known me forever," Tony said, smirking.

Lucas climbed on top of him, bracing his hands on Tony's chest and ground down, their hard cocks rubbing together and wiping the smirk right off his face. "Feels like it," he said. His tone was impudent, teasing, but there was a look in his eyes—Tony couldn't help but think: *this is it, this is what you've been waiting for.*

He pulled Lucas down, mashing their mouths together, and Lucas groaned again as he laid his entire body out against Tony's.

"You're so fucking sexy," Lucas murmured as he kissed his way down Tony's neck. "I can barely stand it."

"Yeah?" Tony asked with a shudder as Lucas gave a particularly sensitive spot on his neck a long, leisurely nip, scraping it with his teeth when he moaned.

"All this fucking hair," Lucas said, reaching up and stroking it back. "I wanna see it like this, all spread out, and then I wanna ride the shit out of you."

Tony gulped, his dick hardening even further at the visual. "That wouldn't suck for me either."

"No?" Lucas teased, leaning down and giving him a hot, fierce kiss before pulling away, leaving Tony lying there with a raging hard-on and desperation beginning to set in. Would Lucas tease him again? Would he like it as much as he had before?

Maybe, and *absolutely, definitely, positively fucking yes.*

Tony watched as Lucas shed his shorts, and then hooking a finger under the waistband of his briefs, hesitated, staring at him.

"Well?" Lucas said, motioning with his other hand. "I'm waiting."

"Waiting for what?" Tony asked, amused. He stretched his arms and put them behind his head. "I'm enjoying the view."

And he was. Goddamnit, Lucas was a work of art. All lean, bunched muscle and tan skin, and those hooded hazel eyes, gazing at him like there was nothing he'd love more than to just devour Tony where he lay.

"So am I—or I *would* be, if you'd get naked," Lucas teased.

"Oh, is that what you're waiting for?" Tony reached down, fingers drifting across his dick, feeling the rush of pleasure as he stroked it.

"That," Lucas said, grabbing his hand, "is all mine. Now get naked."

Tony decided it would be stupid to ignore Lucas' request, because if he did, god knew what kind of torture would be in store for him. He sat up, stripping off his shirt and pulled down his shorts and his boxer briefs, hissing as his cock, hard and wet at the tip, smacked his stomach. "Fuck, you gotta get over here."

Lucas yanked down his own briefs, his cock bobbing in front of him as he opened a drawer in the bedside table, pulling out a small bottle of lube and a condom. "I'm working on it," he said, grinning as he climbed back on the bed. "You're just Mr. Impatience today."

Reaching out, Tony curled his fingers around Lucas' cock, giving it an experimental stroke, enjoying how his head fell back, and his teeth sank into his bottom lip.

"Just me, huh?" Tony asked.

"Doooon't," Lucas wailed as he gave another stroke. "Fuck, I'm close, and I want this to be good."

"It's gonna be fucking amazing," Tony said, and tried to reach for the lube, but Lucas batted his hands away.

"I'm gonna do it and you're gonna watch," Lucas said.

It wasn't something that Tony had ever thought he'd be into—this *just watching* thing—because it was so goddamn fun to do *more* than watch, but watching Lucas? He could do that all fucking day.

He just hoped it wouldn't take all day, because he was just about as close as Lucas was, and he wanted it to be good, too.

Honestly, he wanted it to be *better* than good. He wanted it to be fucking mind-blowing. So amazing that Lucas would stick around long enough to see just how good they could be together.

Lucas slicked up his fingers and Tony watched as his face contorted with the slight awkwardness, and then as it smoothed right into pleasure, he felt his own heartbeat accelerate.

"You wanna see?" Lucas asked, panting.

He absolutely fucking wanted to see, but he also loved looking at the openness on Lucas' face, how he'd let his guard down when holding it up became too much, and the walls between them dissolved with the wave of heat rising between them.

"I wanna look at you just like this," Tony said, reaching down and giving his own cock a much-needed stroke. He was dying here, dying to get inside, dying to feel Lucas slide down around him, dying for *anything* that Lucas would give him.

"Fuck, fuck," he said, his eyes screwing shut, making Tony's pulse race harder. Maybe he did want to see. What was Lucas doing that could make him moan like that? He wanted to know, wanted to unlock every secret. "You shouldn't say shit like that."

He probably shouldn't. It might scare Lucas off. But then he was here, wasn't he, in Lucas' apartment? At his invitation? Lucas might claim he just liked hookups, but he also liked Tony, and wanted him desperately. Besides, Tony was tired of hiding how much he fucking liked Lucas; might even *love* him.

That word vibrated through him until he was trembling. He *might*, and as Lucas climbed on top of him again, leaning down to kiss him thoroughly, stroking his cock with his lube-wet fingers and unrolling the condom down his length, he thought, *I think I actually fucking do.*

It was a crazy thought to be having right now, but they called it making love for a reason, didn't they?

"I like it," Lucas said, giving Tony's lip a last nibble as he lined up his cock. "I fucking love it, actually. It drives me crazy. *God.*" He gave a little panting moan as he began to sink down, Tony's hands fisting in the sheets as he tried not to move, tried to just *exist* as he experienced the best fucking thing he'd ever felt.

"Goddamn it," Lucas wailed as he bottomed out. "God fucking damnit, I knew you'd feel like this."

"Like what," Tony ground out, trying to leash his own ballooning desire. He was *not* going to fucking come before Lucas even moved. He *was not*. But it felt so good, he thought he could.

Lucas glanced down at him, eyes wide and bright, his damp, sweaty hair pushed back, and he grinned. "Mind-blowing." He pressed his hand against his lower abs, barely brushing his own cock, and just smiled, like he'd wanted this from the moment they'd met, and now he'd finally gotten it.

Take more, take it all, Tony thought blindly.

"I'm gonna move now," Lucas said, his voice dropping to a gravelly murmur. "You good with that?"

It was almost too much to look at this bright, gorgeous guy, and not just *come.* But it was harder to not give him everything he wanted. To not make it the best for him it could be.

Bracing his hands on Tony's chest, Lucas began to ride him, slowly at first, his eyes screwed shut like he could barely even stand it, and then harder, and faster, until Tony didn't know his own name anymore, didn't know where they were at, what he was doing, only that he existed to feel this insanely intoxicating pleasure and to give it in return.

The thought flashed across his mind, and that was all it took for Tony to reach out, blindly, wanting to make sure Lucas knew he was good, that he *cared*, but Lucas batted his hand away. "I'm gonna, I'm gonna," he said in a breathless rush, "I don't need that. But can you..."

Tony wasn't sure exactly what he was going to say, but the thought his dick could make Lucas come untouched burned away all thought, all control, fucking *everything*, and Tony planted his feet and thrust, meeting Lucas' rhythm until he wasn't sure if it was him that was wailing or if it was Lucas. It was him, Tony realized, feeling Lucas start to shudder, his cock twitching and then striping all the way up his chest, it was him who was fucking yelling, and somehow, though he'd never been the noisiest guy during sex, the feeling of Lucas clenching around him made him even louder.

His orgasm hit him like a freight train, and he dug his fingertips into Lucas' skin and just *felt* as he emptied himself out.

When it was finally over, Lucas slumped down onto his chest, and before Tony could think any better of it, he reached out and stroked his back. Trying to reassure Lucas? Trying to reassure himself? He wasn't sure, but what he knew was that something between them had changed. Not only that, but they'd been headed in this direction from almost the first moment, and now it was happening.

"That feels nice," Lucas said drowsily. "I like it."

"As much as you like my cock in your ass?" Tony asked, feeling it deflate even as he said it, and begin to slip out.

Lucas chuckled, and it finally slipped the rest of the way. Tony knew he needed to get up and clean up, and be a considerate partner, and help Lucas too, but *god*, he wanted to lie here for a long time. Maybe even forever.

"I like both," Lucas said quietly. "I like *you*, in case you hadn't realized."

I love you. Tony's hand hesitated on the smooth-muscled planes of Lucas' back. "I like you too, but then I think you knew that already."

"Yeah, but it's nice. Nice to know you're a sure thing."

He was the surest thing in the world, but he wasn't going to be dumb enough to tell Lucas that. Not when everything was so fucking good.

"That I am," Tony said, and finally shifted Lucas in his arms, carefully depositing him on the bed, hoping they weren't making too much of a mess. "I'll be right back. Is the bathroom through there?" he asked, pointing to the door.

"Yeah," Lucas said, nodding. "Are you sure because I can . . ."

"Nope, I got this," Tony said, leaning down to place one more soft kiss on Lucas' forehead. "Let me, okay?"

Lucas' bathroom was as clean as the rest of his apartment. The fixtures were older and well-used, but they were all spotless. Like Lucas was trying to make the best of the cracked bathtub/shower combination and the old, long-stained sink. After Tony tied off the condom and tossed it in the small garbage can and wiped down his own chest, he went looking for something to help Lucas clean up. There was a small closet, and when Tony opened it, there were some towels stacked in it. He pulled out a washcloth, made sure the water was warm-ish, and squeezed out any excess before returning to the other room.

Lucas was still where he'd left him, eyes half-closed, a smile, private smile on his handsome face. "Thanks," he said, when Tony handed him the damp cloth. "You're good at this."

"At what?" Tony tried to play dumb. But he was doing all this for a reason—so Lucas could look back and realize just how much Tony cared about him. That it wasn't just sex. That Tony had real, genuine feelings, and that maybe Lucas might too.

"Not just sex." Lucas flushed. "But the rest of it, too."

"Thanks," Tony said. "I didn't use to be."

"Put that back in the bathroom, and come to bed," Lucas said after he finished cleaning himself, and scooted further up the bed, so he was propped up on the pillows.

"I see," Tony teased. "Missing your post-coital cuddle?"

Lucas flushed even redder. "No, of course not."

"Of course not," Tony agreed. If it made Lucas feel better not to call it what their relationship was rapidly becoming, then he could play along. "I'll be right back."

When he returned, Lucas was waiting expectantly. Tony crawled back into bed and wrapped an arm around Lucas' shoulders, pulling him in close. Lucas went easily, like he'd been waiting for exactly this.

"What did you mean, when you said you didn't use to be this way?" Lucas wondered after a long, but not awkward, silence.

Tony had had a feeling he would get asked about that. He took a deep breath. "I used to think of partners as disposable, not even for fun, just . . . a way to pass the time, to get through each day," he admitted. "I didn't care about their feelings, and I think some of them might have cared a whole lot more for mine. It wasn't fair. I wasn't . . ." Tony hated talking about this, but he supposed they couldn't really *have* a relationship if he didn't come clean about his past. "I wasn't a good guy back then."

Lucas gave a thoughtful hum. "You are now," he said, matter-of-factly, like he'd never once questioned this. Tony's heart swelled in his chest, even as he told himself that it probably didn't mean what he hoped it might.

"That means a lot," Tony admitted. Maybe Brody was a total asshole, but he'd at least given Tony a brief glimpse of what he was missing in his life. He'd shown him that there was more than just random hookups and brief relationships that never lasted.

Now, Tony hoped he could do the same for Lucas—and maybe it wouldn't end in an epic explosion of suck this time around.

"I'm . . . I'm still trying to figure some of this shit out," Lucas mumbled after a lengthy pause.

And the thing was, Tony *knew* it, and he wanted to be patient, even though he'd never been patient in his whole fucking life. But the alternative—rushing Lucas, forcing him to choose what he wanted before he was ready, and almost definitely scaring him off? *So much worse. Absolute fucking catastrophe. Do not pass go. Do not collect two hundred dollars.*

"It's cool," Tony said, tightening his grip around Lucas, his fingertips digging into his skin. Making sure he knew it was a little more than just cool. "I'm good, right here."

"Yeah?" Lucas said, snuggling even closer. "Hey, me too, boss."

Tony fell asleep with his arm around the guy he (probably) loved, and he'd never felt better about it in his entire life.

Lucas woke up the next morning, fully expecting to feel terrified as hell.

Tony had come over to his apartment. They'd had absolutely fucking incredible, mind-blowing, probably-never-going-back-from-this sex, and then he'd invited Tony to stay over. To *cuddle.*

Who was he and what had happened to Lucas Barnes?

But instead of waking up and seeing Tony's hair spread across his pillow and feeling either abject and total fear or the inherent need to flee, all Lucas felt was an exhilarating sense of rightness.

Careful not to wake Tony, he got out of bed, surprised they'd managed to fall asleep with the light on—*no you aren't,* his mind supplied, *it was the best sex you ever had in your whole damn life, it's a miracle you could stay awake for even five minutes after it was over*—and flipped off the switch. Padded over to the little stove and got the coffee going. While the water was heating up, he stretched, feeling the pull of muscles he hadn't used in a while, enjoying the strain, and then he dropped to the floor and started his morning pushups.

He was halfway through, counting as he went, his fingers curling into the hardwood boards of the floor when a voice startled him.

It wasn't like he'd forgotten Tony was here—Tony practically felt like a permanent imprint in his mind at this point, someone he couldn't forget even if he'd wanted to—but he'd gotten lost in his morning routine.

"Now, *this* is a view I wouldn't mind seeing every morning."

Lucas smiled, because yes, he *was* doing naked pushups. But then he'd been naked when he woke up, and who wanted to bother with clothes, anyway?

"Please tell me you do this every morning, so I can at least fantasize about it," Tony continued. Lucas hesitated for a second, his muscles straining as he paused, tempted for the first time in basically forever to not push through and do his regular set. "But seriously," Tony added, "don't let me stop you."

So instead of giving in and stopping, Lucas finished, standing up and wiping the dampness on his forehead with his forearm. The coffee was just beginning to bubble.

"You want breakfast?" he asked Tony, who hadn't moved from the bed.

Six months ago, Lucas would have just about *died* before bringing a guy breakfast in bed, but Tony? Yeah, he could do that. He even *wanted* to do it, because he could already imagine the smile on his face when he did.

"Just coffee," Tony said. "And maybe one of those energy bars you're so famous for?"

"Really?" Lucas was surprised. "Are you sure? I can make . . ."

"I actually really liked it," Tony interrupted, his face flushing. "Maybe I've been craving one since the stakeout."

"I think you're a big fat liar who lies," Lucas teased as he went over to the big wide bookcase in the corner where he stored all his supply. "Which flavor? You want to try something new?"

"What do you have?"

"Dark chocolate peanut butter, sea salt caramel pecan, I've got the blueberry cobbler one from earlier, and also a mixed berry, if you're into something fruity this morning. Oh, and the pina colada flavor. I've been experimenting with this one. It's got coconuts and pecans and some dried pineapple."

"Ooooh," Tony said. "I wanna try *that* one."

"Looking for some more pineapple in your diet?" Lucas teased. "I wouldn't argue with that." He tossed the bars onto the bed, and Tony's smile was so bright it could've lit half of LA. It took Lucas' breath away. Was it any wonder that he kept pulling him closer instead of pushing him away?

"What do you want in your coffee?" he asked as he poured two cups.

"Black," Tony said, between mouthfuls of energy bar. "Black is totally fine."

Lucas raised an eyebrow and glanced over at where Tony had propped himself up against the bare bones headboard that Lucas had found on Craigslist. "Are you sure? I make it strong."

Tony grinned. "Just the way I like it, baby."

Lucas couldn't help it then; he threw his head back and laughed.

"Come back to bed," Tony said, and Lucas couldn't think of a single reason why he shouldn't. Not anymore.

CHAPTER FOURTEEN

ONLY AN HOUR LATER, they were showered and on the way back to the truck. Tony helped Lucas load a bunch of boxes of supplies into the trunk of his Mini, and then when they finally got on the road, Tony shot Lucas a pleading look.

"I'm hungry again," he said, "can we stop at McDonald's? I want . . . no, I *need* . . . a Sausage Egg McMuffin."

"What?" Lucas supposed he shouldn't be surprised.

"You know what that is, don't you?" Tony asked, grinning.

"I do," Lucas reluctantly admitted.

"But you wouldn't eat one." Tony stretched his legs out as much as he could in the passenger seat—which was not much. "I've got a long morning cleaning and helping you. I need sustenance."

"What about the bar you just ate?"

"I worked up an appetite after it," Tony said, and *yeah*, they kinda had. In the shower. And out of it. Usually his bars were enough to keep him satisfied, because he'd designed them that way, but even he could admit that with all the physical exertion he and Tony had shared, he was feeling a little empty himself.

"Okay, you win," Lucas said, abruptly turning. It wasn't like he really knew where a McDonald's was, but okay, *yes*, he did. Once in a while, everyone had to treat themselves.

"Yes," Tony said, giving a quick fist pump. "I knew I could wear you down."

Lucas rolled his eyes. "It wasn't that hard."

"Oh, yes it was," Tony retorted, and Lucas laughed *again*. It was like he just couldn't help it when Tony was around. He didn't think he'd ever laughed so much in years; it felt like his old, slightly bitter, very-too-cool-for-school self was slowly melting away, and he was learning again what it felt like to *live*. To laugh. Maybe even to love.

Nope, Lucas told himself as he pulled into the drive-through, *that is one fucking step too far.*

But the truth was, he wasn't at all convinced it *was* a step too far.

By the time they made it through the drive-through, and to the food truck, they were only running an hour and a half behind, but Lucas found he couldn't make himself care that he was behind schedule. With Tony's help, he'd get what he needed done today, and without the confirmation yet from his potential distributor, he didn't want to overstock, anyway. Besides, if he was going to angst about running late, then he'd have to find it in himself to regret the way he'd spent the morning and with Tony grinning beside him, mouth full of McDonald's, he actually *couldn't*.

After parking and unloading, Tony leaned against the counter and glanced at Lucas. "Clean first?" he wondered.

Lucas looked around. He was kind of a notorious clean freak—surely Tony had noticed that although his apartment might not have been the nicest, it was *clean*—but the truck was still definitely clean enough for him.

He crossed his arms over his chest and shot Tony a knowing look. "Did you concoct this cleaning plan so we could duck out of here early last night?"

Tony flushed. "Of course not. This could totally use a deep clean. Right? I mean . . ."

"You totally did," Lucas said triumphantly. "What would Wyatt say?"

"Wyatt would be very pleased at my dedication for spending my day off cleaning," Tony said, now searching for the shreds of his remaining dignity.

Lucas grinned. "I'm sure that has nothing to do with me being here."

"Nope, not at all, you're just . . . a distraction."

"A distraction, huh?" Lucas asked, and rose up on his tiptoes to give Tony what felt like their thousandth kiss of the day. And it still was barely nine in the morning.

Lucas thought it was definitely the good kind of relationship when you couldn't keep track anymore.

The kiss heated up, Lucas leaning between Tony's legs, and he probably could've continued just like that forever, but the drive that had kept him going, even when he was sick, even when he was exhausted, reminded him they weren't here to make out. They were here to work.

He broke off the kiss, but instead of moving away, he rested his head on Tony's chest. "I guess we should've been tougher on ourselves and made some kind of rule about no truck PDA," Tony said, his voice muffled by Lucas' hair. "Because now I want to do it all the time."

"Me too," Lucas admitted. Maybe the reason he wasn't more terrified of falling for this guy was because the guy seemed to be falling right along with him.

"I didn't expect any of this when you showed up that first morning." Tony's voice was wry, and maybe he hadn't—god knew Lucas hadn't—but it had happened all the same.

"Even when you were sure Wyatt set us up?" Lucas asked slyly.

"My brother wouldn't be this smart," Tony grumbled. "He's incapable of it."

"Actually, I think he's pretty cool." Lucas liked him, and he hadn't been sure he would, the first time they'd met in the restaurant supply store. He'd been sure that Wyatt would end up being stuck up and snobby, but instead he'd been kind and he'd offered Lucas a job.

"Ugh, not you too," Tony teased. "When is someone gonna like *me* best?"

Lucas laughed. "Would you be surprised if I said I did?"

Tony's arms tightened around him. "No," he said, his voice suddenly raw with honesty. "No."

Slowly, they broke apart, Lucas stepping back. "Okay," he said, surprised at how his own voice was trembling, "okay, good."

Tony turned away, like it was too much to look at each other just then, and Lucas found he couldn't argue with that. The emotion felt too big to be contained in this tiny space. "I guess we should get going on your bars, then, and do some cleanup after."

Lucas cleared his throat. "Yeah, we can do that."

Tony was not laboring under any ridiculous assumption that he was actually *helping* Lucas with the energy bars. He had a very solid, very efficient process already in place, and all Tony was doing was asking a thousand questions and essentially distracting the shit out of him.

Finally, Lucas had relegated him to chopping up the dried fruit and nuts. "So," Tony asked, glancing over at where he was mixing a huge pot of oats, grains, and seeds with some honey and a few binders, "basically, you've made me into Jeremy."

Lucas looked up, surprised, and grinned. "Maybe? But you're a very good *sous*, so don't be too upset."

"I'd hope I'm a little better than him," Tony said, running his knife one more time over the pecans scattered across his cutting board.

"Where did you meet him?" Lucas asked, continuing to stir. "Are you almost done with those pecans, I'm gonna need them and the pineapple in a sec."

"Yeah, yeah, I'm just about done," Tony said, picking up the cutting board and carrying it over to Lucas' pot. Carefully he slid in the pecans and then dumped in the dried pineapple he'd chopped previously. "I met him in Napa, when I worked at the Napa Tavern up there. He was on the line with me and he did a decent job back then."

"Why did he move to LA?" Lucas wondered. "It's weird, especially if he was all set up in Napa with a good job."

"You know," Tony said, leaning against the back counter, watching as Lucas added a few last touches to the mix in his pot, "I really don't know. I didn't ask." And now he realized he'd been a shitty friend *not* to ask. Jeremy had started showing up in LA one day, maybe six months after he'd moved himself, and it had been right when he'd needed a friend the most. Right after the breakup. When he'd been going out of his mind with hurt and rejection and anger. When it had been sometimes too painful to see Wyatt and Ryan up close. He'd enjoyed getting out of the house and grabbing a beer with Jeremy. It had felt like normal in a sea of shit—a reminder that although it felt like his entire foundation had changed and then slid away, there were people who still cared about him.

And he'd taken all that attention and not even bothered to ask why Jeremy had moved.

Tony groaned. "I think . . . I wonder sometimes if he moved here for me. And I stupidly didn't ask, because at that point I'd just broken up with my ex and things were rough. I should have. I was a bad friend."

Just last night he'd told Lucas that he used to be a waste of space, and Lucas had argued that he wasn't anymore. That he'd succeeded in turning his life around. But now, suddenly, he wasn't so sure. Had he just been leaning on Jeremy and using him and not really *caring* why he was around? Taking and taking instead of ever giving?

Maybe he wasn't as good a guy as he thought he was.

And that thought *stung*—and not just because Lucas might judge him for it.

"Listen, we all go through tough shit sometimes," Lucas said, hefting the pot up and beginning to pour the molten mixture into the prepared pan. Normally, Tony might find himself distracted by how effortlessly Lucas lifted what was a very heavy, very full pot, and the way his muscles bunched as he carefully, deliberately held it still and steady. But Tony was still feeling the sting of his realization.

"Maybe," Lucas added, "Jeremy was going through some shit too, and he didn't want to talk about it. It's not your fault if he wouldn't open up to you. Friendship is a two-way street."

Tony was touched that Lucas was trying to make him feel better. He wasn't the kind of guy who judged—and maybe *that* was why Tony loved him.

Because yeah, standing here in his tiny food truck kitchen, watching him carefully spread out energy bar mixture in a pan, making sure it was perfectly even, Tony was pretty damn sure he did love him.

He knew he could be real around him, show him his true self, and Lucas wouldn't run; he'd embrace any of it and all of it—anything Tony wanted to give him, probably.

Lucas glanced over at him, looking concerned. Probably because he'd been struck dumb, even though the realization had been barreling down on him for a while now. "Are you okay? You look . . . weirded out?"

Was he weirded out? Not really, actually. It wasn't all that surprising. He'd known almost from the first moment that he'd seen Lucas that he was attracted to him, like he hadn't been with anyone in a long time. And then, when they'd spent time together, he'd only liked him even more. It turned out they fit together in so many unexpectedly fantastic ways that he never could have imagined.

"I'm good," Tony said, and discovered that it was actually true. He *was* good. Things were better than good, they were fucking *outstanding*. He'd fallen in love; he was fairly sure that Lucas was falling right alongside him. Could they get any better?

"Good," Lucas said, eyes crinkling with amusement. "Just checking. You wanna help me out over here?"

"Yeah, yeah, of course. What do you need?"

Lucas grinned and shoved the empty pot at him. "Clean this?"

Tony glanced down at the sticky, messy interior—still stuck with bits of energy bar. "Really?"

Lucas shrugged unrepentantly. "You said you wanted to help . . ."

"I did say that," Tony said, with a begrudging sigh. "Fine. I will wash your pot out for you. Maybe we should get you another one. So you know . . . you don't have to keep rinsing it out to make another batch."

Lucas was already gathering the next set of ingredients and didn't look back at where Tony had started the hot water running in the small sink. "It's what I can afford," he said.

And it wasn't like Tony hadn't wondered that. There was a reason he was using Tony's food truck and not an actual rented commercial kitchen space. It was why he'd agreed to work for Tony and Wyatt in the first place—because he needed *this* space.

"Shit, I'm sorry, I know," Tony apologized. "I'm . . . the king of foot in mouth, apparently."

Lucas flashed him a quick, easy smile, and the sudden tenseness inside Tony relaxed a fraction. "It's totally cool. And you're really not . . ." Lucas hesitated. "You're like . . . the most fucking charming guy on the planet. You make everyone feel good. There's a reason people line up at your truck, and it's not just because your fish tacos are bomb."

Tony's hands, in the middle of scrubbing out the pot, froze. "You really think so?"

Suddenly, Lucas was right there, right at Tony's elbow, with the cutest disgruntled expression on his face. "You think I *like* it when all our customers flirt with you?"

"No?"

"I don't," Lucas said with absolute certainty. "I *really* don't."

"Oh, okay, well, it's apparently hard to turn all this charm off," Tony teased. "Should we put up a sign? 'The guy with the silly man bun is taken'?"

Lucas stared at him for a long second, and then nodded, sharply. "Yeah, yeah, you should."

Tony kept scrubbing the pot, all too aware of how fast his heart was beating. He hadn't quite meant to say it that way, or that directly, but then he had, and Lucas wasn't running. *Yet.*

"But then," Lucas said, his tone of voice deceptively casual, like they weren't discussing real commitment, "then Jeremy might get the wrong idea and quit after all."

"I thought you wanted Jeremy to quit," Tony joked.

"I mean . . . when we're busy, and there's only two of us? That's really not very fun. I don't have even a second to spare to stare at the really cute guy with the man bun."

"Ah," Tony said knowingly. "Well, we can't have that. So no sign?"

"Maybe . . ." Lucas paused. "Maybe if we both knew that the sign was *there*, but not there, you know?"

"So what you're saying is that the sign isn't *here*, not really, but like it exists in a non-temporal plane?" Tony wondered.

Lucas rolled his eyes, but then he sighed and reached up, pressing a quick kiss to Tony's cheek. "Yeah, sure," he said. "That works for me."

Tony's heart stuttered. He was surprised it didn't just explode with the joy surging through him. "Yeah, me too," he said, copying Lucas' tone, like this was all no big deal, instead of *the biggest deal of all time*.

Lucas floated through the rest of the morning on a mixture of disbelief and sheer, fucking happiness. He'd told himself so many damn times that relationships weren't for him, but this thing with Tony? He'd fallen into it, and they'd already been halfway there by the time he'd realized where they were headed. All he knew was that the more time he spent with the guy, the more he craved. The more he just plain fucking *liked* him. At first he'd thought it was just sexual. Tony was so hot, it was understandable to confuse that, but when Lucas was over the moon just spending the day together, hip to hip in the truck kitchen? It couldn't possibly just be sexual. It was a hell of a lot more than that, and now, he knew it.

He didn't know exactly when things between them had begun to shift—maybe they'd never really been where he'd thought they were, and they'd been shifting from the first moment—but last night, he'd realized everything was changing. And this morning? It was undeniable; he'd *known*.

"Hey," Tony said, as Lucas finished their fourth batch of bars. "I'm starving. I'm gonna go grab some wraps for us for lunch. Sean is parked only a few miles away, and he makes killer sandwiches."

"Yeah, that'd be perfect," Lucas said, wiping his hands on a towel he'd tossed haphazardly over his shoulder. "And after lunch we can start on the big cleanup?"

"Works for me," Tony said. "What do you want?"

Lucas thought of what he'd eaten for breakfast. "Something with lots of veggies?"

"Sure thing," Tony said. "I'll be back in a few."

After Tony left, Lucas wrapped up the last pan of energy bars, stowed it in the fridge, and checked the others. They were cooling, but not ready yet to cut into bars. He finished cleaning up, and then pulled out his phone, checking his email first.

As he clicked through the junk mail, he froze when he got to an email from the distributor he'd desperately wanted to pick up his energy bars. He'd been *counting* on the deal going through, even overstocking more than he personally felt comfortable with, ordering additional supplies and putting a definite strain on his business account, all with the assumption that it *would* go through and he'd end up signing on the dotted line.

Except that wasn't what was happening.

Lucas felt a desperate frustration surge through him as he read through the email. "We're sorry to let you know that we've decided that SoYou Energy Bars aren't a good fit for the Pacific Foods brand." Lucas read it out loud, slowly, sure that he was missing something, that there was some kind of silver lining, some kind of sweet kicker at the end that wouldn't mean this wasn't the end of all his hopes.

Maybe Pacific Foods wasn't the only distributor, but they'd been the best fit for him, and he'd worked so hard, hoping that this would finally be it, the culmination of all his hopes, all his late nights and early mornings, all the weeks where he had to figure out how to creatively get by on a twenty tucked into his worn wallet. And now?

It had all been for fucking nothing.

He slumped against the counter, squeezing his eyes shut, but still seeing the damning words flashing in front of them, over and over.

He couldn't fucking believe it. How had he gone from owning the fucking world, to having the world fuck him over in mere minutes?

"Hey," Tony said, his footsteps and voice announcing his arrival before he'd made it up the stairs, "hey, I got you some kind of veggie bacon tempeh thing that Sean promises that you're going to *love.*"

Lucas tried to school his expression into something less devastated, but there wasn't enough time, and *fuck,* he loved this guy, he couldn't hide in front of him, even if he wanted to.

Tony stopped dead in his tracks, in the middle of the kitchen and stared. "What happened?" he demanded. "Are you okay?"

He opened his mouth, trying to figure out the way to say, *it all went to shit,* but nothing came out, except this horrible, wretched sob. He'd been holding it in for so long, all this terrible hope, and now that it was burning up, he couldn't contain it anymore.

Tony crossed to him in a single step, and pulled him into his arms, not questioning anymore, just holding him. To Lucas' surprise, even though everything was still fucking shitty, there was something about Tony's arms around him, his unconditional support that comforted him somewhere deep inside. That told him he would be okay, even though he had no fucking clue how that was going to happen.

"Hey, hey," Tony said, slightly pulling away, one large, warm hand stroking his back. "Hey, what's going on?"

Lucas realized with acute embarrassment that he'd left a big wet spot on the shoulder of Tony's t-shirt. He'd honest-to-god *cried,* and on his brand-new boyfriend. Wiping his eyes, he tried to figure out a way to tell Tony some of the truth without all of it, but before he could say a word, he realized that wasn't going to work at all.

He fucking *loved* him. He was almost sure Tony was feeling something like that, too. He deserved to hear all of Lucas' truth.

"Can we . . . I don't know . . . sit down?" Lucas asked. It was a stupid question, because there weren't exactly many places to sit, but this was a long story.

"Sure," Tony said, and plopped right down onto the floor mats. "You're right," he added when Lucas gaped at him. "It's pretty clean after all."

Lucas gingerly sat down next to him, close enough to touch, but apparently that wasn't near enough for Tony, because he reached out and snagging him around the waist, dragged him another couple of inches closer.

"Now, tell me," Tony said, eyes warm, his expression concerned.

"I . . . it's a long, crappy story," Lucas said. And Tony just nodded, like he'd expected that it would be.

"I told you my parents cared more about my mom's stupid cats than me, right," Lucas said self-consciously. It was never easy to admit this; that his own parents had thrown him away like he was trash, all because of who he could love—who he *did* love.

"Right," Tony said steadily, anger crossing over his face. But he said nothing else, just let Lucas continue at his own pace, when he felt comfortable.

"So . . . I was only seventeen. I had a job, but I didn't have enough money. I spent, I spent a lot of time at shelters, underneath overpasses . . . it was a really fucking hard time." An understatement, but he'd triumphed over the shitty circumstances fate and his parents had thrown in his face. "I met Ria then, got a second job at her gym.

She let me sleep there, and things got better. I got into that healthy kind of lifestyle, and I felt *good*, and it turned out that I enjoyed feeling good. I worked in restaurants too, sometimes. Started out doing dishes and cleaning up after hours, and worked my way up to a sub for the line, even without finishing high school," Lucas said wryly. "I . . . lied a lot to get jobs, but I didn't lie to get this one."

"I believe you," Tony said, pulling him even closer, until he was cradled against him. "God, I am so sorry your parents were such shit, and you had such a hard time."

"Me too," Lucas said softly. "I worked so hard. Worked so many jobs. Sometimes it felt like I didn't even sleep. And it was all because I'd found a goal. To have my own place, my own *space*, no more crashing on someone else's couch, no roommates to bother me, a place I could be safe, a place I could call all mine."

"And you got it," Tony said, squeezing him hard. "You did it."

"It's not much, but it is mine," Lucas agreed. "It might be nicer, but I also didn't want to depend on anyone else for a living ever again, just me, and Ria helped me put together a business plan. I created the energy bar recipe, I perfected it, I made a bunch of different flavors. Started selling them. But I needed to take it to the next level; it was time. I had found this distributor who could get them into grocery stores, and I stupidly thought . . . I thought this was *it*. I had finally done it. Dragged myself up, done something that I could be proud of. I had a lot of help, but it was mostly me. A ton of late nights. Early mornings. Scrimping. Saving. And then . . ."

Lucas took a deep breath.

"Then, I got an email today, while you were gone, they aren't interested. They don't want the bars." He choked back another sob. It didn't feel real yet that after all this time, after everything he'd done, it had still fallen apart.

"Oh god, oh god, I am so sorry," Tony said, and pulled him onto his lap, until he could hold him again, surround him with all the love that Lucas realized he desperately wanted. "That is utter shit."

"It kinda is." Lucas sniffed back another round of tears.

"Are there other distributors you could try?" Tony asked.

"Yeah, but . . . this one was the best fit. The others, I'd have to compromise ingredients probably, and they wouldn't get them into stores I think would do the best job selling them. This just . . . this was it. This was the right fit."

"We're going to figure this out," Tony said.

"Don't tell your brother. Don't ask him for a single dime, okay?" Lucas felt very suddenly, very fiercely sure that he didn't want Tony to go running to his brother, to his seemingly bottom-less bank accounts. He'd done this almost entirely by himself up to this point, and he wasn't willing to beg now, not when he was so close.

"I didn't mean that," Tony said slowly. "The bars . . . they're vegan, right?"

"Yeah," Lucas said. It was something that had been important to him when he'd been developing them—he wanted anybody to be able to eat them, regardless of dietary restrictions and lifestyle choices.

"Wyatt wants to start a bunch of new trucks. You heard him. He is super into this new vegan/vegetarian thing we've been trying on this truck. The specials have been selling out like crazy, you know that. What if we started a new truck like he suggested and sold the bars on it? Like our very own kind of mini-distributor?"

"You'd start a food truck for me just because . . ." Lucas didn't want to finish that sentence, but it was definitely *because we're involved, now.*

"I wouldn't be doing it for that reason." Tony's gaze was very serious. "I'd be doing it because you have a really good fucking idea, and I think it could make you *and* us some decent cash. It'd fill a niche I think you've already proved needs filled."

"I'd . . . I'd have to think about it." Was he willing to tie himself so closely, personally *and* professionally, to Tony? His first instinct was *yes, yes, yes, hell fucking yes,* but that didn't mean it wasn't right to take some time to consider his options.

Tony's plan *wasn't* what he'd always wanted. He'd wanted his bars more universally accessible than that, and maybe this wasn't the end of that dream, but maybe just another link in the chain. He'd get there, but it would just be a little slower, and a little different path than he'd expected.

"I think you should take all the time you need," Tony said.

Lucas knew he would, but he also knew that he would probably come back to Tony in a day or two or maybe even a week and tell him he wanted to do it. That he'd actually fucking *love* to go to work with Tony every day, to hang out more with Wyatt and his husband. It would feel like . . . and it suddenly dawned on Lucas. He had Ria, of course, and a handful of other casual friends, but Tony and his brother and his husband might end up feeling more like a family than he'd had in years.

"You're basically incredible. You know that, right?" Lucas mumbled into Tony's shoulder.

He couldn't see Tony's smile, but he could *feel* the strength of it. "Apparently, according to you and most of our customers, I am." He paused. "But the only one I give a damn about is you."

CHAPTER FIFTEEN

"I've missed you," Tony said as he boxed Lucas in, hoping to get at least one mind-blowing kiss in before Jeremy showed up to work.

Lucas grinned. "It's been two days. Not an eternity."

"What, and that wasn't you last night, texting me about how you were jacking off, thinking about my cock, and desperately wishing it was inside of you?"

The text had been so fucking hot, so explicit, so devastating, that Tony had nearly hopped on his motorcycle despite the time and driven over there. It hadn't been late, but they'd both been tired—Lucas because he'd pulled a double shift at Ria's, and Tony because he'd been forced to work with Jeremy all day. Still, the text had seriously flustered him, and it hadn't helped that Jeremy had been mopey, and also that their credit card machine had gone down with a few hours left in the dinner rush, and the truck had been forced to switch to cash only.

Tony *knew* Lucas hadn't turned him down because he didn't *want* to see him, but he'd still had a momentary freak-out that he'd pushed too hard, too fast. Lucas had been quieter since his breakdown, but Tony understood it. There were a lot of things on his mind. They'd agreed to be in a relationship, which he knew was new for Lucas, and then right on the heels of that, he'd gotten the rejection from the distributor, forcing him to reevaluate how he wanted to run his business. That was a lot, and Tony had been hesitantly giving him some space, but then that text had come in and all bets had been off.

Lucas' expression turned coy. "It might've been."

"Were you satisfied with what you got instead?" Tony wondered, crowding him a littler closer, and feeling Lucas' body melt into his.

"Not even close." Lucas reached up and closed the distance between them, planting a searing kiss on Tony's mouth. He tasted a little minty, like he'd just brushed his teeth, and also a little like coconut and pineapple, like he'd eaten one of his pina colada–flavored energy bars this morning.

Tony deepened the kiss, and wondered if they might have time not only for the kiss that was currently blowing his mind into tiny pieces and *also* making his dick hard, but if they might have the time to do something about it.

Lucas rubbed his own hardening dick against Tony's shamelessly. "Fuck everything," he murmured when Tony lifted his head for a brief second. "Let's go to bed."

"What's everything?" Tony wondered.

"Jeremy, the truck, the schedule," Lucas murmured, and that was when Tony knew he didn't even mean it.

"That *really* must have been unsatisfying last night," Tony teased, stepping away. Lucas shot him a peeved look, but then it melted into a sweet, carefree grin.

"It was pretty good," he admitted. "I could even show you later. Do a whole reenactment. If you wanted."

And yes, Tony wanted. Tony wanted so much that he nearly agreed with Lucas and said *fuck it* to everything else he had to do today.

"A reenactment of what?" Jeremy asked as he walked into the kitchen. "Do I even want to know?"

"Um, definitely not," Tony said, and Lucas smiled.

"Yeah, you'd hate it," Lucas agreed.

"Ugh, you two are the worst," Jeremy said. "All happy and shit."

"Where we at today, boss?" Lucas asked, obviously trying to change the subject. Which, really, was better, because the last thing they needed to do was make Jeremy's mood worse by continually rubbing in how happy they were together.

"Lunch downtown. And then the brewery again tonight."

"We're getting into their regular rotation, aren't we?" Lucas asked. "We've been there a couple of times now."

"Yeah, I think we'll be busy tonight. God bless the beer drinkers, they all like to snack," Tony said, and then the rest of his brain kicked back into gear. "Shit, I should check the credit card setup, make sure it's working again this morning. I don't want to have to go cash only again."

And that was *also* the moment he realized that last night, he'd been so goddamned distracted by Lucas' text, that he hadn't done anything with their unusually large amount of cash except lock it away in the upper cabinet, intending to drop it off at the bank on his way home. But then he'd forgotten about it completely, and with the stupid thief on the loose, that had been incredibly fucking dumb.

Heart in his throat, he reached over to the cabinet, heart sinking as he saw the telltale scratch marks on the stainless steel. Someone had definitely broken in here. Tony had a feeling if he looked at the front door, which he'd barely noticed in his eagerness to kiss Lucas, he'd see the same kind of scratching around the lock.

He pulled the door open, and it went easily, like it had never been locked. The entire pouch of cash—the one he'd absolutely meant to deposit at the bank—was fucking gone. Whoever had taken it hadn't even left the bag.

"Fuck," Tony ground out. "Fuck, fuck, fuck."

Losing the money hurt, but what hurt more? The fact that not only was this fucking thief continually targeting them, but that he'd *let* them take a bunch of money that should have been sitting safely in their bank account.

"What is it?" Jeremy asked, peering around Tony's shoulders. "Did you leave the cash here last night?"

It was painful to admit it. Even more painful because how silly the reason was—*I'm in love and I was distracted and desperate and missing him so much and then he said the exact same fucking thing and it was like my mind just . . . blanked out.*

"Yeah," Tony said shortly.

"Wow," Jeremy said softly.

"What happened?" Lucas said, peeking his head into the truck. He must have ducked out to deal with the daily delivery, and Tony had been so upset he hadn't even noticed.

"Someone broke in again," Tony admitted. "And I stupidly left a bunch of money for them to take."

"But how would they know it was even here?" Jeremy wondered. "It *has* to be an inside job. How else would they know we had to switch to cash last night?"

Tony didn't miss how Jeremy's gaze narrowed, and who it narrowed on. "It was you, wasn't it?" Jeremy said, pointing a finger at Lucas. "You weren't with him last night, T. I know you went back home alone."

He knew that because Tony had been sulking about it. Definitely not his finest moment.

"Of course it wasn't me," Lucas said easily. "I didn't even know you had a lot of cash. Tony didn't tell me that the credit card machine went down."

He hadn't. He'd been way too busy trying to convince Lucas to let him come over and give him the dick he so desperately wanted.

"I don't want *any more* accusations being thrown around. Not against my boyfriend; not against *anyone*," Tony said in a hard voice. "This ends here. This is *my* fault. I left the cash here."

"But . . ." This time it was Lucas who spoke up, but Tony shot him a look that surely spoke volumes about how much he did not want to fucking deal with this right now.

"No more," Tony ground out. "I don't want to hear another fucking word about it."

And thankfully, Jeremy stayed quiet this time. Tony stomped down the stairs, anger at the situation, and at himself still billowing inside him. How could he have been so goddamned stupid?

His first phone call was to a locksmith that Gabriel had recommended awhile back. There would be no more shoddy, easily picked locks on *his* truck. He would make sure nobody else got in.

His second was to Wyatt.

"Hey," Wyatt said when he answered. "Everything okay?"

"I'm getting some better locks put on the truck," Tony said shortly, hoping that Wyatt wouldn't ask why, but knowing that was an impossible pipe dream.

"Someone broke in again," Wyatt stated.

"Someone broke in again," Tony agreed.

Wyatt sighed. "What did they take this time?"

Tony leaned back against the side of the truck, watching Lucas going through the delivery out of the corner of his eye. "Some cash," he admitted. "But it was one hundred percent my fault. I got . . . distracted or something. And the credit card machine had gone down, so we had more than normal. I meant to swing by the bank on my way home, but I forgot the bag and just left it on the truck. Normally . . . probably not a huge deal but ever since this goddamned thief started targeting us? A much bigger problem." Tony's voice cracked at the end. God, he was so angry at himself.

"It's fine, I'm sure we'll be fine," Wyatt soothed. No accusation whatsoever. "We'll get the new locks. And yeah, maybe it really is time to move on from that lot. There's no security. There's barely some lighting there at night. That's it. We need to find a permanent home."

"Yeah, we do." Tony remembered how Ash had mentioned a friend who was selling some property in a suitable spot. Maybe that was something he and Wyatt needed to look into. "I've actually got an idea for that. We can talk tomorrow?" He'd text Ash for the details and have them, because Wyatt would want to know.

"Breakfast is at eight," Wyatt said. "Unless you're staying with your new guy . . ."

"I'll be there," Tony said. "I just . . . I'm really fucking sorry, okay?"

"You don't have to apologize," Wyatt said.

"Yeah, except I kinda do. I totally fucked up."

"We all do that sometimes. It's not the end of the world," Wyatt said with a rueful chuckle. "I promise."

"Yeah, but . . ." *But when I moved down here, and we became partners, I promised I wouldn't do it anymore. I told myself I was gonna be better, and I was. I* am.

"No buts," Wyatt said. "I mean it."

"No buts?" Tony tried to muster up some of his usual sass and bluster. "But that's my favorite part!"

Wyatt laughed. "God, TMI. Seriously. TMI. Tell your boy about that, not me."

"I'll see you tomorrow morning," Tony said. He remembered when he and his brother could barely say more than a handful of non-confrontational words to each other. They'd come so far. They'd become partners, they'd even become friends. Frankly, he'd been worried that maybe this fuckup would mean the return of all their old shit, but *no*, they were better than that.

Tony hung up and when he looked up Lucas was standing there, an unusually determined look on his face—and he looked determined a *lot*.

"That was Wyatt?" Lucas asked.

"Yeah," Tony said shortly. He didn't think he was ever *not* in the mood to see Lucas, but he didn't think he was in a mood to see *anyone* right now. Maybe he and Wyatt were okay still, and he'd been reassured that they'd be fine without the cash, but the sickly remnants of self-recrimination and guilt were still lingering.

"I want to talk to you," Lucas said.

"That's what we're doing," Tony replied flippantly.

Lucas frowned. "You know what I mean."

"Yeah, yeah, what's up?" Tony said, giving in, because that was kind of how this morning had gone so far. First, being interrupted by Jeremy, and then the cash going missing, and now Lucas wanting to make an issue out of something that Tony was really sure he did not want to deal with.

"Jeremy," Lucas said firmly. "I know you don't want to talk about this. I heard you earlier, but fuck, Tony, you know it has to be him. He's the thief. He has to be."

"Not you too," Tony said, scrubbing a hand over his face, wishing that his gut feeling hadn't been quite so spot on.

"I mean it," Lucas insisted. "It's been him the whole time. I wouldn't even be surprised if he was the one who gave the onion dip recipe to the Basket guys. I don't know why. Maybe he needed the cash. Maybe he wanted your attention. Maybe he wanted to discredit me. I don't know. But he's the thread that ties all this together. He *knew* the cash was there. He was the only one besides you who knew it was."

There was a part of Tony that couldn't *not* listen to Lucas, and not only listen, but understand and believe every single word he was saying. What he said made logical sense; who else would have known the cash was there? Even someone who had noticed their cash-only sign would assume that it'd get deposited. But he and Jeremy had left together, and he might have noticed that Tony had forgotten to grab it. And Jeremy had motive. He'd turned around at least twice now and directly accused Lucas right after the thefts were discovered. Like that had been the plan the whole damn time.

But on the other hand, Jeremy was a goddamned *friend*. He'd been there for Tony when it felt like Tony didn't have anyone else. He'd listened to him crying in so many beers, Tony had lost count. He'd been there, always. Maybe he'd been a little weird or creepy, and maybe Wyatt got a bad vibe off him, but Tony couldn't judge. Why would someone so loyal, who had been in Tony's corner from day one steal from him?

Tony shook his head. "No," he said, and then again, "*No.*"

Lucas rolled his eyes. "You cannot fucking believe that it wasn't him. Not after all of this."

"I can, and I will. He's my *friend.*"

"I'm telling you . . . as your *friend*, and don't think I missed that reference earlier, *your boyfriend*, that he's sketchy as hell. I really think you need to talk to him about it. Fuck, he might even admit it. He's that eager for your attention, even for some goddamned reason, your *negative* attention."

"I don't want to talk about this anymore," Tony said, cutting him off. "I'm getting new locks installed. It should stop whoever it is."

Lucas threw up his hands in frustration. "I'm not trying to turn you against your friend, okay? I'm . . . will you just *listen* to me, and to yourself?"

"No," Tony said shortly and turned to go back into the truck, but Lucas caught his arm.

"I care about you," Lucas said, and Tony was stopped short, not just by the firm grip that Lucas had on him, but the wretched edge to Lucas' voice. "I fucking care about you so much. Maybe I shouldn't. Maybe it's too much, too soon. But I fucking love you, you idiot, and it's killing me you're going to keep trusting this guy who doesn't deserve it. Because *you* deserve fucking better."

Tony wasn't sure he'd heard what he thought he did; his heart was racing too hard, too loud. "Did you just say you love me?"

"I do," Lucas said, dropping Tony's arm and crossing his own across his chest. "Fuck, I shouldn't, but I do. I didn't want to tell you, not like this, but this is *killing me*. I can't just stand there and pretend he isn't fucking you over."

"What if he isn't?" Tony wondered. He was still a little stuck on Lucas' love confession. He'd known that he was feeling it, and he'd known Lucas was right there along with him, but he sure hadn't wanted to have it confirmed this way. It felt like a bittersweet revelation.

"I don't know, then he isn't, but I swear to god, despite the lack of proof, there isn't anyone else it could be. I've known it was him from day one, and he's not done anything to prove he can be trusted."

Tony remembered the guilt he'd felt when he'd realized he hadn't always been the best kind of friend to Jeremy. And still Jeremy had stuck around. How could he repay that by accusing him of stealing? He just couldn't, no matter how much Lucas wanted him to.

Even if he loved Lucas the way he loved him.

"Remember how I felt the other day? How I felt like I'd been let down and the world had eaten me up?" Lucas' expression had gotten increasingly frantic, like he knew Tony wasn't going to listen, but he felt compelled to try anyway. And yeah, Tony got that. Because that day, he'd wanted to do everything and anything to make Lucas feel less like a failure.

"I wanted to help you. I still do. That hasn't changed." Tony reached out for him. "God, I know how you feel. You see a problem, and you want to fix it. But maybe this just isn't something that can be fixed or solved or whatever."

"It can," Lucas said stubbornly, tugging himself out of Tony's grasp. "I fucking can't believe you won't even talk to him. We've been building towards this . . . I don't even know what it is . . . I guess, yeah, it's a relationship. It might've been, anyway. But how can I keep going when I don't think you trust me?"

"I do trust you," Tony said, feeling the beginnings of alarm at the sudden bitterness in Lucas' voice, in his eyes. "I fucking trust you a whole lot, okay? And I love you too, if you'd give me a chance to say it. I've loved you, god it feels like from the moment I thought my brother had set us up and I was pissed about it."

"You don't trust me," Lucas said with an ugly finality that scared the shit out of Tony. "If you really trusted me, you would listen to me. At least about this."

"Fuck, please, I don't want to fight about this," Tony said, reaching for him again—but Lucas still pushed him away. *Turned* away, even, and the desperate ugliness that had been creeping in bloomed into something like panic.

"I can't do this right now," Lucas said. "I can't be around you. Not when you're determined to be blind and Jeremy is determined to do whatever it takes to have you. Even if it means taking your friendship and your loyalty and pissing all over it."

"What does that mean?" Tony knew how desperate he sounded. Knew how desperate he felt. He couldn't lose Lucas now, not after he'd finally found him.

Lucas looked at him with hot, angry eyes. "I don't know. But it means I can't be here today." And he turned and walked away.

"Fuck, fuck, fuck," Tony yelled to nothing and everything, all at once. "Fuck, I can't believe this is fucking happening."

The noise must have caught Jeremy's attention, because suddenly he was there too, making everything just a little bit worse. "What's going on?" he asked. "Why hasn't Lucas brought this stuff up yet?"

"Probably because Lucas is pissed off and just left," Tony bit off. "We'll have to manage without him today."

"Well, that's fucking great," Jeremy said. "What an asshole."

"Yeah," Tony said, and unfortunately didn't mean it at all, not even a little.

"What are you doing?"

Lucas looked up from where he was trying to mop up all his sweat to see Ria standing in the doorway to the spin room, hands on her hips, a perplexed expression on her face.

"What am I doing?" Lucas asked slowly. He wasn't mad anymore, though he'd been so angry for the last few hours, the fierceness of it sizzling bright and hot inside of him, it had gradually burned off with time—or maybe it had burned out because Charles had pushed him harder and farther than he even liked to push himself.

When he'd left the truck after his fight with Tony, his first and only thought had been to come to the gym. It had always been the best way to get rid of any painful, frustrating emotions that he didn't want. The moment he'd stepped inside and realized one of Charles' spin classes was about to begin, he'd thought it was painfully ironic. But then, instead of detouring to the other side of the gym where all the weights sat, he'd found himself stopping at the reception desk where Jasmine, Ria's partner, was sitting.

"Hey," he'd said. "Is there a spot open for the spin class?"

Jasmine had looked at him like he'd just sprouted a second head. And yeah, maybe spin class wasn't normally his thing, but he could do different things, right? He could go wild and crazy and go to spin class and he could fall in love.

Maybe none of those things were advisable, but he'd done them, anyway.

He remembered all too well seeing Tony here, standing in this very room, and looking like he'd just been wrung out, and now he was feeling it himself.

"You never go to spin class," Ria said slowly. "Ever. You think it's masochistic."

"It is." He'd definitely verified that he'd always been right about that. "It fucking sucks."

Ria looked him up and down. "Jasmine said you had a wild look in your eye, and I thought she was having a weirdly poetic day, but no, there's something off with you. What's going on? Is it that guy?"

"What guy?" Lucas asked feebly, tossing his sweaty towel near his gym bag. It didn't quite make it and it drooped over the edge. But he was absolutely *not* willing to bend down to make sure it ended up where it belonged. He might die first. He'd definitely make some kind of inhuman groan if he did, and he was *not* going to do that in front of Ria, who'd never let him live it down.

"Oh, don't be dumb," Ria said. "I know about the guy. I know you've rearranged your schedule so you can pull more shifts at his truck. I know you're sleeping with him."

He was, and the sex was fantastic. But that wasn't even the tip of the iceberg with Tony.

"I love him," Lucas said, and hated the way his voice broke at the last word. He did, and it *sucked*, even as it was astonishing and mind-blowing and wonderful. Only he would fall in love with some stupid asshole who wouldn't listen and was unbelievably more stubborn than Lucas himself.

He didn't think he'd ever seen Ria surprised, but she looked shocked now.

"Of course you do," she said, her face breaking into a huge, triumphant smile. "I should've known it would only be love that could drive you to spin class."

"You should put that on all the marketing," Lucas said with a heavy sigh. Maybe he wasn't pissed anymore, but he was still frustrated. He was still worried. Part of him wanted to figure out where the truck was and go there and watch over Tony's back, so that Jeremy could never fuck with him ever again. The other part of him knew he wasn't nearly ready to deal with the fact that Tony hadn't really trusted him. Not the way he wanted—the way he *craved*—to be trusted.

"So what happened?" Ria asked.

"We just got into a fight," he admitted. "It's . . . actually so stupid. Well, *he's* the stupid one."

Somehow, impossibly, her smile grew. "You really do love him."

"I said so, didn't I?" Lucas reached down anyway, and with a grunt shoved his sweaty, dirty towel into his gym bag. "I'm going to go pour myself into the shower now and try to pretend the last hour didn't just happen."

"But it did," Ria said, following him out of the room, "and trust me when I tell you that tomorrow, you'll definitely not be able to do that."

"I'm in shape," Lucas said stubbornly. "In *great* shape. I'll be fine." This was the same thing he'd told himself during the spin class, AKA the torture session, and yet, he still felt like stomped-on ground beef.

He shouldn't be feeling this way, but even spin class was enough to make him love Tony more. It had been a visceral reminder that Tony—who was hot as fuck but admittedly not exactly athletic—had done it, and he'd done it for him. And love, despite all his annoyance, bloomed inside him anyway.

"I'll remind you of that fact tomorrow," Ria said unapologetically. "Should I expect you for your training sessions?"

"Yeah, I'll be here," Lucas said. He was supposed to have the day off the truck anyway, and it would be good to take a few days for them both to calm down. He didn't want to break up—God knew it had taken him long enough to find anybody he *wanted* to be with the way he wanted to be with Tony—but he also didn't think he could be in the same tiny cramped space with him right now.

"Good." Ria patted him on the back. "Now, go chill out and don't spend too much time thinking about your guy. *Or* moping about him. You guys are gonna be just fine."

As Lucas headed towards his car, he realized he knew two things for sure: *one,* spin class was not for the faint of heart and *two,* he really, really wanted Ria to be right.

CHAPTER SIXTEEN

Tony had experienced lots of terrible, shitty days in his life. The first time that his nana hadn't recognized him. The day she'd died. When Brody had told him he wasn't sticking around. The fight he and Marco had gotten into the day he'd left Napa.

None of them had felt as bad as this one did.

He'd been sluggish all day, dragging, mind occupied by the argument, distracted by the way they'd confessed their love. He didn't know about Lucas—he wanted to claim he didn't know what the fuck Lucas was thinking, but that wasn't true, was it?—but he hadn't ever intended to tell him he loved him that way. He hadn't wanted to make it an enormous deal, because that wasn't really his way, and it definitely wasn't Lucas' way, but he'd wanted it to be so much more than something he spat out in anger.

And I love you too, if you'd give me a chance to say it. I've loved you, god it feels like from the moment I thought my brother had set us up and I was pissed about it.

Because that was why he'd *really* been pissed, wasn't it? Because he'd taken one look at Lucas, and it felt like everything inside of him that had been lying dormant and still and cold had come back to life in one painful moment, between one breath and his next. And he'd understandably worried that Wyatt trying to interfere would only ruin everything before it could even begin.

Except Wyatt hadn't ruined it; *Tony* had.

"Are you done cleaning that one counter yet?" Jeremy asked, his tone not unkind. And that was the worst, wasn't it? The moment Jeremy had realized Lucas had left, that he and Tony had argued, he'd perked right up. Tony's worst day had apparently shaped up to be one of Jeremy's best.

That only gave more fuel to Lucas' words. Had he been right? Tony didn't know, and he wasn't even sure it mattered anymore.

All he knew was he wasn't willing to watch him walk away again, and on the flip side, he knew he couldn't sacrifice his friendship with Jeremy over him, either.

That was the problem, wasn't it? By drawing a line in the sand, Lucas had boxed them in, leaving them on opposite sides. And yet, he wasn't even furious at him for doing it. Might even be able to acknowledge that he'd have done the exact same damn thing. That was what made it all so fucking impossible.

"I'm almost done," Tony said. He pulled out his phone for the hundredth time today, his heart sinking another painful inch when he saw his inbox was empty. Maybe it didn't matter who was right, and who was wrong. He still wanted a do-over.

Before he could rethink it, he typed and sent a quick text. **I want a do-over,** it said. **What do you think?**

Shoving his phone back in his pocket, he tucked a strand of hair that had escaped his hair tie *all fucking day* behind his ear. "Damnit," he muttered.

"What is it?" Jeremy asked.

"I just wish I'd brought my bandana." They might be almost done for the day—they were just finishing cleaning up from their last stop—but Tony felt like he was about ten seconds from taking the nearest knife and just slicing all his hair off. And he *knew* that wasn't the reaction he should be having to a stray piece of hair that wouldn't stay where it was supposed to. It was just this fucking *wretched* day.

"Oh, I think I might have one in my bag," Jeremy said. Tony ignored how eager he sounded to help. It was a flashback to *before*, before Lucas had shown up to work that first day.

"Oh, thanks," Tony said. He set his cleaning rag down, and went down the stairs, opening the passenger side of the truck, where Jeremy usually stowed his bag. And sure enough, when he unzipped it, he found some folded bandanas, right on top. He couldn't be a hundred percent sure, but he was fairly certain that at least one of them had been his at one point.

He wants your attention, even if it's your negative attention.

Tony pushed Lucas' words away. He didn't want to hear them now, not when with each passing moment, they seemed more and more true.

He grabbed the bandana on the top of the pile and was about to zip the bag back up when he felt a crinkle of paper. He didn't know why he stuck his hand back in and dug for it—*yes; he did.* He'd done it because even though Lucas didn't think so, he absolutely *did* fucking trust him, and he was at least half-sure that he was right. Tony just didn't *want* him to be.

Yanking out the paper, he stared at the instantly recognizable slashing black lettering on it. It was a copy of a recipe. Not the onion dip, but one of Lucas' recipes. In this case, the way he'd prepared the jackfruit pulled pork. Tony even remembered why they'd thrown this copy away—Lucas had misjudged how much room the lengthy list of spices would take, and Tony had teased him about how tiny some of his instructions had gotten towards the bottom of the page. Lucas had pouted, but had pulled out a fresh sheet and started again. That was the recipe that was still hanging up in the truck.

But this one? Lucas had crumpled it up and tossed it in the trash.

Jeremy must have gone digging and retrieved it . . . but that didn't even make any fucking sense, because Jeremy had whined about this particular dish over and over again, until he'd become an annoyingly broken record about it.

Tony *knew* why he'd taken it. It wasn't because Jeremy wanted to make it himself. He was going to do the same goddamned thing he'd done with the onion dip recipe. In a week or in a month, the exact same pulled pork jackfruit would end up on the Basket menu. Tony was absolutely, horrifying, one hundred and ten percent fucking sure of it.

"Fuck," Tony said, the paper crumpling further in his fist. "Fuck, fuck, *fuck*."

He knew then that it didn't matter how much he wanted Lucas to be wrong; he hadn't been.

"Hey, did you find one?" Tony squeezed his eyes shut when he heard Jeremy behind him.

"I did," he said, turning. He shoved the paper into Jeremy's surprised face. "And I found this."

Jeremy stared at the recipe. "What?" he asked stupidly. Not even *convincingly*. And the more Tony thought back, the angrier he got. Lucas had been right about everything. Jeremy had taken the onion dip recipe. He'd taken the cash *twice*, and he'd stolen two pieces of kitchen equipment. Why? So Tony would blame Lucas and fire him?

But the onion dip . . . that had happened before Lucas had ever shown up. Weeks before, in fact.

"Why did you have this? You didn't even *like* the jackfruit pulled pork, so you weren't going to make it yourself, were you?"

"I thought that shit was *gross*." Jeremy didn't seem interested at all in trying to hide his obvious guilt, which only pissed Tony off more.

"You did it all. You stole the dip recipe too, didn't you? You stole it and you sold it to the Basket guys. Why would you sell it to those . . . *colossal dicks*?" Tony yelled, anger suddenly cresting over him in a vast wave.

"You didn't need it, did you? You had so many fucking recipes, and," Jeremy said with a shrug, "I figured that you wouldn't even notice. I told them to tweak it. And I . . . I needed the money they promised."

"And everything else?" Tony demanded. "Was that for money too? Or just because you discovered you could fuck me over, and so you decided, *why the fuck not?*"

"No, no, no," Jeremy said, sounding increasingly desperate and petulant. "No, of course not. I just . . . why did you have to hire Lucas? We were good. We were going to be fine. We didn't need anyone else. It was just going to be me and you this summer."

Maybe under other circumstances, maybe if he was slightly less pissed. Maybe if he hadn't stolen one of his brother's recipes and then one of Lucas', Tony might have relented and tried to understand where he was coming from. Obviously, he'd had a big crush for a long time, and he'd thought this was his big moment. The time when it would finally happen.

But what Jeremy didn't know was that it hadn't mattered if Lucas had shown up or not—it was *never* going to happen. Tony just didn't see Jeremy as anything but a friend.

"Listen," Tony said, trying to tamp down at least some of his fury, "I'm sorry you thought that. But Lucas has nothing to do with the fact that I just don't think of you that way. You're my friend. I would have lent you the money if you'd asked. But instead . . . you *stole* from me."

"I have all the stuff," Jeremy said, jerking a thumb towards where his old beater car sat parked. "I can give it all back to you. It's just some fucking cash, and a few old pieces of equipment. You're rich, you were fine."

"*I'm not rich*," Tony said, grinding his teeth together in annoyance. "You fucking *know* that."

Jeremy threw his hands up in frustration. "Then I'll give it all back, okay? Every goddamned penny, if that'll make you happy. It's all in my car, right now. I'll even throw in the stupid old food processor, which you didn't even *want*." His brash tone and the belligerent look in his eyes made it painfully clear that he wasn't sorry at all.

Only sorry that he'd been caught.

"That isn't what this is about," Tony yelled. "You fucking *stole* from me. I'm your *friend*. I gave you a job when you came to LA. I vouched for you, all the goddamn time. And this is how you repay me."

"That's the whole fucking problem," Jeremy said petulantly. "I moved to LA for you. I listened to you cry over Brody *forever*. And I kept thinking, tomorrow he's gonna wake up and see me differently, but you *never did*. But you still *could*, if you'd just *try*." Jeremy reached out, like he was going to grab him and kiss him but Tony was not letting that happen. Not again.

"I couldn't," Tony ground out, shoving him backwards so he wouldn't touch him. Not ever again. "You were my friend."

Jeremy stared at him in shock, like he hadn't ever imagined that Tony might reject him, might actually physically push him away.

"You were *my friend*," Tony repeated. "Get the fuck out of here."

"What?" Jeremy stared at him. Disbelieving.

"In case you missed it, *you're fired,*" Tony said, clenching his fists, trying to get his temper under control, but every time he thought of how he'd defended Jeremy, to his brother, to Ryan, even to Lucas—only yesterday—it roared through him with new life and new power. He'd never imagined that of all the people to betray him, it would be someone he'd tried so hard to help. Someone who'd been his friend.

But were you really a friend? Maybe you were lying to yourself, the same way Jeremy was lying to himself.

"But you . . . you *need* me," Jeremy whined. Not getting how absolutely insanely pissed off Tony was. And that was the whole problem, wasn't it? He was a victim of his own fucking terrible judgment.

Tony kicked one of the tires of the truck. "Fuck," he swore savagely. "I don't give a fuck. You betrayed me."

"I . . ."

But Tony wasn't done. He interrupted him. "You betrayed Wyatt. You took advantage of Ryan and his goddamn money. You stole from Lucas, who was generous enough to volunteer his own recipe. But worst of all, you fucked me over. Over and over again. Even when you knew how upset it was making me. That's not . . ." Tony took a deep breath. "That's not something a friend does. That's not something I can ever forgive."

"What. But what if I return everything . . . what if I give it all back?"

Tony just stared at him. "Are you not fucking listening to me?"

"I am but . . ."

"No," Tony interrupted him. "No. You need to get out of here. I'll send your final check. We're . . . we're *done*."

This asshole who'd clad himself in faux friendship, he'd nearly cost him everything. His relationship with his brother. His burgeoning relationship with Lucas. *Everything.* He'd even risked the food truck that he and Wyatt had built from an old ramshackle, falling-apart, breaking-down piece of shit. But now that Tony knew, he wasn't going to let Jeremy touch anything else, ever again.

Jeremy looked like he wanted to say something else, to keep arguing, but Tony just kept staring at him, anger brimming inside of him, and so he finally grabbed his bag, turned and walked away. Tony watched when he got to his car. After opening the back door, Tony saw as he rooted around in the backseat. First, he tossed out the sandwich press. It hit the ground with a grinding clank of metal. Probably breaking, but maybe they could get it repaired and then they'd have *two*. Or alternatively, they'd have one for What a Catch and then another for the new vegan truck he wanted to start with Lucas.

The food processor went flying next, the plastic bowl shattering on the hard concrete of the sidewalk, but Jeremy didn't blink twice, just tossing the cash envelope down on top of the remains.

"Fine," Tony grumbled. "Fucking *fine*."

Jeremy shot him one last venomous look, got into his car, and finally drove away.

And maybe he was gone, but the clusterfuck he'd created with his selfishness wouldn't disappear. Not that easily, anyway. There was a lot of shit Tony would have to deal with.

Starting with his brother.

Ending with Lucas.

"What is . . . are you drinking that straight from the bottle?"

Tony froze at the sound of his brother's voice, caught in the light of the open freezer as he'd tipped the vodka bottle back, letting a solid glug pour down his throat.

"Uh," Tony said, ashamed that he'd been caught but not that ashamed. How could he be when there was so much additional guilt and shame swirling through him? It felt like a drop in the fucking bucket.

"Here," Wyatt said wryly, "at least use a glass." He reached over, pulled a pair of short squat glasses from the cabinet and set them down on the counter with a solid click.

"You want one too?" Tony wondered. Had Lucas called Wyatt and told him everything when Tony wouldn't listen? *God, he hoped not.*

"I think I'm gonna need one, if you tell me why *you* do," Wyatt said, plopping down on one of the barstools. "Aren't I?"

"Yeah. Yeah. Probably," Tony agreed. He poured them each a healthy shot and slid Wyatt's glass over as he took a seat next to him.

"So, are you gonna tell me what's going on, or do I have to guess?" Wyatt wondered. "Is it you and Lucas? The money?"

Tony scrubbed a hand over his face and gave a bitter laugh. "Would you believe me if I said it was everything?"

"Yeah, considering you were drinking vodka straight from the bottle."

"Lucas wanted me to talk to Jeremy about the thefts. He was pretty convinced it had to be him, and I didn't want to. We argued about it. He told me he loved me, but that he couldn't be around me, and left." Tony swirled the vodka in his glass. "And then I figured out, after defending that shithole, that Jeremy actually *was* guilty. And when I confronted him, he didn't even fucking deny it."

"Seriously?" Wyatt gaped, just as shocked as Tony had been when he'd finally put the pieces together and come to the right conclusion. "I mean, I thought he was kinda shady, mostly because he wouldn't just *tell you* how he felt. He kept waiting for like a lightning bolt from heaven or an arrow from Cupid or something, and I couldn't figure out why. But I didn't think . . ."

"That he'd steal from us?"

"Yeah." Wyatt stared into his drink. "Especially you. *Fuck.* He was like . . . obsessed with you."

Apparently he'd been the only one who hadn't seen it. "Obsessed enough to steal shit, hoping to pin the blame on the guy I love."

Wyatt put a reassuring hand on his back. "You have no idea how happy that makes me."

"That he tried to get me to fire Lucas?" Tony said ruefully.

"No, that you love him. I know you haven't always been happy since Brody. That it wasn't always easy, living with Ryan and me, but I'm just so fucking thrilled for you, dude."

"That's . . . that's what we're focusing on?" Tony couldn't quite believe it, but Wyatt's gaze was one hundred and ten percent sincere.

"Well, *yeah*," Wyatt said. "You fired Jeremy, right?"

Tony rolled his eyes. "Of fucking course. I sent him packing. I don't think he'll show his face around here again."

"Good, then it's done. He didn't do any lasting damage. And you found a guy you love, who loves you back. Things are looking up," Wyatt reasoned.

Tony reached for the bottle and poured himself another shot. "Then why do I feel like utter fucking shit?"

Wyatt leaned back, letting that reassuring hand fall. He stared at his brother. "Why *do* you?"

"I feel like . . ." Tony threw back the freezing cold vodka and felt it slide, reassuring and numbing, right down his throat. "I feel like I was fucking blind. The whole time. That everyone was just standing around, pulling the wool over my eyes like it was the easiest thing in the whole fucking universe. Like I was too dumb to notice, and they knew it. Like, even though I always meant well, even though I wanted to do the right thing, in the end it didn't fucking matter."

Wyatt stared at him. "You know that's not true, right? You're . . . you're a good guy. I know we didn't always get along. I was a judgmental prick, and you were kinda wild—or else you wanted everyone to think you were. But we grew up, and we found each other again. But I'd never say you were stupid enough for just anyone to fool. You believe in the best in people and that's the thing that makes you special, you know?"

"I think it makes me naïve," Tony said starkly. "I think it makes me weak."

"No," Wyatt said steadily. "It makes you strong."

"It cost me Lucas," Tony pointed out.

"I don't think it did. Not even close. He told you he loved you. Love doesn't fade that fast. And the thing that made him so crazy? I bet it's also one of the things he loves most about you."

Tony looked down at his phone. Lucas still hadn't texted him back. "I don't know." He sighed. "I fucking wish I did, though."

"You've got to give him some time. I think . . . I think this is new for him, yeah?"

That much was something Tony knew. Lucas hadn't started something with him thinking they would fall in love. Tony had hoped they might, but it had still turned out both better and worse than he could've ever dreamt.

"Yeah." Tony nodded. "I . . . I don't think either of us really expected this."

"Oh, I'm sure," Wyatt agreed. "Though, after you fix this, which I know you will, because you love each other, you can thank me."

"Thank you?"

"For setting you up," Wyatt said, finishing his vodka and setting the glass down with a decisive click on the marble countertop. He looked over, grinning stupidly. "You didn't *really* think that was a job interview, did you?"

"God, I hate you," Tony said. "I really hate you."

Wyatt laughed and nudged him on the shoulder as he got off the barstool. "You totally don't."

"I can't believe you were setting me up all along," Tony said, still incredulous.

Wyatt just shrugged. "You would've been pissed, right? This way you weren't."

"I still was, a little."

"Yeah, but you got over it real quick," Wyatt teased. He put the hand back on Tony's shoulder. "Seriously, give him a day or two to calm down, and then apologize. I think you guys are gonna be just fine."

"Just apologize?" Tony said, disbelieving. He'd fully expected needing to grovel. To beg. To say, in a thousand unique ways, that he'd been wrong, and Lucas had been right.

Wyatt patted him on the shoulder. "He's a reasonable guy, and he loves you."

"I love him too," Tony said, staring at the vodka bottle.

"I know you do," Wyatt said. "But it's gonna be okay."

"Thanks, bro," Tony said, and *almost* felt like it might be. Maybe if Lucas would text him back, he might really believe it.

"Don't stay up too late, *and* more importantly, don't drink the entire bottle," Wyatt said. "I'll see you tomorrow. You still down to talk about the lot?"

"Shit," Tony said. "The lot. I forgot to get the details from Ash."

"No worries. We can do it later this week. That is, if you aren't knee deep in the honeymoon phase," Wyatt joked.

Tony shot him a weak smile. "Yeah, yeah, we'll see, I guess."

"Yeah, we will." Wyatt turned and left the kitchen, heading towards the bedroom he shared with Ryan on the other side of the house.

Tony contemplated the vodka bottle, wondering if he should have one more shot before he went to bed—*alone*, his brain supplied—and he nearly reached for it, but then his phone dinged.

It was Lucas. With his heart in his throat, Tony opened the text. **I want one too,** it read. **Soon.**

His heartbeat accelerated rapidly, relief cascading through him in a breathless rush. He hadn't fucked everything up, not the way he dreaded he had. But when the first euphoria passed, he found he didn't actually *feel* better? Maybe because everything was still so up in the air. Maybe because instead of saying, *yes, let's talk about it now, come meet me,* Lucas had said *soon.*

For a split second, Tony considered texting him back, telling him he'd figured out Lucas had been right all along, that it *had* been Jeremy, and that he'd also been right about confronting him. As soon as it'd been clear that Tony knew, Jeremy had folded like a shitty hand of cards.

But that wasn't the kind of thing he wanted to say over text. It was an apology, and Lucas deserved a better version than just a throwaway text message. He deserved some real thought; he deserved some real groveling.

Tony needed to figure out how to make that happen. He grabbed the vodka bottle and headed out the back door, towards his cottage. Some major brainstorming was going to happen, because no matter what Wyatt said, he knew just a standard, basic apology wasn't going to be good enough. Not when he'd fucked up the way he had. Not when he'd made Lucas believe that he didn't trust him, even as he told him he loved him.

He needed something big, something not necessarily splashy, but something that really proved how much he trusted Lucas. How much he loved him. How much he was totally, one thousand percent committed to not fucking up at any point ever again.

He flopped down on his coach, set the vodka bottle on the coffee table in front of him, and tried to think of what exactly that might be.

CHAPTER SEVENTEEN

LUCAS WASN'T SLEEPING AT all—he hadn't in two nights, not since he and Tony had argued—so that explained why, when there was a huge commotion at the front entrance to the gym, he barely looked up from where he was helping one of his regulars through a series of squats.

He felt hazy and not quite with it. It wasn't just the lack of sleep; it was the constant circular set of questions that kept flying around his head. *Should I call him? Should I tell him that yes, I want that redo, right now?*

The answer to every single question was always yes, and he'd gotten close a few times, his fingers hesitating over his phone, but he hadn't done anything yet. Maybe because his first instinct was always to apologize, for getting angry, for being frustrated, for believing that Tony had trusted him but not quite enough. And that wasn't fair either. Yeah, Tony had been sticking up for his friend, but he'd also been completely fucking blind, and Lucas couldn't come up with a single circumstance where he should've stayed silent.

But then, if he'd done the right thing, why did it feel like such utter shit?

"What is that?" Lucas' client stood up and wiped his face, gesturing towards the front of the gym where a crowd was gathering.

His first thought was, *oh god, it's Tony, he's doing something insane,* and his second thought was, *oh thank god, we can finally move on from this.* But it wasn't Tony.

In a second it became very clear who was causing such a stir in Ria's front room, and it wasn't because Lucas' stupid boyfriend was doing some kind of stupid stunt. It was because there was an honest-to-god famous athlete hanging out like he came here every day.

Los Angeleans were generally chill. They saw enough celebrities on grocery store runs or jogging in Runyon Canyon to not give much of a shit about anyone in particular, but the exception to this was the handful of professional sports teams that were based in LA. The Dodgers, experiencing a resurgence of popularity and success, were at the forefront of that list. And Ryan Flores? He was the city's new favorite obsession.

"Do you know him?" Nate, Lucas' client, turned to him excitedly. "God, he is *so* cute."

"And *so* taken," Lucas retorted kindly. "Yeah, actually I do. He's . . . well, he's my boyfriend's brother-in-law."

It was the first time he'd said the word out loud. Definitely the first time he'd ever told anyone. And the world didn't end in a giant cataclysm.

"Oh, I didn't realize you were dating anyone," Nate said. They'd been working out together for a while now, ever since Nate had moved down to LA from Napa. He'd been in the midst of a nasty breakup, and wanting to reinvigorate his life, and Lucas had been happy to be there for him. He wouldn't say they were friends, but they were good workout buddies.

"Yeah. It's new."

"So you're dating Tony, then," Nate said casually, still watching as Ryan signed autographs for the entire waiting room. "I . . . that bad breakup of mine? It was Wyatt. The guy who married Ryan Flores."

"You're Wyatt's ex? God, it's a fucking small world." Lucas leaned against one of the weight machines. "That would be a shitty-ass breakup too. For your ex to end up with someone like that."

Nate rolled his eyes. "No fucking kidding. But yeah, I can't blame Wyatt for wanting him."

"Him and everyone else with a pulse," Lucas agreed.

"How did you meet them?" Nate said, his eyes still glued to Ryan. Lucas wondered how cute he really thought Ryan was, and how much of this was regret and envy.

This right here was why he hadn't ever wanted a relationship, and why he definitely hadn't been interested in falling in love.

"I'm working on Tony and Wyatt's food truck," Lucas admitted. "I . . . I wasn't really looking for it. For Tony."

"When it comes to those Blakes, it doesn't matter if you are or you aren't," Nate said, "they'll hook you anyway."

"I guess," Lucas said.

They watched as Ryan finally finished with his autograph and selfie seekers and meandered over to where Lucas and Nate were standing, like this hadn't been his intended destination the entire damn time.

"Hey, Lucas," Ryan said extending his hand. "Am I interrupting you?"

After shaking his hand, Lucas glanced at his watch. He'd known he and Nate were nearly to the end of their session, but when he looked back up, Nate was already halfway across the room. Maybe he hadn't wanted to meet his ex's husband, but he'd definitely decided to split, leaving just Lucas and Ryan. He gave a short wave, and Lucas waved back. This was probably better than trying to explain to Ryan his client was his husband's ex-boyfriend.

"I guess not," Lucas admitted. "We were just about done, anyway."

Ryan sighed and sat down on one of the weight benches. "Sometimes it gets annoying, causing a commotion wherever you go. It'd be nice to be invisible again. I kinda miss it."

"Invisibility has its downsides too," Lucas pointed out.

Ryan glanced up, grinning. "Grass is always greener, isn't it?"

He might be pretty interested in Ryan's thoughts on the intersection of celebrity and his career as a professional athlete, but truthfully, Lucas wanted to cut through all the crap. To know why Ryan had come here at all. "I'm surprised to see you here. I thought it would be Tony, coming down here to grovel."

"Oh, he wants to," Ryan said wryly. "He's almost done it about half a dozen times."

"So he sent you instead?" That was a tactic that Lucas genuinely hadn't anticipated.

"Actually, I sent myself." Ryan reached behind him and pulled out a sheaf of papers. "Tony told me about his idea. Well, he told Wyatt, and Wyatt told me."

"The vegan food truck?" Lucas hadn't really thought about it in days, not since they'd argued.

"Yeah," Ryan said. "It's a good idea. Wyatt said you hadn't decided yet what you wanted to do, but I thought I'd put something together, anyway. I know it would be hard, especially if you and Tony didn't work out, but I still want us to work together. I like the bars. I want to give you a way to sell them, because they need to get out there."

"So this is you making sure I know that the business side of our relationship isn't dependent on the personal." Lucas looked at the papers in Ryan's hand and finally took them. There was no harm in reading what he'd drawn up, right? Also, when a very famous multimillionaire and professional athlete wanted to get into business with you, it would be incredibly stupid to turn them down just because you had a personal connection.

"I'd have discussed it with you personally, without Tony, no matter what," Ryan said, stretching out his legs. "It's not dependent on whatever happens with him. This is business."

Lucas had always respected the hell out of Ryan Flores. Yeah, maybe he'd gone through a bit of a wild patch, but he'd been brave, risking condemnation and being forced out of the sport he loved, all because he wanted to be honest about who he was. That took some real balls. That was before all the charity work he'd done with several local LGBT organizations, even a few shelters that Lucas was more intimately familiar with than he expected Ryan knew.

"Right," Lucas said, tapping the rolled-up papers absently on his thigh. "Tony really didn't send you?"

Ryan shot him a look. "Yeah, Tony is a good guy. I love him. He was kind of the bonus I didn't expect when Wyatt and I got together, but yeah, he doesn't tell me to do jack shit."

Which was sort of what Lucas had assumed, but this was too important to leave to chance—because if he was being really fucking honest with himself, he wanted both. He wanted the food truck, and he also wanted that do-over with Tony.

"I didn't think so, but I had to check," Lucas said.

Ryan nodded approvingly. "I thought I liked you, and now I know for sure."

"Thanks," Lucas said dryly.

"Look over the contract," Ryan said. "My business manager's number is on there, if you have any questions, and so is mine, if you feel more comfortable reaching out directly to me."

"I will. I've got a spin class this afternoon, but I'll make the time to read it."

"You teach spin?" Ryan wondered. "Is that why Tony tortured himself that one day?"

Lucas chuckled, remembering how charmed he'd been that Tony had suffered through it, all for a potential glimpse of a guy he'd liked. *Him*. He'd done it for *him*. "No," he said, "but I've been taking the classes the last few days. It's kinda helping my temper."

"Yeah, I get it. Sometimes you just want it to hurt. I'll see you around, dude." Ryan stood up and started to leave, but then, like he'd changed his mind, turned back. "Actually, if you have the time, I want to tell you a story, if you have another minute."

Here was the entreaty he'd expected Ryan to make the entire time. Maybe Tony hadn't sent him, but he was still on Tony's side. *And so are you*, his heart reminded him. *You love him, too.*

"Yeah, sure. Nothing but time." This time it was Lucas who sat down on the opposite weight bench, but Ryan didn't follow suit.

"You heard that parrot, right, when you were at our house that one morning?" Ryan asked, and Lucas nodded. "Well, god, that fucking parrot, it's been wreaking havoc on my relationship. Wyatt thought I should let it go, but I didn't want to. Somehow, that stupid parrot was like . . . the first thing that had really gone wrong in a while, and I thought I needed to do something to stop it. And yeah, it was incredibly fucking dumb, sending a cease and desist letter to a *bird.*"

"You really did that?" Lucas said, cracking a smile for the first time in days.

Ryan shrugged. "When you're really in love, and you're desperate to preserve what you have, when you're terrified something will destroy it, even a bird looks way worse than it is."

"But you and Wyatt are solid," Lucas said.

"Yeah, well, apparently I'm the last one to realize that," Ryan retorted wryly.

"So the parrot didn't cease and desist?"

"Not a bit. But it doesn't matter. It's just a bird. Yeah, it's obnoxious. But a few squawks can't destroy our marriage. At first it was because I swore I wouldn't let them, but the truth is, they just *can't.*"

"Am I supposed to be taking something from this cautionary tale?" Lucas wondered.

Ryan laughed and slipped his silver sunglasses back on, probably because he was about to wade through a whole new set of fans that had gathered in the waiting area. "Well, obviously, don't be an idiot and try to cease and desist a parrot. That's the most important takeaway. But also . . . something is only capable of destroying your relationship if you let it."

Lucas took his break after Nate, grabbing an iced coffee from the little shop down the street he liked and sitting out on their patio, carefully reading through Ryan's contract. He made a few notations, but from what he'd taught himself about business, it seemed very solid. He should probably spring for a lawyer to at least take a look at it, before he agreed to sign it. Because he already knew he was going to. This was the opportunity that he'd never, ever expected, but once it had fallen in his lap, how could he ever turn it down?

After he finished with the contract, and his iced coffee was gone, he sat there for a long time, reading the last set of texts he and Tony had exchanged. Obviously Tony hadn't said exactly what he wanted to "do-over" but Lucas had what he believed was a damn accurate hunch, because he wanted the exact same thing. He wished that he hadn't told Tony he loved him in anger. Wished that he'd been less frustrated and way less fed up when Tony said it back.

All he would have to do was to text him. Or call him. The conversation with Ryan had proven how willing Tony was to talk.

And Lucas *missed* him. They hadn't known each other that long, but life without Tony adding color and excitement and *fun* seemed bland and lifeless. He missed him like he was a limb he hadn't realized he *needed*, but turned out was vital to existence.

A calendar entry popped up on his phone, right as he'd been about to type out a message about meeting tonight. *Spin class*, it said, *starting in ten minutes.*

Shit, he'd totally forgotten that he'd signed up for it this morning, despite his still-sore muscles from the last one. He'd felt better after it, exhausted and emptied out, and he'd hoped that if he did another one, it might burn out the last of his anger and his frustration and he could maybe finally get some fucking sleep.

For a moment, he considered canceling it. He could probably convince Ria to give him his money back. But maybe it wouldn't be a bad thing to go, to wear out the last of his resistance, and *then* text Tony.

He stood and tossed his cup into the recycling bin and headed back towards Ria's. From the back room, he grabbed his bag, and after changing, ducked into the back of the spin room, right as Charles cued up the music.

He picked a bike in the last row, one of the last unoccupied, and took a deep breath, centering himself for the hell to come. *The hell you signed up for,* his brain squawked.

"Welcome to spin," Charles shouted over the PA, and Lucas was swinging his leg over the seat, when a telltale head of hair in the next row over caught his attention.

That was Tony. It *had* to be. He'd recognize that hair and man bun anywhere. Also, there was the awkward way he was pedaling. It was all a dead giveaway. *Plus*, that little voice in his head muttered, the one who sounded so much like Ria, *you told Ryan you'd be here this afternoon.*

Lucas knew the last time Tony had come to spin, he'd only done it because of Lucas. Was he here again for Lucas? Or had he come because he'd somehow decided the masochistic style of the class actually appealed to him?

Considering he'd told Ryan where he would be, Lucas was almost certain it was the former and not the latter. After all, since the one time, Tony hadn't seemed interested in going back. He'd asked about yoga—probably because he really seemed to appreciate how bendy Lucas was—but he definitely hadn't said a word about spin.

Charles was barking out another set of instructions, but Lucas hadn't moved, dazedly staring at Tony's back.

And suddenly, it seemed very stupid to not ask him *now*, before he had to go through an entire class wondering and not *knowing* why Tony was here.

He got off the bike and skirted around Tony's bike, watching as his eyes widened when Lucas stopped in front of him. "Hey," he said, raising his voice so Tony could hear him over the pounding music.

Tony jerked in surprise. Maybe he hadn't come here to find Lucas, because he sure seemed shocked to see him.

"Fuck, it's you, it's you," Tony breathed out. He moved, maybe to get off the bike, but instead of waiting for the pedals to stop, he just launched himself off, getting tangled, and nearly falling right onto Lucas.

He caught him and they stood there for a long second; the music pulsing and the lights flickering, surrounded by a bunch of people who weren't even paying attention to them. "I'm sorry," Tony said before Lucas could figure out what to say. "I'm so fucking sorry."

"It's okay," Lucas said, because he discovered that it *was*. Tony was a loyal guy. He would always go balls-to-the-wall for everyone he cared for, and that had included Jeremy. He'd been torn, between what he knew might be true and what he desperately didn't want to be true. Lucas realized that now.

"No," Tony said, shaking his head and raising his voice as Charles cranked up the music volume, heading out of the warm-up period. "No, I was so fucking wrong. I was . . . I fired Jeremy."

"You didn't have to do that." *Not for me. I don't want you to resent me for it.*

"I caught him," Tony said flatly. "He'd stolen one of your recipes. And you were right, when I confronted him, he told me everything."

"I didn't want to be right," Lucas said.

Tony's eyes softened. "I know."

"Excuse me." A voice cut through their bubble. "Are we bothering you?"

Lucas looked over and saw that Charles' gaze had narrowed in at them. He knew there was nothing that the instructor hated more than people who took his class and then didn't take it seriously.

"Uh," Tony said. "I just need . . . I just need to do this real quick."

Charles looked downright pissed off. "Oh, then, by all means," he said, his voice echoing through the room, the snide edge in it apparent, "if we're bothering you, don't let us interrupt you."

Tony looked back at Lucas, grinning. "I think we're pissing him off."

"It's high time someone did," Lucas said.

"I know I said I wanted a do-over, and you said you did too, but then you said soon. So I was trying to wait, and I . . . I'm just total shit at waiting," Tony confessed. "When Ryan said he'd found you at the gym and he'd said you were taking spin later, I thought, *what the hell.* I didn't hesitate, I just came."

"What the hell, I'll just torture myself a little and hope that you might see me?" he wondered.

Tony blushed. "Yeah, yeah, something like that. It was . . . crazy. If it's too soon or too much or . . ."

"It's just right," Lucas interrupted him and leaned in, wrapping his hands around his neck, tugging him down, until their mouths met in a fierce, passionate kiss.

"Unacceptable," he heard Charles roar, and he chuckled into Tony's mouth as they kissed. He'd missed this as much as he'd miss breathing. He hadn't even known he *wanted* it, but then Tony had shown up and made it so fucking obvious just what he was missing.

"Maybe," Tony said, after breaking their kiss, "maybe we should take this outside."

"You should," Charles yelled. "You absolutely fucking should."

Lucas laughed. "I think we might have pushed him just far enough."

"I think so too," Tony agreed seriously.

Tony watched as Lucas grabbed his bag, and after doing the same, he followed him out of the spin room, and then outside to the empty sidewalk in front of the gym, chuckling as Charles made more noise about it being about fucking time.

He wasn't wrong. It was about fucking time.

Lucas didn't even look mad that he'd shown up, *and* he'd kissed him.

"You came to spin class again," Lucas said, as soon as they were outside.

"Yeah," Tony admitted. "I . . . I would've done a lot more, just for a chance to talk to you again."

Lucas smiled. "Really? Even suffer through Sadist Charles and spin class?"

"Yeah, actually. Way worse. Though I probably shouldn't admit that."

"You really shouldn't, you know," Lucas said, reaching out and taking his empty hand, tangling their fingers together, squeezing gently. "I might use that against you."

"I trust you," Tony said softly. "And I really do, you know. I mean it. I *do* fucking trust you."

"I know," Lucas admitted. "I know that now. I'm sorry, I'm sorry I said that you didn't. I was just . . . so fucking frustrated that you wouldn't listen. But I shouldn't have let Jeremy and his petty shit get between us."

"And I should have listened," Tony admitted wryly. "I still can't believe he did that to me."

"He was an idiot," Lucas said. "I'd love to punch him in the face."

"No argument here, and if he comes around again, I won't stop you." Tony took a deep breath, and took a risk though, with Lucas smiling up at him like that, it didn't feel like a risk so much as the first step of the rest of their lives. "Are you ready for that do-over?"

Lucas tilted his head, considering Tony's question. "I think so, yeah."

"Okay," Tony said. He dropped his gym bag and took Lucas' other hand, his blue eyes burning with sincerity. "I want to go on a thousand stakeouts with you, even if we never catch anybody, I never want to fight again, even though we probably will. There's nothing I wouldn't do to help you succeed, even take a backseat if that's what's necessary. I want to cook next to you, for as long as you'll let me. And it would be the greatest honor if you'd let me love you, too."

Lucas stared at him. "You mean all that."

"Every word. I love you. I'm probably more trouble than I'm worth, I know it . . ."

But before Tony could get more words out, Lucas flung his arms around his neck and pulled him against him, tight and close. "You're the exact right amount of trouble," Lucas said fiercely into his ear. "I won't have you insulting the man I love, okay?"

"Okay," Tony agreed easily. "You got it, boss."

EPILOGUE

"Hey, boss," Dean, one of the guys Tony and Lucas had hired for the new truck, called out. "Do you have the gazpacho done yet?"

Tony glanced up, met Lucas' amused hazel eyes, and tried very hard to ignore the way his cock seemed to react to the nickname that Dean didn't understand yet was reserved for one guy and one guy only.

"Yeah, boss," Lucas said, leaning right into his space, his voice dropping low, driving Tony just a little crazier, "where's the gazpacho?"

"It's . . ." Tony took a deep breath, trying to focus, but it was hard, because now he knew why it felt like his brother never got anything done when Ryan was around. "It's coming. Right now."

"Doesn't feel like it," Lucas cooed. And *yes,* maybe they had made several *very* necessary rules about PDA, both in the new truck and the old one, but that didn't stop Lucas from being fucking adorable and hot as fuck just by *breathing* and *existing*.

And talking. Talking was a real problem.

Tony took a deep breath. "Don't you have sandwiches you should be making?"

"Oh?" Lucas asked innocently, when that was the very last thing he was. "Am I bothering you?"

Tony squeezed his eyes shut. "Do you want this gazpacho or not?"

"Yeah, we need it, *right now*," Dean said, because he was new and so had no idea what kind of games Tony and Lucas liked to play—and if Tony could keep himself under control, he never would. But that was apparently going to be a lot tougher than he'd ever anticipated.

"Yeah, yeah," Tony said, forcing himself to focus as he gave the gazpacho one last pulse in the food processor and then poured it into the clear plastic cup, drizzling the cilantro oil over the top and sprinkling with the homemade corn chips.

After giving it a once-over, he slid it across the counter to Dean, who called out the name. Lucas shot Tony a very unimpressed look. "I think you must have forgotten how to work the new equipment," Lucas teased. "Is it very difficult?"

"Focusing when you want me to not focus? Impossible, it turns out," Tony ground out, but Lucas just laughed.

"I'm going to have to talk to Dean about it, aren't I?" Lucas said as Dean called out more orders. They were set up in front of the Funky Cup for their inaugural evening, to work out all the kinks. While Tony was grateful that Shaw had let them park here, and excited that they were finally selling the food they'd worked so hard to develop, there was also a part of him that would've liked to spend the night the way they'd been spending so many recently—wrapped up together, with Lucas the only one calling him boss.

"It should be me," Tony objected. Lucas had zero shame and Dean, who seemed like a good guy, didn't need to be scared off by his boyfriend's oversharing.

"You're just afraid I'm going to tell him it's a kink of yours," Lucas teased.

"Absolutely fucking yes," Tony said. "That is one hundred percent what I'm scared of."

Lucas' dimples emerged as he grinned. "You're gonna pay for that."

"Later, I hope," Tony said, not even sounding a tiny bit afraid.

Lucas slid one of his jackfruit pulled pork sandwiches across to Dean. "Do you want me to do it right now?"

Everything inside Tony tensed, and Lucas burst out into laughter. "You should see your face right now!"

Dean glanced behind him, in the middle of taking orders. "What's going on?"

Tony straightened. "Um, nothing."

Dean smirked. "Yeah, it sounds a lot like foreplay back here. Is this gonna be a problem?"

"No, absolutely not," Tony squeaked at the exact same time that Lucas said, "All the fucking time."

Dean rolled his eyes and turned back to the next person in line. "Get your shit straight, *boss*," he said, and even that usage, when he was so clearly annoyed with Tony, made his heart leap in his chest.

Lucas sighed. "I am gonna have to talk to him."

"Try to keep it . . . G-rated, okay?" Tony said as he started another batch of gazpacho.

"Sure thing, boss," Lucas teased, his eyes glinting right before he turned back to the grill.

Fuck, Tony thought, *I love him so much.*

"Looks like it's been a huge success," Ryan said an hour later, when the line had finally cleared out and they had run out of enough of their menu that Dean had pulled the shades down on the truck. They'd decamped to the fire pit in the back of the bar, to discuss how the opening night had gone.

"I can't complain," Lucas said. "Dean even said he took some orders for energy bars."

"That's fantastic, I knew this would be a great fit," Wyatt enthused.

Lucas glanced over to where Tony was standing with Gabe and Sean and Tate, who'd all stopped by to help support their friend—*friends*, he corrected, *they're* your *friends now too*. And that was something he'd never quite imagined when he'd run into Wyatt Flores at the restaurant supply store. He'd ended up with several hotel pans, a job, a boyfriend, and an extended group of friends and even a few he'd call family.

"Yeah," Lucas said, "I can't believe how it all turned out."

Ryan turned to his husband. "You wouldn't have anything to do with this picture-perfect fairytale ending, would you?"

Wyatt just blushed and shook his head, though Lucas had a feeling that Wyatt had known, or at least had *guessed,* that he and Tony would hit it off. But how could he have guessed that they'd fall crazy in love with each other? Or that it would turn out that his meat-loving boyfriend would end up so surprisingly into the vegan recipes that they'd developed for the truck together.

Wyatt couldn't have predicted it all, especially the serendipity of how it all fell together into one slightly disorganized, but incredibly happy jumble.

Lucas definitely could never have imagined it, because he'd never thought any of this was really for him, but it turned out that some things were worth breaking the rules for.

"You look like you're thinking really hard," Tony said and Lucas glanced up, noticing that Tate had gone back into the bar, and Sean and Gabriel were now having a hushed conversation. *That* was not exactly serendipity, at least not yet, but Lucas knew that Tony had high hopes that his two friends would figure their shit out soon.

Tony dropped down next to him on the bench and wrapped one arm around Lucas, pulling him tighter against him. Something that Lucas never would have liked before, feeling tied to someone, but now he welcomed the pull of it. Love was funny that way.

"I was just thinking how lucky I am," Lucas said softly. "Lucky *and* happy." At first he'd been afraid of anything even remotely sappy, but with every sweet glance Tony gave him, and with every hushed declaration of love, he'd felt a wave of happiness crest through him. And he'd learned that he felt even happier when he told Tony exactly how he felt, too.

Now, six months into their relationship, he wasn't afraid anymore, only eager to see what the future might bring them.

"Maybe you'll get even luckier," Tony said, grip tightening on him. "I can't wait to take you home tonight."

"Gross," Wyatt said, and Ryan cackled with laughter.

"Just payback," Tony said, grinning.

"I've never been happier that you live in the guest cottage," Wyatt said.

"Hey, me too," Tony agreed. "Better put your earplugs in tonight."

Wyatt chuckled, like he thought Tony was kidding—and maybe he did—but Lucas knew he was serious, knew it from the way Tony's fingers dug into his side, from the heat in his gaze as he watched as Lucas took a drink from the beer bottle in his hand. He felt his stomach tighten in anticipation, because there was nothing he loved more than making Tony scream—and letting him return the favor.

"Did you hear from Marco?" Wyatt asked, changing the subject. "Is he coming or not?"

"He didn't return my text," Tony said, frustration leaking into his voice. "Who the fuck knows what's going through that kid's head."

"I could look into it," Ryan suggested.

"Would you?" Wyatt said, turning to his husband with a grateful smile on his face. "It'd be a lot better time spent than worrying about that parrot."

"If I remember, it was *you* who was so worried about the parrot," Ryan retorted.

"You *both* were," Lucas inserted and everyone burst into laughter. "You were about to get your lawyer to muzzle the stupid thing."

"Not my finest moment," Ryan admitted wryly.

But Lucas kind of thought this one was, surrounded by people he cared about and who cared about him, with the lights twinkling overhead, a cold beer in his hand, his own goddamn food truck sitting by the curb, and even an employee whom he was going to have to tell to stop calling his boyfriend—his fantastic, loyal, stubborn, sexy-as-hell boyfriend—boss because at some point Tony wasn't going to be responsible for his actions.

"To a great night," Tony said, raising his beer. "And to a lot of great nights to come." As Lucas clinked his bottle with Tony's, he realized he couldn't have put it any better himself.

He leaned in, whispering in Tony's ear, "You sure about that, boss?"

Tony's kiss might've been beer-flavored, but underneath it, he tasted like home.

To read a steamy bonus scene about Tony and Lucas' making one of Nana's famous dessert, Sex in a Pan, click here.

To continue the Food Truck Warriors series with *Hit the Brakes*, Tate and Chase's story, click here.

or you can always check out the complete Food Truck Warriors box sets here: Part One and Part Two.

INTERESTED IN READING MORE OF
BETH'S BOOKS?

CHECK OUT A FULL LIST OF TILES
BY SCANNING THE QR CODE
OR VISITING HER WEBSITE

WWW.BETHBOLDEN.COM/BOOKLIST

WANT TO FOLLOW BETH?

MAKE SURE YOU NEVER
MISS A RELEASE?

SCAN THE QR CODE BELOW
OR VISIT HER WEBSITE
FOR A SOCIAL MEDIA LIST,
NEWSLETTER SIGNUP,
AND SO MUCH MORE!

WWW.BETHBOLDEN.COM/ABOUT

www.ingramcontent.com/pod-product-compliance
Lightning Source LLC
Chambersburg PA
CBHW070406310726
48977CB00003B/585